Under the Salvadoran Sun

A Novel

Sher Davidson

LA PAGE
PRESS

Portland, Oregon

To Millie,
Enjoy — so
great to meet
you &
J Sher
Davidson

Published in the US by LaPagePress, Portland, Oregon, USA

For information about special discounts on bulk purchases, please write the author at her contact page on her website: www.sherdavidson.com.

Cover art: Fernando Llort
Cover design: Margot Boland
Interior layout and formatting: Margie Baxley and John Edwards

To the people of El Salvador where
I have visited, worked and loved.

As someone with a deep commitment to our partner communities in El Salvador, Sher Davidson writes from experience and from the heart. Humor and insight, coupled with real life experience, give Angela's story a grounding in reality. Weaving history and geography with storytelling, Davidson takes us with her on a life-changing journey.

Yael Falicov
Executive Director of
EcoViva

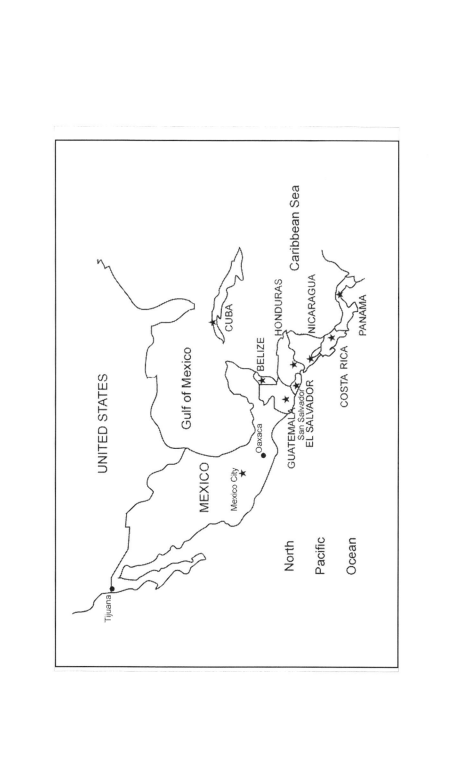

PART ONE

I would prove to man that they do not stop falling in love, as they get older. They get older as soon as they stop falling in love.

—Anonymous

Memories can be like a submerged brook running under fragile ground.

— Owen Sheers, *Resistance*

Remembering
El Salvador 2000

Ten years ago, on a hot and humid March day, Angela Larson looked up at the San Salvador Cathedral, admired the brightly colored paintings on its pure white façade, and sighed with relief. She had finally arrived. The cathedral was the culmination of a long march commemorating the anniversary of the death of martyred Salvadoran Archbishop, Oscar Romero. People from all over the world participated to show their solidarity with the Salvadorans.

A tall, slim and attractive woman of fifty-three, Angela felt out of place in the crowd of shorter, copper skinned Salvadorans. At five feet eight, she towered over most of them. Her olive complexion shone with moistness from the hot sun, and her light blouse clung to her. She was here on a mission, searching for a new purpose for her life. After raising children and a successful career as a sculptor, she hoped she could make a difference in the world. She and her architect husband, David, seemed to be more at odds with each other than ever before. Their marriage felt like old crystal, fragile and riddled with cracks, threatening at any moment to break apart into a million fragments.

When her friend, Sandy, invited her to join a group of volunteers with a NGO (Non-governmental Organization) to plant mangroves and fruit trees in a rural coastal town in El Salvador, she had jumped at the chance. The timing for this trip was auspicious. Not only was it the anniversary of the death of Romero, it would give her time to think about her marriage and how to reconcile their differences and to rekindle the passion they once had. Maybe a time of separation would be good.

A helicopter hovered low over the crowd of marchers. Angela grabbed the arm of her new Salvadoran friend, a teacher from the Spanish Language School she attended the week before she was to meet the group.

"Don't worry," he said. "We're used to this. It's only to intimidate us."

Repression and political unrest still existed in this post civil war country. As in so many other Latin American countries, the majority of people were poor. Living off the land they could barely scrape by, and there were few social services. Though the war had brought about land reform, the country was still rife with problems of power, corruption, and unequal distribution of wealth.

On this day, hundreds of women sat outside the cathedral with photos of their loved ones, victims of the war whose bodies had never been found. They called these victims the "Disappeared." A shroud of sadness hung over the crowd.

It was here and then that Angela first laid eyes on Liam, the man who still lingered in her mind and heart. He stood on the steps of the cathedral, passing out crepe paper flowers to the marchers and speaking Spanish with the women. Their eyes met for one of those interminable moments—when the mind races to find a fragment of memory that will tell it why a face looks familiar, if only because one wants it to be.

"Angela," a voice had called out. "We're over here."

Distracted from her gaze at the stranger, Angela turned to see her friend Sandy and the group waving to her by the southwest corner of the steps to the cathedral, where they had agreed to gather. Angela ran over to meet them. Sandy embraced her.

"How was the march? I'm sure glad you're OK," Sandy said. "We saw the military helicopters and weren't quite sure what was happening."

"Oh, I'm fine—just a little weary, but it was inspiring and I'm glad I did the march," said Angela, her mind elsewhere. "It's good to see all of you. Sorry you had to wait." She looked back at the steps of the cathedral, but the man she had seen was no longer there.

Everyone seemed anxious to start out for La Liberdad, a town on the Pacific coast, where they were to have a four-day orientation and time to get to know one another.

"C'mon, the bus is over there," Sandy said, as she pointed to an old yellow school bus, owned by the Seattle-based NGO, which sponsored the trip. "We've got a two hour drive to La Liberdad."

Sandy and her husband, Jake, had been on the board of directors of the NGO for years. They had led many groups doing aid work and building solidarity with the people of El Salvador, and they knew the country well.

"We'll spend four days there for our orientation and then go on to the Bajo Lempa, the rural area where our project planting mangroves on the coast, and fruit trees around the schools, will begin," said Jake. "Hope you're all rested."

Later, after their arrival in La Liberdad, Angela was surprised when she exited her hotel to go meet the group for dinner. A man she recognized approached her.

"Excuse me, but didn't I see you earlier today at the front of the march to the cathedral in San Salvador?" he asked with a quizzical smile. "You looked so intense and moved by the event, I couldn't help but think how much I would like to meet you. You ran off too soon."

Surprised by the stranger's forthrightness, Angela continued to walk. "Well, thank you," she said, "but I'm sure your thoughts were on more important things."

He continued, "Sorry, if I'm being too forward but, really, I noticed you and wanted to meet you. You might say I recognize a compassionate soul when I see one. What brings you to El Salvador?"

Stopped short by the man's earnestness, Angela paused in the road and said, "Oh, I've been interested in visiting the country since I first met Salvadoran refugees while working in Nicaragua during the Contra War, in the eighties. I'm here with friends on a tree-planting project. I'm on my way to meet them now." *Damn, I gave him way too much information.* She looked at her watch and began to turn away. "Will you excuse me, please? I really don't want to keep my friends waiting."

"Oh, of course. Forgive me, but I would like to see you again. Would you care to join me later for a walk on the beach? The water's beautiful in the moonlight."

This guy's coming on strong, Angela mused. She moved her left hand, with its wedding ring finger, up to brush back a strand of her long hair that had fallen into her eyes.

"Thank you for the invitation, but I'm very tired tonight after that march this morning, and not up to going down to the beach."

He persisted. "Well, then how about an early morning swim? The surf's great."

Actually, earlier that evening, when Sandy showed the group the beach pathway, she mentioned that the surf was rough and they should watch out for the huge rip tides.

The stranger continued: "I'll be walking down to the beach about seven in the morning if you'd care to join me."

"Thank you, I may be up for that, but I'm not sure." She hoped this sounded noncommittal enough.

"By the way," the man asked, "What's your name?"

"Angela ... and yours?"

"Liam, Liam O'Connor. I'm delighted to meet you. Well, then see you tomorrow."

Angela didn't answer, but waved as she turned to walk down the road in search of the restaurant Sandy called a *pupuseria,* named for the national dish. She had explained that *pupusas* were like small tortillas stuffed with mashed beans, cheese, and sometimes pork, even squash blossoms. Sounded good.

As Angela walked along the road, a mixture of broken up asphalt and dirt, strewn with trash, she thought about what had just transpired. Was she crazy? At her age, how could she still have felt that near-electrical impulse that sexual attraction once created? Liam O'Connor's face had character, and his tall, lean frame displayed an almost schoolboy awkwardness, the way he rocked from one foot to the other, his hands in his pockets, shoulders tense. At the same time he spoke with a great deal of confidence … an interesting mix. Her curiosity was getting to her, and she even went so far as to resolve she might just wake up early enough to join him at the beach, in the morning.

That is how it all began—the affair that she had never fully recovered from, the guilt that had hung in her heart like a heavy stone, and the memory of him and their days in the sultry heat, under the Salvadoran sun.

Chance Meeting
El Salvador 2010

Now ten years later, Angela was wiser after the ordeal of caring for her husband during an extended illness, and widowhood. She began to awaken from her year of grieving, and once again to look for a new direction for her life, a way she could do something significant. Her heroes, like Martin Luther King and Nelson Mandela, inspired her belief that one person could make a difference. She wanted to return to Central America, a place where she had felt needed when she and her husband worked repairing a hospital during the Contra War. Her daughters disapproved.

"It's only been a year, mother," Arial said. "Why are you so anxious to return to Central America? You and daddy did your part. We'll worry about you traveling alone, and Dad would have, too."

"You forget, dear," said Angela, "I traveled alone to El Salvador ten years ago and was able to accomplish something as well as build new friendships. I'll be fine—try not to worry. It's important to me to see my Nicaraguan and Salvadoran friends again."

Though not as adamant as her sister, and distracted by her own boyfriend problems, Katherine, the youngest daughter, concurred. "We'll really miss you mother. Losing one parent is enough. How long will you stay?"

"Only a month, dear. You mustn't worry," Angela said.

Angela knew her own heart. She knew that revisiting these places of her past, where she had grown to love the people and to feel like she was doing some good in the world, was just what she needed.

A month later Angela began her pilgrimage, stopping first in Guatemala, then Nicaragua and finally on to San Salvador where she checked into the same hostel where she had once stayed before she met her NGO group. Unpacking, she couldn't help but be nostalgic.

Tomorrow, she planned to attend a lecture about building non-violent reconciliation and self-sufficiency in this country still scarred by civil war. The presenter was a man she had once met and looked forward to seeing again, though she doubted he would remember her. She informed the manager at the hostel that she would need a taxi the following morning.

The next day, awaking with a start, Angela realized she had overslept. The hostel's manager tapped at the door.

"*Señora,* your taxi is here."

"*Gracias.*"

Angela hurried to dress, and pulled her hair back

from her face into a ponytail. Arial told her that wearing her hair back showed off her high cheekbones. Peering in the mirror, she pinched her cheeks, wiped some gloss across her lips and slipped into her sandals. Then she put on a pair of simple beaded earrings her friend, Adriana, had given her. She never liked to wear much jewelry when she traveled in Latin America. Somehow, it seemed like rubbing wealth in the face of the poor, as well as inviting theft. Grabbing her brightly colored, woven Guatemalan bag, she headed out to the lobby and then the waiting taxi.

Angela looked up at the San Salvador cathedral, breathed deep with anticipation, and hurried to cross the street. As she clutched her bag close to her, she stepped out into the traffic of honking cars and trucks, carts pulled by burros and vendors hawking their wares. Approaching the steps of the cathedral, she stopped short. There, casually leaning against a parked red pickup was a man she recognized. She could clearly make out his form and facial features—it was definitely he.

Recognition permeated every fiber of her body, as Liam turned his eyes towards her. His direct gaze penetrated her. It reminded her of their first encounter when his stare threw her off guard. It was as if he peered right through her, she thought—not the way that makes women squirm uncomfortably, like they're being undressed, but a look that registers with some element of oneself. With a look of surprise, Liam smiled broadly and began to walk toward her, his tall and lanky frame moving with ease. He seemed somewhat thinner than she remembered, and his hair had taken on a salt-and-pepper hue. With a nervous gesture, she pushed a wisp of hers back, away from her eyes.

Angela had only a moment to catch her breath before Liam stood and faced her with a boyish grin of recognition—as boyish as a sixty-something-year old man can muster. The flirtatious glint in his eyes was disarming, but at the same time exciting. How amazing they should once again meet at the steps of the cathedral. For a moment she felt uneasy, as she recalled the years of guilt about their affair. With her Italian Catholic upbringing, it had been hard to justify their brief transgression.

"Wow—how can this be? Angela, it's really you," said Liam. "You're still as beautiful as I remember. What in heaven's name brings you to San Salvador this time?" He reached out his arms to embrace her. She pulled away and looked up into his limpid blue eyes.

"I could ask the same of you. You're the last person I expected to see here." Her heart beat faster than the hurrying feet of the folks running up the steps to the cathedral entrance. She and Liam were barely conscious of the crowd as it brushed past them. They stared at each other for several moments, until Liam took her arm and steered her into the imposing edifice.

"We better go in if we want to get a good seat," he said. "We can talk later. You came to hear Father Rutilio, not me, I presume?" Liam winked.

Though Rutilio was no longer a priest, Angela noted how Liam always addressed him as "Father," a sign of special reverence for a man he loved and admired.

"Do you remember when I introduced you to

Rutilio?" asked Liam.

"How could I forget?" Angela said, still catching her breath from this surprise encounter. "When I heard he was going to speak here, I arranged to stay over a couple of days before going to the Bajo Lempa. I'm sure he won't remember me. We met so many years ago."

"Don't be too sure about that. Father Rutilio rarely forgets anyone, especially someone as attractive as you. You know these Latin men."

Angela smiled with a nod.

They found seats on a crowded bench near the pulpit. Pressed beside one another, their shoulders touched, and the years since they were last together evaporated.

Father Rutilio approached the pulpit, glanced in Liam's direction with a warm smile and began to speak. Angela's mind was elsewhere, whisked back to her first trip to El Salvador and her time with Liam ten years earlier.

More Memories
El Salvador 2000

On that morning in La Liberdad, when Angela heard Liam's voice call out from the roadside below her second floor hotel balcony, she hadn't yet decided to go to the beach with him. She awoke with the sound of his voice, pulled the sheets up around her naked body, and walked to the open window to look down at him. There was Liam, dressed in swim trunks, a red-and-orange towel thrown over his shoulder. He looked up at her.

"Well, are you going to join me at the beach? Liam asked. "It's seven thirty-five, a perfect time for a swim."

"Sure, I'll meet you down there." said Angela. She felt pursued and had to admit it was nice for a change. It had been a long time since her husband had shown such interest.

"Fine, but you'll have to get by the guards. This is a gated beach, and I have the secret password. I'll wait for you there."

Angela slipped into her one-piece black bathing suit, the one she thought most flattered her figure, applied blush to her cheeks, and tried to rub away the wrinkles around her deep-set dark, brown eyes—impossible— pulled her hair back into a ponytail and grabbed a towel. On her way out, she stopped at the room next door, tapped lightly and told Sandy she was off to the beach, and to join her there, if she'd like. Descending the narrow staircase, she walked out the door to the street.

The Salvadoran morning was already an oppressive ninety degrees with high humidity. The coastal streets were filled with new sights, sounds, and smells. Latin music mixed with the voices of people setting up their stalls of coconuts, fruits, and other items to sell. Children peered out of doorways from windowless huts, and tired-looking women bent over wood-burning stoves. Nearly naked toddlers ran here and there, and chickens clucked as they pecked at the ground. Noisy, rattling pickups loaded down with sugar cane, rusted metal, boxes of produce, and other sundry items rumbled down the dirt road. Burros, loaded with firewood, a commodity becoming more and more scarce in this second-most deforested nation in the Western Hemisphere, plodded along. Trucks kicked up clouds of dust, but no one seemed to care. Street smells invaded the atmosphere: human sweat, scents of tropical flowers, and motor-oil.

Angela slipped by the throngs of people and took the narrow pathway Sandy had shown her the night before. It was lined with a few straggly palms, and she had to be careful not to trip on garbage and old concrete bricks, seemingly cast there for no other reason than that a city dump did not exist. For a moment, she was reminded of the poverty she had seen while working in war-torn Nicaragua. Her visit there, a week ago, proved it hadn't changed much either.

Gingerly, Angela made her way around the debris and watched a gecko, as it slipped with speed in between the stones to avoid being stepped on. She headed for the beach, and the heavily guarded gate one had to pass through, to get there. This was part of the small resort reserved for tourists and off-limits to the locals who had their own less well-cared-for beach down the road. It was all the same coast, but with class separations as obvious as many beaches in the United States. She remembered that in some states, one could encounter signs saying: "Private Beach, Keep Out." Angela resented that great wealth could buy private access to environmentally endowed areas, then make them off-limits to those less fortunate. All was not equal in the world. She remembered the prejudice her grandparents suffered as non-English speaking immigrants from the old country. She bristled for a moment with the indignity of it, but knew she probably could not change it. Better to save her energy for the things she could change.

Liam waited. He looked relaxed, but a bit comical in his clunky hiking boots and his bare, hairy legs sticking out of swim trunks, perhaps one size too big. He wore a light cotton plaid shirt, half open down to his waist. The wrinkled shirttails flapped in the gentle morning sea breeze. His glance darted her way, his eyes crinkled in a smile. She couldn't help but laugh to herself and feel her whole body excited by the possibilities this meeting might present. The fact that she was a married woman, with daughters and grandchildren, was far from her mind at that moment. All she could think about was the beach, the beauty of the morning, and the anticipation she felt as Liam took her arm.

"*Hola, señora*, after you!" he said. Then with a schoolboy's embarrassment, "Excuse the silly shoes." He pointed down to his over-worn, dark brown hiking boots. "I forgot my flip-flops back home and wear these boots everywhere."

Angela laughed and felt her body relax. "No problem," she said, with a smile. "I forgot mine, too."

They walked through the gates as Liam gave the guards his "secret password" in Spanish. He quickly pulled off his boots and took Angela's hand pulling her towards the surf.

"You'll have to excuse me if I don't go out far—I'm not a strong swimmer any more," said Angela, "but I have fond memories of body surfing with my dad in Laguna Beach, California, in my younger years."

"So you're a California girl," Liam said.

"Just born there. I've lived in Seattle most of my adult life. I went to school at the University of Washington. Where are you from?"

"I'm a Boston guy. Irish immigrant—couldn't you tell by my name and accent?"

"No, I didn't pick up on that. I loved the Irish when I traveled there."

"That's good for me," said Liam.

They approached the deeper water, and Angela held back.

"Don't worry," Liam said. "I'll grab you if you begin to go under." He winked at her, grabbed her arm and pulled her along.

The ocean was bathwater warm. Its salty spray splashed their bodies, and Angela felt whisked back to her youth. As a huge wave headed their way, she tried to pull away from Liam's strong grasp, but the wave inundated them. She could feel the pull of the outgoing tide. Liam's strong arms wrapped around her torso, held her back and lifted her up from the receding surf. Spluttering from the salt water she had taken in, she was reassured by Liam's hold on her.

"Wow, that was a big one!" said Angela. She wiped the salt water out of her eyes and moved away from his hold. "Thank you. You saved my life."

"It was a pleasure. Are you OK?"

"Oh, yes, now I am, but for a moment I felt like I might be dragged out to sea."

As the outgoing surf lapped at their feet, Liam pulled her close again. A tremor went through her. She felt self-conscious and laughed as she broke away from his grasp.

Liam smiled. "Let's take a walk down the beach. I want to show you something."

As they walked along in the soft, damp sand, wet with sweat and seawater, their shoulders brushed against one another from time to time. They moved apart a bit and then closer together, as in a dance, each feeling drawn to the other with the rhythm of the waves coming in and going out.

Together Again
El Salvador 2010

"So my friends, this is our job—together, we can build peace and sustainability in the world." Rutilio ended his speech to loud applause.

The resounding noise of clapping hands awoke Angela from her memories. As charismatic as Rutilio was, she realized she had heard little of what he said. Sitting close to Liam, it had been hard to concentrate and to ignore the memories of the past.

Liam fidgeted, moved his arm from behind her shoulders, and began to applaud. He stood and invited Angela to approach Father Rutilio, who was immediately surrounded by a throng of admirers.

Rutilio was a stout man with broad shoulders, built like a solid wall you could depend on. His deep brown face under a shock of pure white, was creased with wrinkles from his broad smile. His piercing dark eyes seemed to hold mysteries from his past. He shook the hands of the people who approached, and hugged others with a warm embrace. As the crowd thinned, he looked up and motioned to Liam and Angela.

"Well, well, who has Liam brought this time? We finally meet again. Angelina, isn't it?" asked Father Rutilio.

Embarrassed, Angela hesitated…

"Father Rutilio, this is my friend, Angela," said Liam. "I introduced the two of you in El Salvador ten years ago. Do you remember?"

"*Sí, sí,* of course I remember. I never forget a pretty woman's face."

Other people began to approach the lectern, and Angela felt the soft pressure of Liam's hand on her back as he began to move away.

"Let's give the others a chance to talk to Father Rutilio?" Liam said. "We can meet up with him later."

Before Angela could reply, Father Rutilio said: "Yes, let's have lunch together. I hope you're going to be here for a few days, Angela."

"I'm leaving for the Bajo Lempa in two days. I want to visit my friends there. I think you know them. I'd love to see you again, though, before I go," said Angela.

"I remember now." He paused as if awakening to the past. "I recall the work you did planting mangroves there. I know the people have not forgotten you. Let's ask Liam to arrange a get together before you leave San Salvador. He'll want to tell you about our projects in Suchitoto, won't you, Liam?"

"*Sí,* Father. *Hasta luego,*" said Liam.

Liam guided Angela towards the doors of the cathedral. As they walked out into the hot, bright sunlight of San Salvador, he stopped for a moment on the stairs.

"By the way, I forgot to ask—where are you staying?"

"Oh, I think you know the place, the hostel, *Nueva Vida*," Angela replied.

"Perfect. That's where I am, too. Coincidence is everything in life, isn't it?"

With a smile, Angela nodded in agreement. "I must admit I'm still in shock that we should meet here. I never thought I'd see you again—you remember how we parted."

"How could I forget—it was an unhappy day for me."

"You know, I never could get you completely out of my mind," said Liam, as they got into his pickup. "The short time we spent together was, well, you know, something magical. We have a lot of catching up to do. How about getting a drink and a bite to eat at the hostel's patio bar?"

"Sounds good. I'm starved. I didn't get a chance to eat before I left the hostel this morning. I would like, though, to change into something a bit cooler. Can you wait while I go up to my room when we get back?"

Liam gave her a sideways glance, as he maneuvered through the San Salvador traffic. "I think I can wait ten minutes—after all I've waited ten years for this moment."

Though she was now a lot older, Angela was still captivated by this man. Maybe he was just what she needed now. She wondered if he was still married—and hoped not.

As they got out of the pickup, Angela said "Meet

you on the patio."

"Fine. I'll find us a nice secluded table," said Liam.

Looking Back
El Salvador 2000

While Angela changed, she recalled those heady days of their romance, meeting on the beach and struggling to find time for each other away from her NGO group, before they had to leave for the Bajo Lempa and their volunteer work. She remembered the third day in La Liberdad, when Sandy reproached her about the time she was spending away from the group during their orientation.

On their way to breakfast, Sandy said: "The purpose of these few days here is to get to know each other before beginning our work in the Bajo Lempa. I'll be frank, Angie, some of the group are starting to grumble about you being such a loner, and the fact that they still hardly know you."

Angela bristled and then smiled to herself. She had never been much of a joiner and admitted she liked to spend long hours by herself. As was true with many artists, she relished her solitude—her time with her creative muses. She was accustomed to spending lots of time alone in her Seattle studio. Sandy's interrogation about what she had been doing for the past three days with Liam made her uncomfortable. After all, she was an adult. It was none of Sandy's business. She stopped herself from blurting out her resentment, sucked in her breath, sighed and looked down with embarrassment.

"I'm sorry, Sandy. It's not been my intention to avoid the group. I want to be up front with you. As you know, my reasons for agreeing to come on this trip were twofold. I'm truly interested in getting to know the people of El Salvador. Their history touches me, and I want to be of help in this project. But, at the same time, I'm trying to sort out my priorities at this stage of my life, and to find a way to reconcile my marriage, which has been in deep trouble for the past few years. I hope you can understand."

Sandy hesitated. "I know you told me some of that at the Latin American conference in Seattle. But really, I have to be honest. I know you have been spending a lot of time with the guy you met the first night we were here. You introduced him to me in the lobby of the hotel. Isn't his name Liam?"

"Yes, you're right," Angela said. "I have to admit he has provided a kind of salve for my wounded ego. He's fun to be with, and interesting to talk to. He knows a great deal about El Salvador, having been down here many times working on projects in the same region as we are going to, the Bajo Lempa. I thought I might glean some information from him about the area." Knowing she was not being totally transparent, Angela rationalized that part of this was true. Liam had told her much about the history of the region, and what the current situation was there.

"Liam has been coming down here for several years, bringing pickup trucks full of humanitarian aid collected by his church," said Angela. "He is familiar with the area where we are planting trees. He knows lots of people there."

Sipping her coffee, Sandy studied Angela. "I can tell you are drawn to him, Angela, and I have no doubt that he is very knowledgeable about the country. I don't want to pry. Just be careful you don't get hurt."

Ambivalent, Angela resented Sandy's prying, but at the same time she admired her friend's candor, as uneasy as it made her feel. Could it be the guilt she felt for even entertaining the idea of spending more time with Liam in the Bajo Lempa? He had said he would follow her there.

As they walked out of the *pupuseria,* Sandy hugged Angela. "You do remember, we're leaving tomorrow at seven a.m. sharp. It's a long ride, and we have a busy next two weeks ahead. I suggest you get some sleep tonight."

"Don't worry," Angela said. "I'll be ready to go, on time, tomorrow morning." Angela glanced at her watch, remembering she had promised to meet Liam at their "secret spot" on the beach at ten. "I have to go now, but I'll see you later, perhaps on the beach. *Ciao.*"

"*Adios,*" Sandy said. "See you later."

Angela remembered how she was not only falling in love with Liam, but with the country. How infectious were its sights, sounds, and smells. Everywhere people were engaged in surviving. Men carried produce on their backs or firewood on their heads. Young girls, barely past childhood, dressed in cotton skirts and tight-fitting T-shirts, carried babies wrapped in colorful *rebozos* on their hips. Boys in jeans and baseball caps sold everything from wood to coconuts. Everyone worked from dawn to dusk. People smiled, talked and jostled with good nature. Pickups, taxis, and mini-buses filled with passengers passed and honked at one another.

She could never forget their last day together on the beach in La Liberdad, before she had to leave with the brigade for their work project in the Bajo Lempa. They met in a more secluded area under a deserted *palapa* they had found the first day they were there. Liam had a surprise for her.

"You said you had always wanted to ride horseback on the beach, didn't you?" asked Liam.

Angela nodded, remembering her love of horses as a young girl. Her parents could never afford to buy one for her, but her best friend sometimes took her for a ride on hers. What did this deliciously mysterious man now have up his sleeve? "Well, I found you a horse." He pointed to a man standing off to one side, a shaggy straw hat pushed back on his head. He was holding a rope that was attached to a handmade bridle looped around the most sorry-looking specimen of a horse Angela had ever seen. She almost laughed out loud, but then, on second thought, decided that might be rude.

"Oh, what a surprise," Angela said.

"Go ahead," Liam said. "The *señor* will lead you

down the beach, and when you feel you're ready to go on your own, just go for it."

Angela walked toward the old man, greeted him and carefully stepped up on his interlaced hands, as he helped her onto the worn and frayed blanket thrown across the horse's back. The horse looked so skinny and malnourished that she feared he might collapse under her weight. She looked back over her shoulder as they walked toward the surf. Liam smiled and waved.

"*Buen viaje!*"

After a brief saunter, Angela motioned to the guide that she was fine and could continue on her own. She certainly didn't feel threatened by this sickly looking animal, and was sure he didn't have the ability to lope. She just let the old nag plod along down the beach, hardly believing that she was actually riding a horse. Angela turned after some meters and came back, feeling too guilty to burden the animal any longer.

The old man smiled and said, "*No, está OK. Adelante.*"

She had seen Liam slip the man some money and felt it was now a matter of saving the man's pride, so she continued in the other direction a while longer, then feigned tiredness, and returned. The man helped her down from the horse. Liam ran up to greet Angela and they embraced, laughing. He slipped the man a few more coins.

"*Muchas gracias, señores,*" she said to both Liam and the horse's owner.

"*Adios, Señor y Señora,*" said the old man. He nodded, tipping his weathered straw hat again and took the reins, leading his beast of burden down the beach to find another willing customer.

Angela and Liam watched as the man disappeared down the beach, pulling his sorry specimen of a horse behind him.

"We're the privileged ones," Liam said, "staying in our hotel with its gated beach. This poor devil lives in a nearby village where man and beast never seem to have quite enough to eat. The hotel allows him to bring his horse down here to make what he can from the unsuspecting tourists."

"Their poverty is obvious," said Angela. "How do they continue to be hopeful? It's a good reminder, when I'm at home, of how little others have in the world. I think about it sometimes, but then go on merrily consuming and enjoying the benefits of our developed country."

"Don't be too hard on yourself," Liam said. "At least you're here trying to make a little dent for change, trying to do something to help. By that very act you're showing your compassion. Remember, it's not only the large acts of magnanimity that count. We can't all be Bill Gates. Each small act is like a grain of sand. That's what Rutilio always tells me. You and I are just a small part of a bigger whole. It all counts."

Angela looked into Liam's eyes and saw the sincerity with which he spoke.

"C'mon, let's go for a run on the beach since you didn't exactly get your run for my money with the horse," said Liam. He grabbed Angela's hand and they ran until they were out of breath, laughing, as they collapsed on the hot sand.

During the day, Liam told Angela how he had

met Father Rutilio in the US during the war, when he spoke at Liam's liberal Catholic parish in Boston. He explained that after the Peace Accords were signed, he and Father Rutilio returned to El Salvador together to offer humanitarian assistance to the small villages in the Bajo Lempa, which had suffered from the war, devastated by massacres and dislocation of the people. He had been coming to El Salvador for the past eight years. He stopped himself in the midst of a long soliloquy: "Oh, sorry, you don't want to hear all of this …"

"Yes, Liam. I do," said Angela. "Please go on."

Liam looked directly into her eyes with his disarming smile, and reached for her hand, interlacing his fingers with hers.

"Yeah, well, as I said, after that first talk Father Rutilio presented at our parish, I was truly taken with his charismatic personality and his stories of his country. Admittedly, I had been looking for a project to sink my teeth into. My electrical contracting firm no longer grabbed me, and I had a good team who could pretty much run things on their own. I guess I was going through a sort of midlife crisis," under his breath, Liam said, "At least, that's what my wife, Mary, called it."

Angela felt awkward at the mention of his wife, and slipped her hand out of his. She began to draw pictures in the sand. "You haven't mentioned her before—I guess I thought you were single."

"I'm married, but we aren't in love anymore; we often live separately. She's not well though, so I try to stay near and help her with the serious stuff."

Angela wasn't sure what that meant and didn't really

want to know more now. For a few moments, they were quiet and just watched the surf, allowing its sounds to fill the empty spaces between them.

Finally, Angela said "Go on. I really want to hear more about what you've been doing in El Salvador."

"I've continued to make annual treks down here hauling bicycles—the *campesinos* in the Bajo Lempa use the wheels for their water pumps, and sometimes the good ones are kept for just getting around. Few people can afford a vehicle, let alone the gas to run it. I brought down all sorts of stuff. I made sure it was what the people could use. I still do it, and now Rutilio is getting me more involved helping with projects in the villages of Bajo Lempa. I like bringing the pickups down and then leaving them for the people to use. I usually fly home for a few months and then return."

Angela was impressed with Liam's efforts to help the Salvadorans.

"Liam, I'm truly grateful for all the information about the area you've shared with me. I hope we'll connect in the Bajo Lempa somehow, but I feel a bit uneasy about where our relationship is heading. We are both married, and I'm traveling with people who know that about me. I must be discreet."

Liam smiled. "Don't worry, I know that. I, too, want to preserve our self-respect, but we can't hold back the river."

Not quite sure what that meant, and maybe not wanting to know, Angela lay down on the blanket Liam had brought, shielding her eyes with her arm from the sun. She was getting good at rationalizing her growing feelings for Liam—perhaps, she told herself, it was a kind of providence of the heart. Liam lay down next to her. Their hands touched, and the two were quiet for a while, leaving each to his or her own thoughts.

"Let's just enjoy our short journey together while we have the time," Liam said.

Angela had a vivid memory of their last night together, when they managed to steal some time for one night at the hotel in La Liberdad, awash in passion. Now as she thought about it, and how guilty she felt afterwards, she remembered vowing that David and the girls would never know. It would remain her secret. She had carried her guilt around like a stone in her heart, heavy and unyielding. It had weighed her down for months after her return from that first trip to El Salvador, whenever she made love to David.

As more years passed, memories of Liam became just a sliver of thought from time to time, disappearing as quickly as they came.

On that last night together, they had walked on the beach in the moonlight. After a quick swim in the ocean, they had made love and Angela was torn between reluctance and desire.

Funny, she thought, how when you are on a trip, far from those who inhabit your daily life—it is as if you are given a clean slate, where you can rewrite the script—for just a little while. She teased herself into feeling this "freedom" with Liam, on the beach where the tide had risen and wiped the sand clean of all previous marks. It allowed for certain self-delusions. The magic of mutual attraction could not be stopped. They were drawn to each other as a magnet is to metal. Much of it, she rationalized, was their common interest in helping the people with their struggle for justice in an unjust world.

Now, ten years later, was it an accident of fate, or God's will, that they should meet again? She didn't know, but she wanted to take full advantage of this fortuitous reunion with Liam. As she waited for Liam to return to the table, she fluffed up her hair and smoothed her skirt. She hoped he wouldn't notice the wrinkles she had acquired over the years since their first meeting.

The Bajo Lempa
El Salvador 2000

"May I get you something, *Señora*?" The voice of the young waiter caught Angela's attention by surprise, as she sat under the canopy of the jacaranda trees and listened to the sounds of tropical birds, Latin music in the background and the soft chirping of the tree frogs.

"*Sí, una cervesa, por favor.*" A cold beer is just what she needed.

"*Sí, Señora.* I'll be right back."

Angela's mind wandered. She was looking forward to seeing Adriana and her family again after all these years of separation. She had lived with Adriana and her family for two weeks, in the year 2000, while planting mangroves along the coast near their village. How well she recalled the details of that time spent in the Bajo Lempa.

When the brigade first arrived in the Bay of Jiquilisco, Angela could see in the distance a small isthmus where the mangroves had been devastated by the pounding of hurricanes and the desperate bombing the fishermen did for a day's catch. She learned later that the NGO, with the help of the villagers, was trying to stop this practice. The mangroves were an important resource for the fisheries.

The mayor of the small village arrived and introduced some of the villagers and fishermen who would be taking them out to the mangrove area. Standing by were six women wearing aprons over neat cotton dresses; some had small children clutching their mothers' legs, as they looked with curiosity at the strangers who came to help them. One of the women reminded Angela of her daughters back in Seattle. The two women smiled at each other while the mayor explained to the group that they were to meet again at the community center the next morning for an orientation on planting the mangroves. A local agronomist, supported by the NGO, would be there to train them.

"Now it's time to introduce you to your host families," he said, motioning for the six women to step up beside him, while the translator explained to the group what was happening.

As each woman was introduced they were paired up with one or two of the brigade members. Soon it was Angela's turn, and the mayor turned to the young woman who had smiled at her. The mayor introduced them, and explained that everyone could now go back to their host family's houses where they would be staying.

Adriana walked up to Angela. "Hello, Angela. I'm

happy to meet you. She spoke a bit of broken English, rare for a Salvadoran woman in this area, where most didn't have an education beyond sixth grade.

"*Igualmente,*" Angela said. She was proud that she remembered the word, commonly used in introductions, she had learned in her Spanish class.

The two women shook hands, and Adriana motioned her to follow. As they walked along the beach, Adriana explained a little about the village. Most of the villagers lived off the small plots of land they had in the surrounding area, and some worked at the local shrimp farm and fished from the bay. The children attended a nearby school. Angela could see them as they came home now in the late afternoon, trailed by cows arriving from the fields. She smiled at a lanky boy with long legs, passing her on his burro. His feet almost touched the dirt road, as he prodded a calf along with a stick. The air was filled with smoke as women prepared food over wood fires and men in straw hats or baseball caps carried fishing nets up the beach to home.

The two women arrived at Adriana's house, a typical drab-gray, one-room concrete-block structure with a corrugated roof and a porch topped with palm fronds. Two colorful hammocks were strung across the porch. A young girl languidly swung in one, her leg draped over the side. She looked up from the paper she was reading and smiled shyly at Angela.

"*Hola,*" she said.

"*Hola,*" Angela replied. "What's your name?"

"Sofia. I'm Adriana's sister."

Angela smiled. "*Mucho gusto.* I'm happy to meet

you, Sofia. My name is Angela."

"*Mucho gusto*," Sofia said, and went back to her reading. Motioning to Angela to follow, Adriana showed her where the outhouse was located down a pathway behind the house. As they walked back, Angela saw an older woman patting tortillas between her hands and stoking a fire under a large, flat metal pan. A toddler played in the dirt beside her. As Adriana and Angela approached, the little girl looked up and ran toward Adriana, who leaned down to pick her up.

"Mama, mama!" Mother and child hugged each other with affection, as Adriana pointed to Angela:

"*Mi chulita,* this is my new friend, Angela. Say hello to her." Adriana introduced the child to their guest. "Angela, this is my daughter, Cici."

"*Hola.*" The little girl looked down with shyness and cast her eyes back at her grandmother. Adriana's mother came forward with a broad smile. She reached out her hand to grasp Angela's.

"*Mi nombre es Isabel*" Adriana's mother said. She withdrew her hand to her apron pocket as quickly as she had offered it. Her shyness was evident. Her short, small frame was bent from the backbreaking work of gathering and cutting wood for the cooking fires, helping Adriana's father with the small farm they had, and preparing the meals for the family.

Angela nodded with a smile. *"Mucho gusto."*

Adriana proceeded to tell Angela about her family and their daily routine. She showed her the hammock, next to hers, where she would sleep for the two weeks she would be in Jiquilisco.

"You can join us on the porch at night. My papa likes to play his guitar and sometimes our friends stop by to talk and tell us about their day," said Adriana. "You'll have to excuse my papa. He likes to tell stories of the war, about Romero, the archbishop who spoke to the people with his homilies every week over the radio, and gave them courage."

"I have a lot to learn about the history of your country," said Angela.

Adriana explained that her husband, Jorge, like so many of the other young men in the village, had "crossed over" to *El Norte*, the States, to find work in order to send monthly remittances back to his family.

"Before Cici was born, I spent a year in the states with Jorge. I was very frightened to cross over. Many of our people die trying to make the crossing, either from the heat of the desert and no water, or just from the terrible trip north through Mexico. If they make it over, the *migras,* the name we call the border patrol agents, stop them and they are thrown into big buildings where they are held for days—I think you call them detention centers. For us, they are like prisons and we are ashamed to be treated like criminals, just because we need work. I worked in the states picking strawberries and other fruits in the fields on the central California coast. That's where I learned a little bit of English—from a young *gringa* girl my age. She was the daughter of the landowner, a Mexican immigrant whose father went to the states many years ago, worked hard and eventually was able to buy his own land and start a farm. He was kind to us."

Angela listened, reminded of how often she had

heard these stories of the difficulties the immigrants had surviving, not only the border crossing, but life in the US, making too little money, maybe just enough for some food and a shared room in a rundown motel or apartment building. She remembered when she and David once delivered mattresses to migrant workers, who picked apples in Washington.

Adriana continued: "When I learned I was pregnant, Jorge and I came home to the Bajo Lempa. He soon realized that he had to go back to find work so he could support our family. I begged him not to go, but things were tough. Like most of my friends who have husbands, fathers and brothers in the States, we all try to keep positive and hope that they are fine. I want Jorge to come home so Cici will know her father."

"I can understand that," said Angela, feeling empathy for this young wife and mother whose fate was not hers to choose.

"I have to go and help now with the cooking," said Adriana, "so make yourself comfortable and I'll see you in a little while. We usually eat about six o'clock before dark. Adriana went off towards the small lean-to kitchen where her mother and Cici were engaged in the friendly chatter of a grandmother and grandchild."

Angela dug down into her backpack for a towel to wipe the sweat from her body. She pulled off her shirt and found a lightweight tank top to pull on, hoping she'd feel cooler soon. The heat was sweltering that night. Angela had a hard time sleeping, but as dawn approached it cooled down, and she had to pull a blanket up around her. She awoke to the clucking of the chickens, pecking the ground around the casita. Adriana's mother, Isabel, had received a micro-financed loan from the NGO. With the loan she had bought a half dozen hens and a rooster, then sold the eggs they produced, and raised the baby chicks to sell to her neighbors. When Isabel spoke about her business Angela could hear the pride in her voice.

The aromas of the freshly made coffee and *pupusas,* which came from the lean-to, enticed Angela to the breakfast table. After eating and before leaving to plant mangroves with her NGO group, Angela pushed the old wooden chair back from the table, got up and cleared her plates to the lean-to, washing them out in the big concrete *pila*, a fixture in every Salvadoran outdoor kitchen, where water is stored for brushing teeth, bathing and washing clothes and dishes.

"*Hasta luego.* I'll see you later," said Angela, as she set off to meet her group of volunteers on the beach.

After greeting each other, the brigade climbed into the long, narrow motorized skiffs that whisked them out to the area where they would spend the morning, their feet submerged in mud, poking the "candles," the word for the young mangrove shoots, into the ground, row after row. It was not hard work, but the bugs, and rising heat of the day made it tedious. In the afternoons, after they returned from tree planting, they met with some of the village committees and learned about the other projects supported by the NGO. Angela was impressed that it was local people who directed these, the grassroots coordinating committee made up of representatives from the surrounding communities. They discussed future sustainable environmental projects for the region.

The days passed quickly and by the end of the week Angela felt like a member of Adriana's family. One day, as she came back from planting trees, she heard a familiar voice.

"*Hola!*" someone called out from down the beach.

Angela recognized the voice of Juan, a good friend of the family, as he pulled in on his skiff. He was returning from a run out to where they were still planting more mangroves. She strained to see him from under her broad-brimmed sun hat. They walked toward each other and shook hands. Juan walked with a limp, a reminder of the battles he fought during the war on the side of the National Liberation Front (FMLN), named after their hero, Faribundo Marti. Better known as the *guerillas*, they struggled to gain rights for the peasants of the country, and to right the injustices of the hundreds of years since the Spanish conquistadors.

"*Que tal?*" Juan asked.

"*Bien, muy bien.*" Angela wiped the sweat from her brow and swatted a fly with her hat. "I heard about the party Adriana's having tonight for Jesús' birthday. Are you coming?

"Sí," said Juan. "We're going to the community center afterward. You and your friends are invited to come and watch a DVD your *amiga* from the NGO brought down to us from San Salvador. It's about one of the members of our community, when he was a boy during the war. He now lives in the States. He made this film in memory of his uncle and the rest of his family who were killed. I think it might be sad, but it will help you understand more about our people and our history."

"*Gracias.* I would like to see it," Angela said.

"*Bueno,* see you later." Juan walked off down the beach to his boat.

That evening, they all sat around laughing and joking, on the porch, in front of Adriana's house. They teased Papa about his graying hair. Angela felt sure he wasn't even as old as she was. Age didn't seem to matter to these people. They had other priorities, like putting food on the table, caring for their community, and dealing with the disasters, such as hurricanes and floods, which frequented their small village on the coast almost yearly. Several in the village had been lost in Hurricane Mitch.

"Hey, Angela, you speak better Spanish now. *Bien.*" Adriana's father complimented the progress she had made while staying there.

" *Muchas gracias!* I like to try."

"I understand you marched in memory of Romero, before you came here, Angela. *Que bueno,*" said Jesús. "During the war, thousands of people in our villages were slaughtered or 'disappeared' by the military men from the government. One time, I remember, a whole village near here was wiped out. Soldiers killed the infants first, by beheading and putting their heads on the ends of their bayonets. They said they were saving the future from communists—but we didn't even know what communism was. Most of us couldn't read and write. We listened every week to Romero, who gave us faith and courage to go on."

Angela felt a lump form in her throat at the graphic

description Jésus offered of the offences of the war. She found it hard to hold back tears.

Jesús took up his guitar again and began to strum a tune. The mood changed from the dark memories to a lighter, happier present. Juan and Adriana began to sing along. Cici entertained them, swaying to the rhythm of her grandfather's music. Music seemed to come naturally to these people, their release from day-to-day hardships.

As Angela looked up at the stars, her mind wandered once again to Liam. She had not seen him for a week. She missed him, and wondered if she would see him again. He had promised her he would find her. In another week and a half, she had to leave El Salvador. She knew, what would be, would be, "*Que sera, sera.*"

After Adriana put Cici to bed, she invited her papa to go to the community center with them to see the DVD about the war. "Are you coming, Papa," she asked.

"No, I've had enough of war in my life," Jesús said. He looked down as if conjuring up more unpleasant memories. "But you go ahead, Adriana, with the others. It's good for you to understand what happened in this country, so it never happens again. You were only small children. Thank God you were spared."

Angela and Adriana, Juan and Sofia walked down the dirt road. It was dark except for the stars lighting their way. They could hear the sounds of the night, the cicadas in the surrounding vegetation, the hum of neighbors talking softly on their front porches, the music from the few radios in the community. On the way, they stopped for Sandy, Jake, and a few of the others in the brigade.

As they approached a large concrete-block structure, where community meetings were held, Angela saw several people gathered there. When they entered the center, she hung back with Sandy and Jake, as the Salvadorans greeted one another, and hands flew up in high fives. The lights went down, and the black and white numbers of the DVD trailer appeared on the screen. There was tension and scuffling of nervous feet in the room. Then, as the title, *Innocent Voices,* appeared, everyone became silent.

The next hour-and-a-half was filled with soft sniffling sounds from the spectators, as they witnessed the incredulous truths of the war in El Salvador. Some slipped quietly out the back door. It was hard to watch this story of torment and sadness, of how the national armies came to villages and recruited boys as young as twelve to fight in the war against the *guerrillas,* the FMLN. Both sides were guilty. Angela sat silently, stricken by the truth of the film, which showed what she already knew—the history of the US military collaborating in the training of the soldiers, and the US government essentially turning a blind eye to the torture of innocent people in the civil war. Adriana reached over and clasped her hand, and in the soft light of the room, both their faces were wet with tears.

As the film ended, Angela, overwhelmed with emotion and shame, rose and ran out before the lights came on. Adriana followed her and they embraced.

"Mi *hermana,* my sister. I'm so sorry." Angela choked out the words. It was all she could say to the young woman whose family had been so kind to her.

How could she explain that her fellow citizens had been ignorant of what was happening? But there was no need to explain. Adriana was younger than Angela's daughters, and yet seemed to have the understanding and depth of a person many years beyond her age. The two women just stood in their embrace.

As they separated, Angela felt the presence of another and looked up suddenly into the eyes of Liam. Had he been standing on the steps watching and waiting for her to notice him? She fell into his arms weeping. He held her for a few minutes while she gathered her composure.

The others slipped out into the night. Only Adriana remained, and Angela sensed her confusion about who this man was, and whether or not she should leave them or wait for Angela.

"It's okay, Adriana," Angela said. "He is my *amigo*, Liam. Liam, this is Adriana."

"*Mucho gusto*. I think you're the man who brought us the bicycles last year—isn't that right?" said Adriana.

"Nice to meet you, too, Adriana," said Liam. "And you're right. I'm the one who brought the bicycles down last year. I hope your friends are finding them helpful. I know your father is using the wheels from one of them to pump water from his well. That's a clever innovation." Then in Spanish, Liam explained to Adriana not to worry, that after he and Angela had a few minutes to talk he would accompany her back to the house.

"There's no need to wait," he said.

"*Bien. Buenes noches*," Adriana said. She met Juan and the others at the foot of the stairs and they disappeared into the darkness.

Now, as he pulled back from Angela, Liam gazed into her eyes and asked, "Are you OK?"

Angela managed a smile as she wiped her face and blew her nose. "Oh, Liam, it was so sad, the film, I mean, and then I never expected to see you here. I'm so glad you arrived."

"I told you I would find you, but I didn't anticipate you would be drowning in tears. Let's take a walk." He pulled her close, slipped his arm around her waist, and the two took off towards the beach. Angela hoped no one in the village, or in the brigade, would see them. Strolling toward the beach, they could hear the gentle and soothing sound of the surf. The light of the moon hung over them, like a fine fragment of silk.

Liam stopped for a moment, turned toward Angela, drew her close and leaned down to give her a long, deep kiss. Her heart pounded. She could feel the fire between her legs.

"Oh, Liam, what are we going to do?"

"I'm not sure yet. But for now, we're going to enjoy this." He continued to hold her, caressing her hips and pressing his lips to hers, exploring her mouth with his tongue.

She knew it was time to head back to Adriana's *casita*. She pulled away from Liam's embrace, and offered an apology.

"I really shouldn't worry them. I must say good night. Where are you staying? Can we see each other tomorrow?"

"I'm staying just up the road in a small shack owned by one of Father Rutilio's friends," said Liam. If I'm not being too presumptuous, I'll stop by in the morning for coffee. I know how good it is here!"

"Oh, you're welcome, I'm sure. I'll be glad to see you."

Angela slipped her arm in Liam's, and he walked her back to the *casita*, kissing her good night before heading for his pickup, parked just up the dirt road. As he walked away, Angela's heart was filled with a mixture of joy, sorrow, and guilt, all melded together into an alloy of emotions she no longer recognized nor could control.

The ubiquitous roosters crowed early, and whether she liked it or not, Angela finally succumbed to the fact that it was time to roll out of her hammock and face the day. She quietly slipped back behind the house to the outhouse, then dressed and came around to the outdoor kitchen, which was more like what she called a camp kitchen at home. Adriana's mother was already patting the *pupusas* between her hands with the familiar sound of *slap, slap*. As each small circle of corn flour dough was ready to fill, Isabel scooped up some frijoles and cheese, placed it on one pupusa and pressed another over it, pinching the sides together. She then plopped it onto the big round metal plate, called a *comal*, which rested on the grill. The air was filled with the smell of burning wood, animal fat and pupusas. Angela could hear the cowbells, as the cattle were led out to the neighboring fields, and the village awakened to a crescendo of familiar sounds.

The aroma of freshly made coffee filled Angela's nostrils and added to the sensations, which would forever remind her of mornings in El Salvador.

She looked up as she heard Liam's pickup approach and watched as he parked, got out and walked up to the porch with that sensual gait his long legs allowed, greeting everyone in Spanish.

"Buenos días, amigas!"

Adriana introduced him to her mother as *"Angela's amigo."* He was invited to have a seat and join them for coffee. In the presence of Liam, the air seemed electric to Angela. She hoped it wouldn't be too obvious to the others that she was falling in love.

Saying Good-bye
El Salvador 2000

Towards the end of the week, Liam managed to get Angela aside. Their brigade was leaving early the following morning to go back to San Salvador, where they would catch their planes for the States. Angela knew they needed to talk. It had been hard the last few days to find enough time together alone and now she didn't know where this was all leading. Would he beg her to stay? Could she? She didn't know.

Liam and Angela walked down the beach away from the crowds of people. After moments of silence with just the sound of their shoes' heels brushing the sand, Liam started.

"Is there any chance you could stay over an extra week instead of returning to the States with the brigade?" asked Liam. "I want to invite you to a peace conference that Father Rutilio has organized in San Salvador. There will be people from all over Central America attending.

It'll be interesting." He stopped, turned, and looked directly into Angela's eyes. "We might even steal some time together, if you could come."

Angela felt her skin tingle with the thought of more intimate time with Liam, but tempted as she was, she knew she couldn't stay. David's birthday was coming up and the family was expecting her to be there for it.

"Oh, Liam, you really shouldn't tempt me. I can't stay. There is too much at stake and I don't see any real chance for a future to our relationship—do you?"

Liam looked down at his feet with chagrin. "No, I guess you're right. But you can't blame a guy for trying, as the old cliché goes."

Angela knew she had a persuasive nature—and if she tried to convince David of a good reason for staying she would probably win, but it was her daughters that she thought of now. Besides, as she had just said to Liam, there wasn't much of a future for them. Neither felt ready to throw away their "other lives."

Liam interrupted her thoughts. "Well, at least let us escape to La Liberdad for a last night's fling? Your plane, you said, doesn't leave until two in the afternoon tomorrow. If you can say your good-byes to the brigade and Adriana's family now, we can leave in an hour."

"I'm not sure, they'll understand my early departure," Angela equivocated.

Liam looked at her, with temptation in his eyes, and pulled her close. Without saying a thing, he convinced her of her own desire.

Changing her mind, realizing how much she wanted to be with him for this last time they may ever have,

Angela said, "Fine, I'll tell Sandy I'm leaving and they won't have to wait for me tomorrow morning. I'll get to the airport on my own. The gossip will fly but I never have been one to worry about that."

"I like your spunk." said Liam. "I'll get my things, and pick you up in an hour at Adriana's."

Angela went in search of Sandy. She found her packing backpacks and boxes into the yellow bus. She approached her, hesitant at first, and then said.

"Sandy, I really want to see La Liberdad one more time. Liam has offered to take me there and then to the airport tomorrow. I'll meet up with all of you there."

Sandy tried to hide her surprise and put her hand on Angela's shoulder. For a minute it seemed she didn't know what to say. With some hesitation she offered a reply.

"I just hope you know what you're doing. As I said in La Liberdad, I don't want you to be hurt. You've done some good work here, and everybody likes you. For that matter, they like Liam, too. He was a great help planting the mangroves the other day. He's a hard worker. It's your choice. We'll see you tomorrow at the airport." As she said this, she reached down and picked up her backpack, smiled at Angela, and continued to load the bus for the trip back to San Salvador.

When Angela returned to Adriana's house, it was hard to say *adios* to her and the family, which had been so kind to her. She explained that she wanted to see La Liberdad one more time, and Liam offered to take her there. She knew it was a weak excuse for her early departure, but also knew that these people were non-judgmental, and that one day she would return, a promise she made as much to herself as to them. Liam pulled up in his pickup and they took off for their last time together under the Salvadoran sun.

Angela waved to Adriana and Cici: "*Adios, amigas*. I shall return."

The afternoon and night were not long enough. It was a breathless time, the first they had with any real privacy. After a quick swim in the ocean, they knew what each wanted the most. They returned to their small motel room.

With their lovemaking there was no inhibition or shyness; it was as though they already knew the feel of each other's bodies and could explore with abandon. As Angela slipped out of her wet bathing suit, knowing Liam was taking in every inch of her, she quivered, and he pulled her to him. She caressed his back and let her hands slide down to his buttocks, while he explored her breasts and the warmth between her legs. She grew wet, as he gently pulled her to the bed and soon they were wrapped in a full body embrace, as if melded into one. Without hesitation, they savored each other's touch and smells, and delighted in all of it. Being with Liam cast a new lens on her life, and it showed her a more open, joyful self, less afraid, less wary of life's unknowns, less in control than she had ever been.

After making love, they talked about the impossibility of their ever reconnecting. Liam could not leave his wife, who suffered from MS, which made her dependent and needing care. Angela, too, doubted she could leave

David. They had been together so long she felt it would be too much for David and their daughters to bear. They had built a secure life, one her parents never had. To divorce now would undermine all she had worked for. She had grandchildren and she could not bear to alienate her daughters or them. She fantasized for a moment: *What if she and Liam could just walk away from their former lives, re-meet here in Latin America, continue to help people together, maybe even form their own NGO and deepen their newfound love for each other?* No, it was not that simple. Too many people would be hurt. Liam read her thoughts.

"No, sweetheart, it's *not* simple. We must not spoil this time we have with 'what if's.' If you ever need me, I'll come if I can, but for now, I think we'll not see each other for a long while, all the more reason to embrace this moment."

Angela thought: *Oh, Liam, why do you have to be so good and so wise? Damn you.* But in the next breath, they were kissing, as they lie in a close embrace, warmth gliding up their legs under the cool sheets of the small bed.

Angela remembered that night well, their hasty ride to the airport the next day, and their final good-by, as she said *Adios* and lugged her suitcase down the ramp and onto the plane for home.

Back Together
El Salvador 2010

Angela sensed Liam's presence and looked up. He slid into the seat across from her, a confident smile on his lips, the air between them electric, as they looked deep into each other's eyes.

"Hey—where were you?" Liam waved his hand in front of her eyes. "You looked lost in thought."

"Oh— I was thinking about when we met and my first trip to the Bajo Lempa," Angela said, with an almost shy smile, her cheeks turning hot. Fortunately, her olive complexion usually hid a blush. "When we parted, I really didn't think I'd ever see you again."

The waiter approached the table and Liam ordered another beer for Angela, and a lemonade for himself, then looked directly at Angela, his intense blue eyes piercing hers.

"I've missed you. So many times I've thought about you and wondered where you were, what you were doing.

I've longed to hear your voice—feel your touch. Tell me what you're doing here now."

As uncomfortable as it sometimes made her feel, Liam's directness was what drew her to him in the first place. There was never any beating around the bush or coyness with him. He was frank and to the point.

Angela looked down and thought about their lustful behavior so many years ago in El Salvador. She returned to his questioning eyes and cleared her throat.

"Well, a lot has happened since we last saw each other. I'm here on a sentimental journey. My husband died a year ago, and I wanted to go back to the places where we worked together in Central America, when we were younger. I visited for a week in Nicaragua and then came here to El Salvador. David never got here but, as you well know, I did and had wonderful memories. It is here I started to discover a new sense of meaning for my life. I guess I wanted to find that again." She paused. "Never knowing I would also find you. "

"I'm sorry to hear about your husband," said Liam. "I understand what you must have gone through. My wife died five years ago." He paused as if waiting for her reaction. "I wanted to contact you, but then, I didn't want to cause problems with you and David."

Angela sighed. *Damn, why didn't he call?* At the same moment, she felt relieved now that she wouldn't have to be "the other woman" committing a transgression against his marriage. She had lived with enough guilt for the past ten years.

Liam leaned toward her. In the background they both heard the soft sounds and rhythms of *Besame*

Mucho. Angela felt the urge to dance, and moved her feet under the table to the rhythm of the music. Her toes in their bare sandals touched Liam's. She continued her story, nervously twisting a strand of her long hair with one finger. She laid the other hand on Liam's, which rested on the table

"Well, you know the love I found here. For the Latinos, I mean. I wanted to return to renew that passion. I started in Mexico and then traveled by bus to Guatemala and Nicaragua. Afterwards, I came here to San Salvador, and when I heard that Rutilio would be speaking at the cathedral, I arranged to stay over an extra day before going to the Bajo Lempa to visit our friends there. I'm sure you remember Adriana and her family?"

"Of course, I have seen them many times over the years," Liam said.

Strange, Angela thought. In her letters, Adriana, had never mentioned seeing Liam again.

"Well, I'll spend a week there and then fly back to Seattle. That's enough about me. How about you? What have you been doing the last ten years?"

Liam paused. "Well, I continued to make my annual treks to bring pickups and bikes down to our *amigos,* and did whatever I could to lend a hand in their struggle for more sustainable lives, however small it was—always too little." He said this with his usual self-deprecating modesty. "In the meantime, Mary and I nearly divorced, but managed to glue our relationship back together. Most of it was my fault. She was a great lady. Unfortunately, she didn't want to travel down here with me. I can't blame her; she was ill much of the time." Then, as an afterthought, he added, "… and of course, you were always on the back of my mind."

Liam's forthrightness touched Angela. She appreciated his honesty about his problematic marriage. Somehow, though, it did not erase her guilt. She remembered how they had both trespassed their marriage vows, unable to resist their mutual attraction in this exotic environment. Could that have been the cause of Liam and Mary's problems? Angela wondered if Mary ever knew about her. She tried to rationalize that it was just a brief encounter between two strangers drawn to each other out of sheer lust. She could empathize with the marital problems Liam described. She, too, had found it hard to stay with her husband after her return from El Salvador. She was determined to redeem herself, to sustain the marriage and try to reignite the flame that was once there with David—for the girls and the grandchildren. They managed to have some good times, before he became ill. Angela looked down at her napkin in her lap, scrunching it as if to squeeze out the sad memories.

Liam continued, "Mary's MS got progressively worse, and much of my time was spent taking care of her as she became more and more physically and mentally impaired."

"Oh, I'm truly sorry to hear that. It must have been difficult." Angela felt ashamed at how lame this sounded. She saw the sadness in Liam's eyes and knew he had respected his wife. She understood, from a deep place of empathy, as she had felt much the same for David when she cared for him during his last year, after his diagnosis of prostate cancer. Love, she discovered, can blossom again when there is need. As she thought about this, she brushed her hand across her damp cheeks. She hoped Liam didn't notice.

"No, she was a good patient," Liam continued. "My big problem was my relentless desire to get back to El Salvador as much as I could. I fought an inner battle and didn't do very well hiding it from her."

Angela heard the "guilt" that Liam's Irish Catholic upbringing fostered in him since his childhood, just like hers. She didn't really believe half the stuff in the church's teachings, now, but the remnants of it were still there. She remembered conversations they had about religion many years ago, when they first met. They talked about the guilt they often experienced. Now, she realized, for her, it was not the fault of her religious upbringing but more a fear of letting down those she loved. Faithfulness to her loved ones was more important to her. She felt torn.

Liam continued, "In a way, I can't help but think she died to free me to follow my wicked ways and restless spirit."

"Restless spirit, yes, but not wicked ways." Angela allowed the warmth she felt for him to seep into her voice as she reached out again to lay both hands on his. They looked at each other for a long time, as they remembered a shared past.

"Well, now, I'm doing a couple of projects in El Salvador," Liam went on. "I'm an informal caretaker of an orphanage. When Father Rutilio returned to El Salvador after the war, he found many destitute children who had lost families during the violence. He started the orphanage in Suchitoto, before getting involved in the Bajo Lempa communities a few years later. Recently, he asked if I could help there. Of course most of those kids have long since grown up, but there are always more who flow into the orphanage, even if they have living families. The families often cannot feed them, so Sister Agnes takes them in."

"Who's she?" asked Angela.

"She's Father Rutilios side-kick, so to speak, an amazing woman. She's been in El Salvador since before the Civil War and is dedicated to these people. I'll tell you more about her later. I hope you can meet her. My job now is to bring humanitarian aid supplies down to them from our church in Boston, and to help maintain the physical structure of an old convent in Suchitoto, which houses the orphans. I'm just the gofer and the handyman."

Angela suspected Liam was being far too modest about the helpful role he was performing at the orphanage.

Liam continued, "My other focus is helping get women and children over the border to rejoin their husbands who crossed over and are working in the States. Ever since Congress debated HR-4437, during the Bush years, things have not been good for our amigos. When they try to cross to the other side, many die. The immigration debate is heating up again. It's harder and harder for the families here, as it is for their loved ones, the so-called *illegales*, there. Father Rutilio spends half his time in Washington lobbying for reform of immigration laws, and I'm his backup man."

Angela was shocked, to hear that Liam was involved in the illegal transport of immigrants, even if his goal to reunite families was a good one. It bothered her, and she looked at Liam with more than a little consternation, withdrew her hands from his and crossed her arms on the table as she leaned in and gazed straight at him.

"Are you saying, Liam, that you transport poor Salvadorans over the border into our country? That's illegal. You could go to jail. That's almost as bad as being a *coyote*. Not only that, those who cross over often suffer more, having to hide from the immigration authorities." Angela couldn't keep the judgment out of her voice.

Liam hesitated. He reached across the table and gave her arms a gentle squeeze.

"I knew this would be hard for you, Angela. It is a debatable subject, but can we postpone the discussion for a while, until after we've had some time to really enjoy our reunion? I hope you will give me a chance to explain why and how I'm doing this. I also hope that I'll be able to convince you to stay in El Salvador with me, and help at the orphanage."

Angela relaxed some. "I apologize. I know I sounded judgmental. I'm concerned for your safety. I do want to hear more." Angela cautioned herself not to prejudge before she knew all the facts. David often accused her of that. "You're so opinionated and always ready to pick an argument," he would say. "Yes, let's wait and discuss this later," Angela said to Liam.

Liam let out a long sigh: "I hope we can find a way to finally be together."

Angela squirmed in her seat, apprehensive about

what was going to happen next. She cast her eyes about the patio and garden. Looking up at Liam, she said, "Ten years is a long time to be separated. I started to write to you once, but then I didn't send the letter for fear your feelings might have changed. I also didn't want to compromise your relationship with your wife. Now, once again we seem to be thrown together."

Liam laughed and reached for her hand, breaking the serious mood she cast over their reunion.

"What's most important now, is that the one I had given up hope of ever seeing again, is really right here, sitting opposite me, and we're holding hands. If you don't move, I may have to get up and embrace you. I propose that we do not waste any more time," said Liam. God knows we may not have a great deal more."

Angela nodded her head in agreement. She reflected on how many dear friends she had lost in the past two years to illnesses that crept up suddenly, just like David's. At sixty-three, it was time to *carpe diem* as she and her friends often said to each other.

"Let's not talk about the future now," Liam said. We need time to rediscover each other. We need to spend the next two days, before you leave, getting reacquainted. Angela liked how Liam insinuated their spending the night together.

After lunch, Angela and Liam made their way to the Open Market in the center of San Salvador. They strolled among its colorful stalls, where Salvadorans hawked their wares, and the aroma of cumin and chilies, from the crackling fires of the cast-iron grills, filled the air. There was a continual hum of human conversation. As parents strolled through the *mercado,* children laughed and darted in and out around their legs. Hungry and haggard-looking stray dogs, rib cages pressed against their thin flanks, lay sprawled on the dirty concrete walkways or approached with begging eyes.

Tired after a long walk, they came back to the hostel, forgot about dinner, and slipped discreetly up the stairs to Angela's room. There, it didn't take long to rediscover what they had missed in the intervening years. The two were still drawn to each other like moths to light. The one sure thing in Angela's life was her desire to be with Liam, now and forever. She dreaded the fact that in two days she would be leaving him again to continue her pilgrimage to see her friends in the Bajo Lempa, and then to return home to Seattle. She didn't know, for sure, where and when they would be together again.

Liam's Invitation
El Salvador 2010

After a night of lovemaking, Angela awoke early. She rolled over, rubbed her eyes and looked at Liam with his day-old grayish beard and mussed up hair. She felt a rush of renewed adoration. Liam was surveying the ceiling, lost in thought. He appeared to be counting the number of seams between the wood planks. All Angela could think about was the wonderful reunion they had the night before.

"Hello, are you there?" Angela ruffled the hair on Liam's chest. "You seem lost in thought this morning, darling. What's on your mind?"

He smiled. "You're on my mind. How can I have more of you?"

"Whoa, didn't you get enough last night?" Angela snuggled up to his warm body and leaned into that crook between his shoulder blade and arm where her head nestled so naturally.

"It was great," Liam said, "but I want you to stay in El Salvador and work in the orphanage with me. That way we could have more time with each other and, also, accomplish what we have both wanted to do for so long, contribute to bettering the lives of our Salvadoran friends."

"What are you suggesting?"

"You would be fabulous with the children," said Liam. "We're worried about the increased gang violence coming in from San Salvador, attracting some of our kids. You could teach art classes and maybe that would engage them enough to stay out of gangs, at least for a while. Do you have to go back to Seattle after your visit to the Bajo Lempa?"

"Yes, I do, and I'm not sure I can accept your invitation. First of all, I'm not confident I would have enough to offer the children," said Angela. At the same time, she was thinking about how she could teach them to work with clay and give them a chance for self-expression. Maybe that would help keep them from joining the gangs. She remembered how in her own town of Seattle, artists had worked with *taggers* to give them more viable and legal means for expression. All this went through her mind, as she lay there next to the man she loved. She knew she wanted to be at his side working in El Salvador, and she had a nagging desire to do something meaningful in what may be the last chapter of her life. Still, she felt some reluctance about making a full commitment to Liam now. After all, they were just getting reacquainted after ten years of separation. Age brought caution.

An even bigger issue was the thought of leaving her daughters. How could she explain to them that she wanted to return to Central America so soon after this trip, and for an indefinite period of time? Even if she decided she could do it, she would have to go home first, get her affairs in order and spend some time with family and friends. Would her grandchildren understand, and could she bear being away from them?

As she mulled over the various possibilities, Liam looked at her with an intense stare. "Hey, where are you? Now, it's you who's lost in thought."

For a few moments, Angela didn't respond but just lay there feeling the warmth of Liam's body next to hers, while the early morning sun crept across the room and over the bed sheets. Liam rose up and leaned on one elbow, looking down at her.

"Angela, you have the abilities and talents to make a difference in these people's lives. I know that. Don't forget, I saw you in action in the Bajo Lempa. You could do art with the orphans. They have so little, and you could bring a gift to their lives, not to mention, to *mine*."

There it was again, that seductive smile and wink. Liam's arguments were convincing, and Angela felt her reservations begin to melt away.

"I first have to return home after my visit in the Bajo Lempa," Angela said with hesitation. "By the way, remember I'm leaving for there tomorrow."

"Fine, I have to wrap up some things here in San Salvador with Father Rutilio," said Liam. "Then I fly back to Boston, where I have a few personal matters to take care of, and also, find another decent truck to bring down. In today's economic climate, it's getting more difficult to find used vehicles to meet the Salvadoran standards for import. The government here does not want us to dump our junk on them, and rightly so. I'll be driving back in a couple of months. I wish you could drive down with me. We'd have quite an adventure. How long do you need to be in Seattle?"

"Oh, Liam, you make it all sound so simple, but, darling, it's not. I'm not sure yet how long I'll be in Seattle. I have to get my house on the market and spend some quality time with my daughters and grandchildren. The past year has been hard on them, adjusting to their dad's death and helping me with paperwork and getting the house in order. Luckily, I have a friend who's a real estate broker. She has promised to handle the house sale for me, but at the very least, I'll need a couple of months to pack up my studio and make sure my galleries are informed that I'm leaving for an indefinite period. As much as I would love to drive down with you, I don't think that's realistic. I probably won't be able to get back to El Salvador until the end of the summer, at the earliest," said Angela, as she imagined the pain of another separation from him.

"Sweetheart, do what you have to do," Liam said. "I can meet you back in San Salvador in August. That's just three months from now. But, promise me you won't stay away from me any longer. We can communicate by e-mail and phone in the meantime."

She loved how Liam "took charge" and made everything sound so easy. In the interim though, she needed time to sort out her feelings. This reunion of theirs had all happened so unexpectedly. Could she commit to him and to the people in El Salvador? Her mind was abuzz with questions and self-doubt colliding with the energy she felt having a new plan for her life.

"Come on. Let's take advantage of another day together before you head off to visit our friends in the Bajo Lempa." Liam jumped up, pulled on his jeans and a T-shirt, then ran his hands through his thinning hair as he made a beeline to the bathroom.

Angela took advantage of his brief absence to get up and pull on her clothes, as she wasn't sure she wanted him to see her wrinkled body too closely in the daylight. As she pulled her cotton shirt over her head, she glanced at her sagging arm skin and looked down at her still slim and muscular legs. Her body had changed a lot over the years, she mused. At least, she still had good legs and a waistline.

Liam emerged. "I'm ready. How about you?"

Angela headed for the bathroom and said over her shoulder, "Just give me ten minutes and I'll be ready."

"That's what I like about you. You never keep a guy waiting—only ten years."

Later that day, they joined Rutilio for lunch at a small café near the old cathedral. When they entered the café, he sat at a small round table in the back conversing with the waiter. He looked up, smiled and waved to Liam and Angela, motioning them to join him. They made their way around the other tables toward his.

"Hola, amigos." Father Rutilio got up and graciously pulled out a chair for Angela. How are you?" He patted

Liam on the back and smiled at Angela, taking her extended hand in his. "How good you could join us, Angela. I'm anxious to hear what you've been doing all these years since Liam first introduced us."

"Oh, not nearly as much as you and Liam, Father Rutilio. I've had my daughters to help and have continued to produce sculptures for my art clientele, but after talking to Liam, it sounds rather mundane compared with the important work you've been doing in El Salvador. By the way, I enjoyed your talk yesterday. I was moved by the stories about your work in building peace and sustainability in the communities throughout Meso America."

"Yes, Angela, it's been gratifying. Please call me Rutilio. You can drop the *Father*."

"Oh, I'm sorry. I'm so used to hearing Liam call you *Father*, that—"

"I can't break him of that habit. Can I, Liam?"

"No, I guess not, Father. It was so engrained in my Catholic upbringing, I still think of you as a priest, *amigo*."

Rutilio smiled "I know, I know."

A waiter approached to take their order and when he turned away, Rutilio leaned toward Angela.

"So, my dear, how long are you planning to stay in El Salvador? I hope we're going to be able to keep you here for a while. Your amigos in the Bajo Lempa miss you."

Angela thought how much she admired this man, and the energy he still emitted at seventy-five years old. She thought back to when they met and remembered she was amazed at how youthful he was. He was full of so much energy it was like Fourth of July sparklers went off every time you were around him. His intelligence and wisdom belied his poor *campesino* childhood with ten siblings, and his story was a fascinating one of self-education and an enlightened career in the Catholic Church. In the seventies, when liberation theology came along, giving the poor and disenfranchised new hope and courage to raise the cry for land reform and change, he was at the forefront. It was priests like him who called the people to action and suffered for it afterward. Many of them were tortured and killed. Rutilio was among those who were tortured. He fled to the U.S. knowing he was on a death list. The threat to the wealthy classes and to the status quo was too much. One could never tell, looking at him now, that death had nearly been Rutilio's fate. He bore no bitterness, and instead, after the Peace Accords, came back to his country and worked at bringing about non-violent reconciliation between the opposing sides in the civil war. As ex-combatants from the right wing military moved into the Bajo Lempa where they now had land, but where they had slaughtered so many, there was fear that another conflict would be ignited. Father Rutilio helped to dampen the fires, and organized the people to work together to improve their lives. While they sat drinking their lemonades, Rutilio told Angela his stories about those times, and about his friend, the Archbishop Romero.

The waiter arrived with their lunch and they continued their conversation.

"We're making progress on many fronts," Rutilio said, "particularly in the Bajo Lempa region where the people are learning new farming techniques to be self-sufficient. Which brings me back to my original question: Are you going to stay with us longer this time? I guess Liam has told you about our project in my old village of Suchitoto, where I first preached liberation theology."

Liam smiled and nudged her leg under the table as if to reassure her.

"Go ahead, Angela, tell him about our plans." Surprised at Liam's presumption that she was committed to returning to El Salvador to join their work at the orphanage, Angela felt uneasy and tried to buy some time before she made her final commitment.

"Yes, Rutilio," Angela said, "Liam has invited me to work with the two of you and help keep the youth from joining gangs. I must admit, it sounds like a good project for me now that my husband has died and I'm a bit freer. But I do have two grown daughters and three grandchildren. It's a big decision for me to leave my home and move to El Salvador."

"Oh, my dear, don't worry, we're not asking you to give up your family, but I know you could contribute much to the orphans. We promise not to keep you too long; well, at least I do." Winking at Liam, he continued, "Liam may have something else in mind."

Angela blushed and wondered how much of their affair Liam had disclosed to Rutilio.

"Yes, I certainly do. I want Angela to join me for as long as she can. I know she has much to offer, and, I have to admit, I like having her around."

"*Bien*, then it's settled. Angela, we'll give you time to clear up your affairs at home, but we'll anxiously await your return. Now let's eat and enjoy this moment together. Can we bow our heads for a moment of thankfulness for this good meal?"

How clever Rutilio was in avoiding any dissonance, Angela thought, as she slightly bowed her head. She had moved so far away from the church since the death of her parents, it was even uncomfortable to say grace, but Rutilio made it seem so natural.

After their lunch, Angela and Liam said good-bye to Rutilio and strolled over to the cathedral to once again admire the beautiful paintings by the Salvadoran artist, Fernando Llort, which graced the façade. Time seemed to be going by too fast. They went back to the hotel, enjoyed a swim and then spent the rest of the day making love and discussing their plans for the future. After dinner on the patio, they turned in early in order to wake in time for Angela to be ready when Juan came to pick her up.

"OK, don't forget our plan, sweetheart," Liam said, as he pulled her close. "I'm counting on you, and the kids in El Salvador are, too. Call me as soon as you get back to Seattle after your visit. Oh, and say *hola* to Adriana and her mother from me, Cici, too. You won't believe, at twelve years old, what a lovely young girl she has become."

"Liam, I'll miss you, but I'll look forward to our reunion in El Salvador. I can't tell you yet, exactly when, but I can almost promise it will happen. I hope all goes well for you in Boston."

As she drifted off to sleep in Liam's arms, Angela realized their future together was pregnant with possibilities. Now was their time, a second chance.

Return to the Bajo Lempa
El Salvador 2010

"Hola, Angela," called out Juan, as he pulled up in front of the hostel the next day. She stood on the sidewalk, after saying good-bye to Liam. Juan motioned Angela to approach his truck and said through the open window, "Just let me park and I'll help you with your bags." He parked, got out and extended his hand in an affectionate shake."

Juan and Angela exchanged greetings for the first time in ten years. It felt like she had never been gone. After Juan helped her into the truck, he picked up her suitcase and the box she had brought with some gifts for her friends.

"I'll take the box, Juan," said Angela, "It's fragile—just some gifts for Adriana and the family. Some things I made." She reached for the box and placed it on her lap as she sat down in the passenger seat of the pickup. She looked up at Juan as he slid into the driver's side, "There's something for you, also. You'll see it later."

"*Muchas gracias.*"

"It's good to be back in El Salvador," Angela said.

"*Sí.* We're happy you've come back, Angela. Sometimes people come with the brigades and we make good friends, and then we never see them again. It's good to know you have not forgotten us."

The time flew by as they bobbed in and out of San Salvador's traffic and were at last on the Intercontinental Highway making their way in the direction of the small village, which evoked so many memories for Angela. Once they crossed the big bridge over the Lempa River, Angela's heart began to beat faster and her hands sweat as she held on tightly to the box of gifts for her friends. She recognized the dirt road turnoff next to the store where she and Adriana sometimes shopped. She knew they were almost at their destination.

As they drove into the village, Angela saw dirt streets still filled with potholes, just as she remembered. Chickens pecked and clucked in the front yards, fat pigs peered out through makeshift fences, scraggly dogs wandered along the road and children ran here and there playing with sticks and balls. The poverty, compared to US standards, was still palpable. At first sight, not much had changed. Streetlights were the only things new. The small village was now on the grid. It would be easier and safer to walk at night. Women were starting their cooking fires and the air was laden with smoke and smells of frying *pupusas*.

When Juan pulled up to the familiar one story concrete-block house, she saw her friends waiting in front. Adriana and Cici ran to the pickup.

"*Hola, bienvenida*, Angela," called out Adriana.

"*Hola*, Angela," said a pretty young girl.

"This couldn't be Cici," Angela said as she got out of the truck and handed the box to Juan. "Why she's nearly as tall as you, Adriana. Is she the same little girl I met so many years ago?"

Cici gave Angela a bashful hug. She had become a winsome twelve-year-old. Angela was sure Cici couldn't remember her, but probably knew her from the photos she had sent Adriana during the years of her absence. She imagined that the family had told Cici about the brigade that came to plant mangroves, and fruit trees around her school. Isabel, Adriana's mother, ran over from her outdoor kitchen, wiping her hands on her apron as she greeted the new arrival.

"*Hola,* Angela. We are *muy* happy see you again," she said in her broken English.

Angela reached out and took her hand. "*Hola, Isabel,* you speak English now—that's great!"

"I've been teaching Mama a little English so she could talk with you and understand more," Adriana said. "We've missed you."

"I've missed you, too," said Angela. "To show you, here are a few things I made for each of you." She reached over to take the box of gifts out of Juan's arms.

"Oh, you mean I don't get to keep the whole box?" he asked.

"No, but maybe you can come back tonight and open your presents with the family when Jesús gets home from the fields."

"*Gracias*, Angela," said Adriana as she reached out and took the box to set it on the porch. Angela had learned that Salvadorans were sometimes a shy people and showed affection in simple ways.

"It's my pleasure," said Angela.

"I have to go now, but I'll come back later," Juan said. "See you later."

That evening, after dinner, they sat on the front porch just as they had done so many years ago. Jesús, older now and looking more tired with his wrinkled, sun-drenched and weathered face, strummed his guitar. In the background, Angela heard distant sounds from radios and TVs, more than she ever heard in the past. Were these signs of progress? Were the people better off, or did they just receive more remittances from their husbands and sons who worked in the US?

Cici brought the box out on the porch. "May we open this now, Angela?" she asked.

"Sure," said Angela. "If it's okay with your mother and grandparents."

"Go ahead,*"* said Adriana.

Cici began to tear off the wide tape that held the box's top down. Once she had it opened, she peered inside and began to lift out small packages wrapped in orange, red and yellow paper. There was a tag on each with the names of her family and Juan.

"You can pass them out, Cici," said Angela. "Each one took their package from Cici and began to unwrap it.

"Oh, *que bonita*," said Isabel. She was the first to open hers to discover the small clay sculpture of a mother and daughter, which resembled Adriana and Cici. "Muchas gracias." Isabel reached out her hand and squeezed Angela's. "You're an artist."

Adriana unwrapped a portrait of Jorge, which Angela had sketched from a photo Adriana had given her of her husband and her on their wedding day. She smiled at Angela with tears in her eyes.

"I love it, Angela. *Gracias.* Go ahead Cici, open your present."

"Oh, *precioso*," said Cici as she fondled a small clay sculpture of a turtle. "*Gracias,* Angela."

The men hung back and Angela prompted. "Now it's time for the men to open their presents, but first, I want to give the one in the bottom of the box to Adriana for her sister, Sofia. I know from your letters, that she is now living in another village with her new husband. I hope I'll get to see her.

"No, Angela, she's no longer in our country. She and her husband, Carlos, fled over the border several months ago. Mama is very sad—we all are, as we have not heard from her for a long time."

"Oh, I'm sorry," said Angela. Not wanting to cast a pall over the gathering, she looked up at Juan and said, "Go ahead, Juan. Open your present."

Angela had created a bust of Juan with his straw hat, the one he always wore when he was on his boat, taking people to the mangroves. Juan looked pleased, as his face broke into a smile.

Jesús was last. He carefully unwrapped the small sculpture of a man with a guitar, turned it over and over and then looked up at Angela with watery eyes. "*Gracias, amiga*," he said. Now I'll sing you a song in English. We have a radio station now, started by the youth. The Seattle brigades raised the money for the transmitter. I don't always like the music the kids play, but I'm learning English by listening to the literacy program, and we can even get local and national news." He picked up his guitar and started to sing, his voice cracking but his words clear. "*If I had a hammer, I'd hammer in the morning, I'd…*"

"Oh, Jesús, that's one of my favorite songs by Pete Seeger," cried Angela.

Jesús looked pleased and Angela knew she had made the right choice to return to her friends in El Salvador. Her heart was full.

Before they all said good night, Jesús said to Angela: "Get up early tomorrow morning and I'll take you out to see the fields. We have our first crop of tomatoes. I'll let you eat some, but," he chuckled, "you'll have to spit out the seeds and save them for us."

So, thought Angela, this was progress.

Still the Same
Bajo Lempa 2010

The outhouse was in the same place. They still didn't have indoor plumbing, but the brigades had helped install compost toilets in the village, a vast improvement for their sanitation. Adriana led Angela out to see them.

"Angela, I have good news," said Adriana. "We finally found my husband, Jorge. You remember how worried I was when I didn't hear from him for a few months? He's working in California, in the flower fields, near a place called Santa Barbara. Do you know where that is?"

"Oh, *sí*, I do. It's a lovely town. My friend Maggie used to live there, and I often went to visit her. Tell me about Jorge. Is he OK?"

"Yes, things are much better now. It was very hard for him in the beginning. He traveled all over having to follow the work after he was let go earlier than promised by the farmer who hired him with the temporary work visa. He was told it was *tiempo libre* and he could work wherever he wanted for the next six months, but he was given the wrong information, and he and his *amigos* were constantly running from the *migras.* That's why he couldn't let me know where he was. He was fearful for us here that the recruiters would harm us or take my parents' home. He was often in great danger, and some people were very mean to him. Now things are better. He came home after the visa expired and promised us he would not go back."

Angela interrupted, "But where is he now?"

"Well, as things got worse here, economically I mean, and we could not seem to make ends meet, he thought more about trying to cross over again. Four years ago, he made it over the border, illegally this time, so he wouldn't have the same problems having to pay back all his earnings to recruiters. Getting a temporary work visa is not all it's cracked up to be in the US, Angela. Thanks to God, this time a nice *Chicano,* whose parents immigrated back in the fifties, gave him a good job as foreman at a huge flower-growing farm. The man knew he could trust Jorge, and he saw that he is a good worker. He has helped Jorge find a way he can possibly get a green card. He is risking much to help him. We are so grateful to him. Jorge still has to repay the debt for the first visa, and his transportation to and from El Salvador."

"Oh, what great news. I'm happy for him now that he has work with someone who is treating him kindly," said Angela. Adriana shook her head in agreement and paused to take a breath.

"Jorge wants us, me and Cici, to join him there. He misses us terribly, and Cici needs her father. My parents are tired. It is hard to support all of us, even with the remittances Jorge sends. My father is too old to be *papa* to Cici, and also take care of the responsibilities of the farm and help my mother. She, too, is getting older now and has a very bad cough. We're worried that it may be from all the years she has cooked over open fires, from the smoke. Many of the women in our village are dying of lung cancer."

Angela listened to Adriana pour out her concerns. Her thoughts drifted back to Liam and what he had told her in San Salvador, that he was helping women and children to get over the border to join their husbands and fathers. She worried that this might be what he had in mind for Adriana and Cici. She recalled his mentioning he had come to know the family well.

"Adriana, I don't know what to say. I hope that Jorge can make enough money to come back to the village. That would be the best. Then he could help your father and be here with his family and his own culture."

Adriana lowered her head and shrugged her shoulders. "Maybe, Angela."

As the two women said goodnight, there was something unsaid hanging in the air, like laundry out to dry on a damp night.

For the week she spent there, Angela could not get Liam out of her mind, or the proposal he had made for her to rejoin him here under the Salvadoran sun, to help the people she loved.

She wanted to talk to Adriana about how she had run into Liam in San Salvador, about her feelings for him, and the possibility that she might come back to El

Salvador to rejoin him. Each time she tried to broach the subject her feelings of guilt returned. She was ashamed to admit that she had loved him since they met the first time she was here, when she stayed with them as a married woman. She could not find the words to justify her transgression, so she decided to keep it to herself and just enjoy the reunion with her friends.

The days passed quickly as they ate together, sat on the porch at night, talked and sometimes sang to Jesús's guitar music. One night they all went down to the beach and were able to help introduce the baby turtles into their ocean home after they hatched. The moon was full that night, and her mind went back to that first night with Liam. She wished he could be here now, experiencing the fun she and the children were having being witnesses to this bi-annual event of nature. When the turtles hatched, they would pick them up gently and put them into plastic tubs, which they carried down to the water's edge. Angela picked up the tiny turtles and placed them in the seawater. She and the children laughed as the turtles' legs moved quickly like children riding tricycles, as they tried to swim out to sea. Often they would be washed back up on the beach, and she scooped them up, wished them luck and sent them out again. Sometimes it took two or three tries to get them launched.

"There you go, little one," Angela said.

"*Felicidades, tortugas,*" Cici and her mother chimed in.

During the week, Angela called her daughter, Arial, to ask a favor for Adriana.

After she slipped her phone card in the slot, and dialed the number, Angela heard the phone ringing at Arial's office; she knew she would have to speak quickly as it was hard for her daughter to take calls at work.

"Hello. Arial Smith speaking. May I help you?"

Angela recognized her oldest daughter's voice.

"Arial, it's Mother."

"Oh, Mother! Is everything OK? I just spoke with Katherine last night and we're working out how we can meet you at the airport on Friday." Katherine was Arial's younger sister. "She's not sure she can leave the island to come with me to the airport. They are very busy right now at the whale center. But we're sure glad you are finally coming home. It seems strange not having either you *or* Daddy to talk to."

Angela's heart sank. She realized maybe she was needed in Seattle more than she thought. That was not always evident before David passed away. She had sometimes felt the girls treated her like an old slipper, someone they could rely on, but kicked under the bed when they didn't need her. Often, when she called one of them, they seemed annoyed or distracted. Maybe that was to be expected. They were in a different stage of their lives: Arial, with her high-pressured job at Microsoft and two energetic 13 year-old twin boys and a daughter just entering puberty. Katherine had a new job at a San Juan Island whale research center and boyfriend problems. They must have felt sandwiched between the needs of their families, their jobs, and their mother. She didn't want it to be that way. She was still in good health, active, and independent, but ever since David passed away it seemed like the girls felt they should spend more time with her, time they didn't always have.

Arial continued, "It will be good to have you back to help with the kids. Things have been hectic here. Dennis is working nights now, and guess what, the twins had strep while you were gone and—"

Angela interrupted her. "Arial, honey, excuse me, I'm so sorry to hear about your troubles. I hope the boys have recovered okay, but I have a favor to ask of you. Will you go by the house on your way home tonight and find something for me, please?"

There was a pause. Angela hoped she hadn't hurt Arial's feelings, cutting her off from her diatribe of familial matters, but she knew she didn't have many more minutes on her phone card, and calling was such a pain in El Salvador.

"Oh, yes, of course, Mother. What do you need?"

"Well, go to my desk in my studio. In the bottom right-hand drawer, I have some travel journals, and in the one marked El Salvador, 2000, please look up Eduardo Nunez's name and phone number in San Salvador. It's in the back of the journal. I think he might be able to help Adriana get some information about her husband's immigration status, and check out how she might legally join him there. Anyway, could you get that number for me, honey, and I'll call you back in the morning before you leave for work. There is a two-hour time difference. I'll call at seven your time, nine o'clock here. Will that work?"

"Sure, Mother. I'll do it *pronto. Hasta mañana!* Love you. Better go now."

Angela was amused by Arial's trying to impress her with a little Spanish. She had encouraged her daughters to study languages in school. Arial was the only one who took to it.

"Until tomorrow then, Ari." Angela used her daughter's childhood nickname. They hung up.

Angela was glad she would be seeing her daughter in a few days, soon enough to face telling her about Liam and her plans to return to Central America.

Angela knew she was still in El Salvador when she awoke the next morning to the smell of coffee, the sound of the roosters, and Adriana's mother calling Cici to get ready for school. The Salvadoran sun was already high and its heat stroked her skin. Angela pulled herself up out of her hammock, and got dressed, anxious for her morning Salvadoran coffee.

"*Hola, amigos.*"

"*Buenos dias,* Angela," they said in unison. "Did you sleep well?"

"Oh, *sí,* as usual, I always sleep well in El Salvador," Angela said with a smile. She glanced at her watch. "Oh, I didn't realize I slept so late. I have to hurry as I promised my daughter I would call her this morning. Please excuse me."

"*Sí,* no problem!" Adriana said. "Remember we're going out with Juan later this morning to look over the mangroves. Meet us at the boat dock about ten. "

"*Oh, gracias.* Thank you for reminding me. I'm really excited about seeing how they've grown."

Angela walked over to the local phone booth on the edge of the village. She put in her phone card and dialed her daughter's number. She knew she was a few minutes late and hoped she would catch her before she left for work.

"Hello?" Arial's voice sounded loud and impatient.

"Oh, Arial, I'm so glad I caught you. Sorry, dear, that I'm calling a little later than I said I would. I hope I didn't hold you up too long."

"No, that's OK. I have the information you wanted. I have to hurry though. Do you have a pen and paper?

"Yes, dear. Go ahead."

Arial gave her mother the information she needed and said, "Have to run now. Bye." The receiver clicked off.

Angela noticed that Arial's voice seemed more distant than the day before, with a note of annoyance. Maybe it was just her imagination and Arial's impatience to get to work.

Eduardo Nunez was a friend of Angela's from the Seattle NGO group. He now worked in San Salvador with the US Embassy, and Angela hoped he could help Adriana find out more about her husband's immigration status now that she knew where he was. More than that she hoped he could help Adriana and Cici get a visa to go to the States to join Jorge. She knew the chances of that were slim, given the current anti-immigrant fever in the US. Perhaps Eduardo had some pull. It was worth a try. She feared for them and Liam, and wanted to head off any attempt to cross the border illegally. She slipped the paper with Eduardo's phone number into her pocket and began to walk back to Adriana's house.

As she walked, Angela reflected on the annoyance she perceived in Arial's voice. Was it directed at her?

Why? Angela wondered what her daughter might have discovered in her studio desk drawer that may have caused her some consternation. She was sure she had put the letter she once wrote to Liam in another drawer, not the same one with the notebooks. Did she? She tried to pass off her worries, telling herself that her daughter's tone was just because she was in a hurry. Her thoughts were interrupted by Juan's voice.

"*Hola,* Angela. We're on our way down to the boat dock." He was walking with Adriana. Angela was grateful for the distraction and looked forward to going out to the *isla* to see the mangroves.

The day passed quickly. Angela was delighted to see how the trees had grown. When they got back to the village, she and Adriana walked to the house together.

"Adriana, I called my daughter this morning and she was able to find the phone number for the man I told you about who works at the American Embassy in San Salvador. I can't guarantee it, but he may be able to help you." She handed Adriana the small slip of paper with the number on it. "I'll follow up with an e-mail to him when I get back to Seattle and tell him you may be contacting him, but to keep Jorge's name confidential."

"Oh, *muchas gracias*, Angela. I hope he can help us."

"I understand how much you miss Jorge, and I hope you and Cici *can* join him, but the immigration laws in our country are very strict, and it is important that you have a visa and enter legally. It's very dangerous to try to cross the border with a *coyote*—many people die trying."

"I know that, Angela, but …" her voice trailed off and she added, "it's not healthy for our family to be torn apart."

"Do you remember my friend, Liam O'Connor, the man I met when I was here ten years ago?" Angela knew she had to finally bring up the subject of Liam. They may already have planned something together.

"*Sí,* I do remember him." Adriana looked down as she walked along the dirt road. "I feel badly that I did not tell you in my letters that he came to visit us several times." She was kicking the dirt as she walked. Then, with some hesitation, she added, "He has offered to take Cici and me to the States where his church will provide us with sanctuary until we can join Jorge."

With this disclosure, Angela sucked in her breath, letting it out loudly. She *knew* it. She could feel it in her bones when Liam first hinted at what he was doing. Her chest rose and fell, as she took deep breaths, trying to think of what to say next to Adriana.

Adriana continued, "I did not know how to tell you. I remembered you seemed very fond of him, but you also spoke of your husband, and I guess I felt, well, that you may not want me to bring up Liam's name in my letters."

Angela blushed and felt moved by the wisdom and discretion of this young woman so many years her junior.

"*Gracias,* Adriana. That was wise of you. I must confess, I grew fond of Liam when I was here in your beautiful romantic country. We were both lonely at the time, and it was good to have a friend to confide in. I appreciate that you did not mention his name in your letters. It may have been difficult to explain to my husband, whom I also loved."

"Please, don't worry. I understand. Have you seen

Liam again? He never mentioned you when he came to visit and my mother and father didn't ask either."

Angela knew the time had come to tell Adriana about her meeting Liam in San Salvador a few days before her visit here. She could not keep it from her any longer.

"Yes, as a matter of fact, something rather extraordinary happened last week just before I arrived here. I ran into Liam in San Salvador. He was there with his friend, Rutilio. I think you know him, too?"

"Oh, *sí*, Father Rutilio has helped our villages much. We love him. How amazing you met Liam again, after all these years."

"Well," continued Angela, "Rutilio and Liam were in San Salvador and we met at the cathedral where Rutilio was giving a talk. Liam and I had an opportunity to renew our friendship. He wants me to stay in El Salvador to help him at an orphanage in Suchitoto."

"Angela, that's wonderful. You would be so good with the children. Are you going to do that?"

"It's hard to leave my family in Seattle, but yes, I hope it will work out." Angela went on: "I must tell you I don't entirely approve of Liam's promise to you." said Angela. "It will be very dangerous to cross the border illegally for all of you: Liam, you, and Cici. I know how much you want to be with Jorge, but sadly, it's against our immigration laws. It would be better if you applied for a visa from the Embassy." Angela knew how naïve she was. No one like Adriana, a *campesino* from the rural countryside, could get a visa to the States now. It took years. In the meantime, families were torn asunder, whole villages disrupted as they became more and more dependent on the remittances sent back from the States, a huge percentage of their country's gross domestic product.

"Angela, I'm not afraid. I must join my husband, and Cici must have her father back." Adriana sounded determined, almost defiant.

Angela knew there was no point in arguing about this now. Better to wait and see what happened once Adriana talked with Eduardo.

"Well, I'm glad, at least, that now we'll see more of each other when I come back to El Salvador."

"So you're planning to return, for sure? *Que bueno.*"

Angela's decision to return to Liam was almost subconscious. She would return to help Liam with the orphans. At least now, that was the way she felt.

The next morning, after coffee, she embraced her friends and said farewell as she climbed into Juan's pickup. Everyone gathered around the truck to say *adios.* They waved as the pickup pulled away, and Angela waved back through the window.

"*Adios, amigos.* I shall return!"

PART TWO

"...sometimes when you just get flying and it all feels so good and you think, 'This is it, this is that path with heart,' you suddenly fall flat on your face. Everybody's looking at you. You say to yourself, 'What's happened to that path that had heart? This feels like the path full of mud in my face.' ...it pricks you, it pokes you... challenging you to figure out what to do when you don't know what to do. It humbles you. It opens your heart."

—Pema Chödrön

Return Home
Seattle

Angela's plane rolled down the runway. As excited as she was about seeing her daughters again, uppermost in her mind was the thought of returning to Liam and El Salvador, where she could begin a new and meaningful life. Could she convince her daughters that this would give her life new purpose? Would they care? That remained to be seen.

She peered out the small window of the plane and thought about Arial and Katherine waiting for her, or maybe just Arial would be there. She knew it was hard for Katherine to get away from her Orca whale-research job on San Juan Island. The two daughters were very different from one another. Arial was the successful, ladder-climbing, businesswoman at Microsoft. Katherine, on the other hand, was the most adventuresome, an artist like Angela. She would plan on going to San Juan Island soon, if Katherine couldn't come to Seattle.

With a jerk, the plane came to a halt, interrupting Angela's thoughts. The pilot turned off the seatbelt sign and everyone stood up simultaneously, grabbing their luggage and belongings to squeeze out into the plane's narrow aisle. Once Angela disembarked, she went up the gangway and walked along the concourse toward the baggage area where Arial promised to meet her.

"Mother, over here." She heard Arial's voice from a distance and looked up to see her waving furiously as she walked toward her mother. She was tall and statuesque like her father, but had Angela's coloring: olive complexion, dark eyes, chestnut-colored hair—well, at least Angela's hair used to be that color. Angela put down her bag and reached out to embrace her daughter as she approached.

"Welcome home, Mother. You look great," Arial said. "I hope you've had your fill of gallivanting around Latin America for a while. The kids all miss you, and we know you must be anxious to get back to your studio."

Somehow this was not the welcome Angela expected. Arial's tone was crisp. What was she implying when she referred to Angela's *gallivanting around Latin America?* Was she jealous?

"It's good to be back, honey, but I must admit I had a wonderful trip. I can't deny I'll want to go back again."

"I hope you don't mean soon, Mother."

Angela decided to avoid this query for now and changed the subject. "Luckily, I don't have to stop at the baggage carousel. Where are you parked, dear?"

"In the first parking structure," Arial said.

As they talked, the two women stepped out to the overcast skies, which blanketed the airport. A slight drizzle came down, typical for a northwest spring. Angela bemoaned leaving the sunny skies of El Salvador.

"I'll go and get the car, and you can wait here. I'll pick you up at the curb," said Arial.

Strange, thought Angela, that Arial seemed to want a little distance already. Angela had only two small carry-ons, both with wheels, and a backpack. They could walk to the car, but before she could say anything, Arial sprinted off and, for a minute, Angela just stood there wondering what she was doing back in Seattle. She already missed Liam and the sunshine.

Her daughter's BMW appeared at the curb, and Arial sounded the horn and motioned for Angela to get in. Angela threw her bags into the back seat and jumped into the front. Arial sped out into the I-5 traffic, north toward Seattle and the family house on Magnolia Hill. Angela knew Arial had always loved their old neighborhood where she and her sister had grown up. It would be hard telling them that she decided to sell the place. Oh, well, she would deal with that later. Now was definitely not the time to tell Arial of her plans to return to El Salvador.

Procrastination had never been her style in the past. During her marriage to David it had been she who made the big decisions, never looking back with regret. Early in their marriage, when they were thinking of buying the house, David had equivocated for days before, finally, Angela called the realtor and said: "We'll take it." If she hadn't done that they would have lost the opportunity to buy in this choice Seattle neighborhood. Now, it seemed harder to make decisions, to decide once and for all what she wanted. Angela had to steel herself to pay attention to

Arial's comments about the family and all her problems with her pre-pubescent sons and 11 year-old-daughter.

"Well, mother, I guess you'll have a lot to share with us, too." There was a pause; Angela was still not sure exactly what or how she would tell them about the trip.

Arial pulled up to the house. "Well, here we are. I'm sorry to say I just have enough time to help you carry your bags in, and then I have to rush. Dennis is expecting me at a company dinner."

Angela felt exhausted and anxious to unpack and sort out her mixed emotions about the next step, returning to El Salvador and Liam. The news that Arial couldn't stay was good.

"That's fine dear. I'm tired and we can get together later in the week, maybe one night after work?"

"Yes, that would be good. I'm anxious to hear about your trip. You must have had quite a time."

What did Arial mean by "quite a time?" Angela tried to remember what she had said to her when they talked on the phone from El Salvador. She sensed, with a mother's instincts, there was something Arial wasn't saying. She couldn't put her finger on it.

After taking a couple of Angela's bags up the stairs and into the entry hall, Arial turned and gave Angela a slight peck on the cheek. "Bye, Mother. See you soon." They waved as the car pulled out to go down the hill.

Angela began to shuffle through the mail Arial had left on the dining room table. All the while she was thinking about how she would break her news to the girls. Explaining she wanted to return soon to El Salvador to work in an orphanage wasn't going to be easy. She didn't know if she would tell them about Liam or not. Really, why would she have to? It had been her secret for so long, and if she kept it no one had to be hurt. She tried to convince herself that, in the end, they would support her desire to return, once they understood that she would be helping orphans. Maybe, they could even come down and see her, help out a bit, too. She doubted that, though. They had never really been that interested in her projects in Central America. Both girls supported their parents' fund-raising events, but never expressed an interest in learning more or much less going there. They had their own lives and preoccupations; helping out in Central America was not one of them. She accepted that and tried not to foist her politics and ideas on them.

For now, she had enough to do. She had to begin preparations for selling the house, make arrangements with the galleries that represented her work, close up her studio. The thought of all this was overwhelming. Angela unpacked a few of her things, then dropped into bed and fell into a fitful sleep.

The Girls Know
Seattle 2010

Two days later, Arial called. "Mother, hope you've had a chance to catch up on your sleep. I thought I'd drop by after work today. I'm anxious to talk to you about your trip."

"Fine, dear, I'll look forward to that," Angela said. "About five-thirty?"

"Sure, that should work. See you then."

The phone clicked and Angela pondered. She couldn't fathom what was wrong with Arial? Why was she so abrupt-sounding? She picked up a vibration from Arial's tone of voice that something was bothering her. While she continued to unpack and catch up on e-mails, she tried not to think about it. She was probably imagining things and worrying too much. Or was it her own guilt worming its way back into her thoughts again? She busied herself with setting out some wine glasses and a bottle of Chardonnay, Arial's favorite.

Arial arrived at five forty-five and immediately began to talk.

"I need to talk to you, Mother, before Katherine gets into the act. Have you called her yet?"

"For heaven's sake, Ari, whatever do you mean by 'gets into the act?' What act? You seem tense and disturbed. Please tell me what's the matter. You seemed distant when you picked me up at the airport. We've always shared everything." *Well, Angela thought, almost everything.* She was sure the girls had some secrets, too.

Without a reply, Arial brushed past Angela and went directly into the kitchen, where they often sat around the table when they had something important to discuss. Angela began to set some snacks out on the table.

"Would you care for a glass of wine? I bought your favorite Chardonnay."

"OK—yes, wine would be good." Arial seemed distracted.

While Angela poured the wine, Arial reached into her purse and pulled out a faded blue envelope, a bit worse for wear with a few tattered edges. She tossed it on the table with a dramatic flip of her hand, and taking a deep breath said:

"Mother, I found this when I was looking for the information on Eduardo you asked for. What can you tell me about it?" Arial's hands were shaking.

Glancing at the envelope, Angela sank to her chair, almost dropping the tray with the glasses of wine she carried to the table. Her heart began to beat rapidly and her mind raced as she wondered what Ari would say next. She recognized the light blue envelope with the frayed edges. She knew it was the love letter she had once written to Liam, but never sent. She had not seen it for eight years. Deep inside she knew now why Arial had seemed so distracted and, in fact, angry with her.

Arial went on: "Mother, I didn't mean to be snooping, but the words on the envelope, *To my love,* attracted my attention and I—well, I don't know why, but I felt it was something that would help me to understand you more, why you have always seemed like you were hiding something whenever we talked about your last trip to El Salvador."

Angela realized that Arial was more perceptive than she had given her credit.

"This is a love letter, Mother, and it's not to Daddy. Please explain this." She waved the letter in Angela's face. "I have laid awake nights since I found it, reading and re-reading it. Please, help me to understand."

"Yes, it *was* a love letter," Angela admitted. "One I never mailed. Before that trip to El Salvador, your dad and I were having deeper problems than perhaps you ever suspected. While in El Salvador, I met a man to whom I was very much attracted. When I arrived home after my trip, I was unclear what the future held."

"But, why didn't you mail the letter, mother? I hope you had an awakening to how wrong you were to have an affair," Arial said, with a judgmental tone.

Angela tried to gather her composure. Taking a sip of her wine, she continued. "I didn't mail the letter because I was worried I would cause pain and damage to another family, the wife and children of the man I fell in love with."

Arial's hand came up to cover her mouth and the expression of shock she displayed. "So he was married. Mother, what were you thinking?"

Arial's words stung. Now, becoming defensive and angry at Arial's audacity to ask her to explain all the details, Angela said, trying to steady her voice, "I rather resent you opening something private of mine without first talking about it with me. Perhaps, it's for the best, and it's time to confront the truth." Taking another sip of wine, she added: "I can imagine what went through your head, why you felt confused after reading the letter. It was a time of confusion for me, too, when I wrote it. But, I can honestly say the last few years, before your dad died, were some of our best, until he became ill. The loss of your father devastated me."

Arial interrupted. "Did Dad know about this? Who is this man you call Liam? Have you seen him since? Is that why you wanted to go back to El Salvador, to meet him again? Did you?" The questions Arial had been storing for the past week tumbled out of her mouth like a cascade of water rushing over rough rocks, and her eyes were moist with tears.

Angela reached out to touch her daughter's hand, but Arial withdrew it.

"You owe me an explanation, Mother—*you*, of all people, who always taught us to be truthful, to stand up for what we believed was right. How could you deceive us? And more, how could you deceive Daddy?"

"You're right, Arial. Please bear with me so I can attempt to answer your questions and explain what all this means."

With a lump in her throat, Angela began the story of her and Liam.

"Ari, as I said, your father and I had been having many troubles for a few years before I went to El Salvador. I loved him and he loved me, but we didn't always see eye to eye. He was supportive about my desire to go on the work trip to El Salvador, and I never intended that it be anything more than a chance to help the people there. I didn't *plan* on meeting anyone and falling in love, but it happened. Your father never knew about it, and I'm glad for that. I only hope that you can try to understand." Angela finished her confession with a sob. She grabbed the box of tissues on the kitchen counter.

"Mother, I *don't* understand, and I *don't* want to hear any more about it now. I don't even want to hear you cry." Arial jumped up abruptly, almost knocking over her still full glass of wine, and ran to the door, slamming it shut.

"Wait, Ari. Please don't go." But it was too late. Tears spilled over onto Angela's cheeks. She tasted the acrid flavor of mascara in her mouth as it streaked down her face. What had she done wrong? All these years she thought it was the best thing to protect the girls from the truth she kept so deeply inside her. Had she made a pact with the devil, reaping the cost now, losing her daughters and everything she held so dear? She reached across the table for the letter Arial had left there, almost crumpling it in her hand and then, as if on second thought, she stuffed it into her jeans pocket.

When she met David in college, he was everything she thought she would ever want in a lover and husband.

Young love was like a shiny new copper kettle, reflecting the innocent faces of lovers before the fingers of time touched its surface, tarnishing it with age, lending it character. The love she and David had found later in their life was good. The passion had gone, but it was replaced by something deeper.

Angela mulled over these thoughts as she sipped her wine and wiped at her damp cheeks. How could a woman her age explain to her daughters, still caught up in their "ideals" of true love and what they thought they had seen between their parents, the vagaries of the human heart? In this age of "deconstruction" could she help the girls to unravel their original notion of their parents' love and find something even better out of the fray, a new definition of mature love that would help them in their own romantic partnerships? She thought of a quote from her favorite French philosopher, Voltaire, in his story *Candide.* That would be "the best of all possible worlds." Helping her daughters realize what she felt, so they could apply the lessons she had learned to their own lives, would be the ideal. She sighed, as she realized, it was probably too much to ask. Maybe she had been wrong to keep her transgression secret.

Angela walked to the window, hoping to catch a glimpse of Arial. Had she changed her mind and was she lingering out front, sitting in her car and rethinking her abrupt departure? She hadn't heard the car pull away— but that was wishful thinking. Arial *had* departed, and Angela didn't know where to turn. Her mind whirled in confusion and despair. Admittedly, she had been somewhat distraught ever since coming back from El

Salvador. Her nerves were frayed. Seeing Liam once again had opened up a chapter in her life that perhaps should have stayed closed. She slumped down in the living room couch and clutched one of the bright-colored throw pillows to her chest—*oh, if only he were here now*. What was she to do? She felt torn between her familial loyalties and the chance for a new and meaningful life with Liam, an opportunity to help their friends in El Salvador.

Maggie—that's whom she needed to talk to. Since returning, she had only talked once to her best friend. Maggie was up to her neck in a real estate deal and couldn't talk long so they had just "checked in" with each other. They made sure each was well and alive and promised to get together in a week when Angela returned from her visit with Kate. She couldn't wait until then. She reached across the stacks of books and magazines on the coffee table and scrambled for her cell phone. She punched in Maggie's number and waited as it rang.

"Creative Real Estate Sales," Maggie's voice recording came on, "Please leave your name and number and the time of day you called. Your call is important to me. I'll get back to you as soon as I can."

"Maggie," said Angela, "I need to talk to you. Give me a call, please, when you have a free moment."

Angela loved the take-charge tone of her friend's voice. Maggie always possessed the confidence and abilities Angela didn't have, except when it came to doing her art. Maggie admired *her* artistic talents. They were a good balance. They had been friends since their college days at U of W, and Maggie, who had no family of her own, had always been like part of their family.

Angela put down her phone and continued to mull over her predicament, all the while hugging the pillow to her. *Maybe I better just accept that it's not worth ruining my relationship with the girls and give up the idea of going back to El Salvador. On the other hand, I have a right to be happy even now that I am a widow.* One question plagued her: How could she redeem herself in her daughters' eyes now that the truth was out? She was sure that Arial had shared the letter with Katherine.

Angela tried to pull herself together. She began to play back in her head the tapes of the past, to try to find some justification for what had happened, some place of self-forgiveness and understanding. She felt so alone, isolated from everyone and everything. Who could understand if her daughters couldn't? A more private person than Maggie, she was reticent to share the really personal. She'd never told her friend about the affair. For her daughters, she wanted to be a model of self-assurance, intelligence and common sense as well as compassion for others. She didn't want to muddy the water for them by disclosing her weaknesses, her flaws. As they became adults there would be time for them to discover those, she told herself. Now they *were* adults. Self-doubt invaded her.

The phone rang. Angela reached for it.

"Hello?"

"Angie, it's Maggie. Sorry I missed your call."

"Oh," said Angela, "thank you for calling so soon. Maggie, I have been in such despair—I haven't known where to turn or what to do …"

"Whoa, honey, what's the matter?" asked Maggie.

"What do you mean you don't know what to do—about what?"

"I'm sorry. I know I'm not being very clear. Neither one of us have had a lot of time to talk since I got back. Remember, I told you on the phone a couple of days ago that I had run into an old friend down in El Salvador. Well, I wasn't entirely truthful. I've kept something from you and the kids for years, and now I know it's time to reveal my secret."

"What secret? Angie, we've always shared so much. Are you OK?"

"Yes, if you mean my health, sure, I'm fine. I've never been better. Can you come over for a while? I'll fix you my best pot of coffee. And I have a small gift for you from El Salvador."

After a short silence, Maggie said, "I'll be right over. I'm closing up shop early today. Hold your horses. Skip the coffee. I'll bring a bottle of wine."

Thirty minutes later the doorbell rang. Angela and Maggie hugged, and then walked into the kitchen, where Maggie promptly opened the wine she had brought and poured two glassfuls. She was comfortable in Angela's house having been a friend of the family for the past thirty years. She had watched Angela's daughters grow up and shepherded Angela through some pretty difficult times in her marriage to David. They understood each other without always having to say much.

"What's this about a secret? You sounded so upset on the phone," said Maggie.

"Remember my trip to El Salvador with the NGO group, the trip you recommended I take when I was having problems with David?" said Angela.

"Yes, what about it? That's a long time ago."

"I met a man, there, Maggie."

Maggie whistled through her teeth. "Don't tell me more. I can guess. You had an affair. Why didn't you ever tell me? Did David ever know about it?"

Angela looked down at her lap, embarrassed. "No, I don't think so. But something quite remarkable happened this trip, in San Salvador. I ran into that same man—his name is Liam—again. It was an amazing coincidence. We haven't been in touch for ten years. He has asked me to join him, in a few months, to help out in a Salvadoran orphanage."

"Oh, my God, Angie. What a story. I suppose Arial isn't too happy about it. Your leaving again so soon, I mean. Does she know about the affair, and that you are going back to join him?"

Angela shook her head slowly, feeling the tears well up in her eyes once again. She didn't like appearing out of control, and quickly tried to gather her composure. She wiped her eyes with a tissue and continued.

"Yes, and that's why I called you. Arial found a letter I had once written to Liam, but never sent—a love letter. It's been a shock for her. Unfortunately, she found out about it before I could talk to her."

"I can imagine the rest, knowing how close Arial was to her dad," said Maggie. "She idolized him."

"When she picked me up at the airport, she seemed different than her usual self."

"I don't know what to say, Angie. I think it's best now to have a heart-to-heart talk with both girls. Of course, they are not going to be happy to hear you might be going back to El Salvador to be with this Liam guy, but you have to follow your own heart and march to your own drum. You know how I think about that. You've always made a lot of sacrifices for your daughters, and maybe it's your time now."

Of course, those were the words Angela wanted to hear, but somehow she still ached with the thought of alienating her daughters.

"I don't expect you to tell me what to say, Mags. Just having your moral support is enough. Thank you for understanding my trespass."

"You know I always understood some of the challenges of your marriage to David, and in a way, I'm glad now that you are free to pursue this love you feel for ... what's his name ... Liam? And the humanitarian work you've always loved, too. Just don't be too hasty. How much do you know about him? What makes you so sure it's not just being 'in lust' and not 'in love?' By the way, why didn't you ever send that letter?"

"He was married, too. I didn't want to cause any pain to his family. We talked about this when we parted the first time. It was hard for us both, but we knew it was for the best."

"Um, my only thought is the guy sounds too good. If he were in love with you, as you were with him, why didn't he take the risk and at least try to see you?"

Angela paused for a long moment. "I sometimes thought about that myself, but seeing him again, all my doubts disappeared. We're so good with each other. Maybe it was just lust then, but it's love now. I'd like to think this is our second chance." Then, changing the subject, Angela said, "Enough about me. How are you?"

"While we're on the man subject, I may have a new fish to fry, also. I met a really interesting guy last week at the broker's conference. We were able to commiserate on the sorry state of real estate sales. He was intelligent, handsome and … you'll be glad to hear … my age, for a change." Maggie had always had a penchant for liking men younger than her by ten or even twenty years, and Angela had sometimes cautioned her that it might be hard to get a commitment from someone so much her junior. Of course, Maggie had ignored her.

The two friends continued to talk, sharing wine, laughter, and confidences. Angela felt good that she had finally disclosed her truth, something she had always dreaded. How shortsighted she had been, thinking that Maggie would not understand or would judge her infidelity to David. Life's lessons came in small but fast doses lately. Learning to trust others and her instincts was a big step for Angela, one she'd have to take if she decided to pursue her new life in El Salvador and put her family's concerns aside.

Making Plans
Seattle 2010

For the next several days, Angela cleaned up her old studio, packing up her tools and materials in anticipation of a possible move. After all, even if she should decide *not* to go back to El Salvador and Liam, she would have to put her house on the market. Living there was too difficult, too much to care for, too many memories. She fingered each of her clay tools, as she wiped them clean to store, and thought of all the years she had sculpted. She had once started a clay bust of her granddaughter, Heather. It still sat unfinished on the workbench, where she had left it. It tugged at her heart to be completed. Would there be time now to do that, with so much to arrange before leaving?

She called Katherine to firm up a date for her visit to San Juan Island.

"Oh, hi, Moma," Katherine answered. "I'm glad you're back. When are you coming up for a visit?"

Moma was the nickname Katherine had given her mother when she was a child. Angela liked the allusion to the Museum of Modern Art, though she knew Katherine had never thought about that at the time.

Relieved that Katherine didn't sound strange or angry with her, Angela began, "Well, Kate, that's what I called about. I'm thinking of next week. Does that work for you?"

"Sure. That works. You can stay at my place. It's not big, but I think you'll like its cozy feel. We have lots to talk about, I know." There was a pause. "I'll cut to the chase, as Daddy always said. Arial shared the letter you wrote to a man we don't know. She was really upset when she found it. It shocked me, too, but I want to say right up front that I'm sure you have a reasonable explanation, and when you come up, if you're ready to talk about it, I would like to try and understand."

Angela let out a sigh of relief at her daughter's admission. "Thank you, honey. I'm glad you brought it up. I'm afraid your sister left here a couple of days ago very upset with me, and I have been feeling quite badly ever since. I can't blame her. I know I have been secretive about this. It's a long story. Let's talk when I come up next week."

"That's fine. *Ciao,* for now," Katherine said. "See you soon."

"*Ciao,* dear." Angela hung up the phone and sat down at the kitchen table to think about what she was going to say to Katherine—it had to be the truth.

Visit with Katherine
San Juan Island

Passengers waiting to board the San Juan Ferry packed the terminal in Anacortes. Angela felt the excitement in the air as she and her fellow travelers anticipated the crossing to the islands. She always loved this moment of boarding and, even better, the moment the big vessel left its slip slowly heading out through the Straits of Juan de Fuca. For her, it was an escape from the mundane, another chance for adventure. Lost in her thoughts, she was startled when someone said, "Hey, lady—hurry up—the line's moving."

"Oh, sorry," Angela said.

She quickly picked up the bag, adjusted her backpack and threw her woven Guatemalan purse over her shoulder, patting down the wrinkled canvas hat on her head. It was David's, from his kayaking days. She remembered, for a moment, their island forays together, while she moved quickly to find her place in the fast-moving line. Children and teens pushed past her, pulling family dogs by leather leashes. Little boys punched one another in jest, and older kids looked on nonchalantly, feigning maturity beyond their years. Young ones clutched parents' and grandparents' hands. The excitement of the crowd was palpable.

On board at last, Angela cast a glance over the vast central area of seats reserved for passengers, hoping to find one where she could peer out the big windows at the deep blue-green water sparkling under the sunlight. She slipped into a good spot, unloaded her baggage, and tried to arrange things so there was room for someone else to sit next to her. As she looked into her big canvas bag, she caught a whiff of fragrant lavender from her garden, the bouquet she was bringing her daughter. They had always shared a love of gardening and flowers, something that didn't interest Arial.

The engines below the ship's polished linoleum deck roared as they started up for departure. She felt a small lurch forward, and the vibration of the ferry, as it left its slip. Angela glanced at the nests on the piers as the ship slid by them: shiny black-feathered, cormorant parents kept watch over their nestlings. She smiled, remembering how she and the girls loved to count the sea birds they saw, trying to name each and every one of them. In the distance, sunlight reflected off the sleek white sails of small boats, like toys floating in a child's bathtub.

Leaving the mainland always made her feel like a child slipping away to *never-never land*, a place far from the world's cares and woes. She sighed and whispered under her breath: *Maybe the timing for this trip is perfect, a time to take account of all the past month's events, meeting Liam again, reuniting with Adriana and her family in El Salvador, and now exposing my daughters to the truth I've hidden for so long.*

Small feet pattered past and a little boy with big curious eyes hung over the back of the vinyl seat, staring at her.

"You look like my grammy. She has gray hair, too."

"Oh, I *am* a grammy. Maybe we all look alike."

"What's your name?"

"Grandma Angela. What's yours?"

"Peter."

"Well, I'm happy to meet you, Peter."

The boy's mother looked up from her magazine. "Don't bother the lady, Peter."

"Oh, he's fine," Angela said, glad for the distraction. She remembered the many times her daughter Arial had gaily chatted with passengers in adjacent seats on the ferry. She was always the most sociable of the girls, bringing home new friends from school for sleepovers with no warning. Her outgoing nature had served her well as she rose in the business world to head up a large department at Microsoft. Katherine was the rebel. She would be the one who ran when they asked her not to, who got her head stuck between the stair railings and raised havoc when they could not get it easily out, screaming at the top of her lungs.

Angela shuddered at the memory. Crossings with Katherine were always filled with some catastrophe or another, but she also had the ability to keep them all laughing.

"How old are you, Peter?"

He held up four tiny fingers, thumb turned in against the palm of his hand.

"Four."

"Wow, you're a big boy for your age," said Angela.

Peter's mother laughed.

"Yeah, his dad's six feet five. I think he's going to follow the family trend for height."

The women chuckled, distracted by another child running by, flip-flops making a loud clatter on the ship's hard deck. Peter turned around, looking back at his mom for approval, and then slipped off the seat to chase the other boy.

"Careful, Peter, not too fast. Watch you don't run into anyone or slip and fall," said his mother.

Warnings. How many times had Angela warned Katherine about the perils of life, often ones she ignored herself. With her rebellious and independent spirit, Katherine definitely was her soul child.

Angela glanced at her watch. She was always surprised at how quickly they reached their island destination, in spite of the slow-motion pace of the ferry, as it plied the waters of the straits.

Her thoughts shifted to Katherine again. How would she greet her? Would it be different now that Arial had shared their mother's secret with her? Would she be opposed to Angela's returning to El Salvador to join Liam? When she briefly mentioned this possibility to Arial over the phone the night before, Arial had protested loudly and hung up on her. As much as it hurt, it also made Angela more determined to take her destiny into her own hands. It was too late now to turn back. She hoped that Katherine would be more understanding. Katherine had struck out on her own at a very early age, defying her dad's wishes. She had drifted awhile, and they worried about her, but somewhere deep inside, Angela supported her, understanding she had to do this to truly know her own heart. Katherine's therapist once said, "One must lose one's life to find it."

Angela remembered the difficult times she and David had with Katherine. The most worrisome were her high school years when she seemed to lose herself for a while and slipped into anorexic behavior, scaring them all as she lost more and more weight. With counseling, she and David acquired tools for understanding. They had many arguments, too, about Katherine's choices of boyfriends. She always seemed to pick up the scabs of society, men with clay feet, who could never stand up on their own. Katherine was a care-giver, always helping to put the pieces of their shattered lives together, holding them up, while they put her down. David and Angela had argued and lamented about the life choices Katherine made. As they struggled to help their daughter, their disagreements had chipped away at their own relationship. Angela wondered if Katherine was more like her than she wished to admit, always wanting to make the world a better place, including the men in it.

As these reflections raced through Angela's mind, she felt a nudge at her back. Her new young friend was poking her.

"Hurry up, Mrs. Grandma! We have to get off now, Mommy says."

"Oh, my, we're already there? I was daydreaming. Thank you, Peter, for telling me."

"What's daydreaming?" Peter looked inquisitive.

"Well, Peter, you've asked a good question, but before I can answer it," said Angela, "I had better gather up my things and get ready to get off the ferry."

"Why?"

"Because, I'm meeting my daughter on shore. She'll be very sad if I don't get off the ferry."

Peter's mother looked at Angela with a knowing smile and grabbed Peter's hand.

"Come on Peter. Stop asking the nice lady questions. We have to get off, too. Your daddy is waiting for us."

"Bye, Mrs. Grandma."

"Bye, Peter. Have fun on San Juan Island."

Angela's eyes scanned the anxious crowd as the throng pressed forward toward the exit signs, moving like syrup poured through a funnel, oozing out into the waiting spectators on the dock.

"Moma, here I am!" Angela heard her familiar nickname.

Katherine waved her straw hat frantically above the crowd in front of her. It was the hat Angela had given her when she thought it had finally had its day. She and the girls had often exchanged clothes and accessories. The oldest things, with the most character, always ended up with Katherine. Arial was too fashion conscious to want Angela's hand-me-downs. She carefully scoured through everything, usually dismissing anything that was not her style or over a year old.

Angela waved and made her way through the crowd until she could feel the grasp of Katherine's outstretched hands reaching for her. The two women fell into each other's embrace. It felt good. Angela sighed with relief. It seemed at least one of her daughters had already forgiven her trespasses.

"Hi, Moma. Here, let me take some of that stuff. Boy, you brought a lot. Planning to set up camp here in *my* paradise?"

Laughing, Angela shook her head.

"No dear, I just brought a few "rags," as your sister calls them. I thought you might be able to use them. Arial sends her love along with a couple of gifts and of course, I couldn't resist bringing you something from the garden and also, from my trip to El Salvador."

"Such as a new man?" Katherine winked. "Come on, my old clunker is parked over there in the parking lot. I almost rode my bike down but thought you might not relish hanging onto the back—only joking."

Angela flinched at Katherine's flippant reference to "a new man," but quickly felt relieved when she changed the subject to the practical information about her car's location. She could only imagine how the girls' cell phones had been vibrating once Arial disclosed finding the letter, and how they discussed, at great length, their mother's clandestine love affair.

"No, dear, adventuresome as I still am, I think tottering on the back of your bike is not my style now."

They laughed together, and Angela loved feeling Katherine's arm slip through hers as they trudged up the slight incline to the car, leaving the jostling crowds behind them. She recalled family camping trips here. Those days had definitely left their mark on Katherine. After college, she seemed determined to make her home here. She had jumped at the chance to move to San Juan Island when her boyfriend, Josh, asked her to come along with him. But things did not go well for Katherine and six months later, Angela remembered, she was having problems with Josh and sobbing on the other end of a long-distance collect call.

When they pulled up in front of Katherine's small ramshackle cottage with its gray weathered shingles and red door, Angela felt relieved. It looked like Katherine had begun to take her own life into her hands and not let herself be led around by Josh, or any other man for that matter. Ironic how she herself was feeling pulled by Liam's desires. The porch steps were covered with wooden planters of flowers, and there were pots of seedlings along the two front windowsills. Katherine was always happiest puttering in the yard. Having a yearly veggie garden was a summer hobby while she was in high school.

"Welcome to my new niche," Mother. After Josh left, I really had fun getting this place settled and decorated with my own things the way I wanted. I'm now free to make my own decisions, and I don't have to put up with him and his crap."

"Well, honey, sounds like you have reached a good place, accepting that Josh wasn't exactly the best partner. Don't worry. There's other fish to fry, as Maggie would say. I know you'll meet the right man, eventually."

"Mother, don't worry. What if I told you I already have found my soul mate, and she isn't a man?"

"Whatever do you mean, Katherine?"

"Well, let's not go there yet. I have loads of stuff

to show you and want to hear all about your trip to El Salvador. We can talk about my love life later."

Katherine smiled and picked up Angela's backpack and set it on a cot in the corner of the cozy living room. A stack of wood sat by the nearby potbellied stove, ready for a fire.

Angela stood in the doorway, stunned by what Katherine seemed to imply—her daughter, a lesbian? Is that what she was trying to say? It had never occurred to Angela. With Katherine, though, there was always a new surprise. Maybe Angela wasn't the only one with "a bomb" to drop on the family. Was Katherine suggesting she was gay? That would remain to be seen. It would certainly help to deflect Arial's judgments away from her mother's life choices. As she mulled over this new development, she stepped into the bungalow, took off her hat and put her arms on Katherine's shoulders.

"Well, honey, whatever you have to say, I'm sure you'll share it soon enough. In the meantime, I'm so happy to see this cute cottage of yours."

Katherine hung up their jackets and went over to the sink to fill a copper kettle with water. "Let's have some tea. I'll make it with the mint leaves from my garden. While we're waiting for the water to boil, feel free to look around. I'm afraid my bedroom is very small so you're going to sleep over in the corner next to the wood stove. It should be warm when the night chill sets in. I hope you don't mind sleeping on the cot."

"You know me," said Angela. "I can sleep anywhere. Besides, it's just good to be here with you. I see you have all your botany books organized on the bookshelf and your grandmother's old quilt looks great on the couch. Wherever did you dig up that coffee table made from branches of driftwood?" asked Angela.

"That's one of Josh's leftovers. He made it, and willed it to me when he left. It's one of the few good things I have remaining from him."

"Did I catch a note of sarcasm, Kate?" Angela said. "You never did tell your dad or me the whole story."

"Oh, no I don't mean to sound bitter, and I really don't want to go into the details now. Let's just say, for the time being, that Josh didn't have much to offer that was positive in my life, and thankfully, I realized that in time."

"Sounds good for now, honey. I'll accept that." Angela decided to stave off any further questions, knowing that Katherine would share more when she was ready. It never worked to push her.

After their tea, Katherine took Angela out to the back of the cottage where she had already started her garden. Around the raised beds were neat piles of agates that she had collected from a nearby beach. She had made a funny female scarecrow with a floppy hat, an old cotton flowered dress, and a comical painted face on the straw-stuffed pillowslip tied at the throat by some old and frayed ship's rope. Artistic like her mother, Katherine once loved helping Angela in her studio.

The two women spent the rest of the day looking around the cottage, putting Angela's things away and having a fashion show of the "rags" she had brought Katherine. The afternoon slipped by quickly.

"Hey, let's go down and watch the sunset from the

beach," said Katherine. "It's not far from here, and it'll be a good walk before dinner. I made some homemade vegetarian soup and even baked a loaf of bread."

"Sounds good to me," Angela said. "Let me put on my boots and grab my jacket. I remember how chilly it can be here on the islands once the sun sets."

They walked to the beach, climbed over some dunes and ran down to the rocky peninsula known as Agate Beach. The sun was just starting to set, and under the vibrant peach-streaked crepuscular sky mother and daughter walked with brisk steps, arm and arm. All seemed well with the world, at least for now.

Talk About Love
San Juan Island

Angela rolled over in her cot, as the bright sunlight swept across the bed through the overhead window. She wiped the sleep from her eyes and looked out into the quiet cottage room. Water in an antique copper kettle simmered on the potbelly stove. She looked over at her daughter, Katherine, who sat on an old braided rug with her knees up, wrapped in the quilt Angela's mother had made for her. With her head resting on her knees she looked down at a small sketchbook in which she was drawing something. Angela couldn't make it out.

As Katherine realized her mother was watching her, she looked up and smiled. "You caught me. I'm doing my morning meditation, drawing the small agates and bird feathers we collected yesterday on the beach. Hope you slept well and didn't feel too cramped on that cot."

"Um, slept really well. The cot was fine, honey. It makes me glad to see you sketching."

"Yes, I find it very meditative. Julia likes to draw, too. You're going to like her."

"Is she the new friend you mentioned yesterday?"

"*Soul mate* is the word I think I used. Come on. Put on your robe. I'll fix you some tea and toast with my homemade bread, and tell you all about her."

Angela threw her legs over the side of the cot, stretched a minute and got up, glancing at her watch where it lay on a pile of books. "Wow, I can't believe I slept so late. You were so quiet, and I guess I needed the sleep. I've been a bit restless ever since I got back from El Salvador last week. Still suffering from a bit of jet lag."

"Let's talk about your trip, too," said Katherine, "I want to hear all the details."

Angela pulled on the warn velour robe David had given her so many years ago, and shuffled off toward the small bathroom. "I'll just be a minute, honey."

The stove fire and the sunshine streaming through the windows warmed up the room. Though Katherine left the windows slightly ajar, it felt toasty and inviting. Angela liked the fresh smell of the sea air. The two women sat hunched over a wooden table in the center of the room, sipped their mint tea and munched on the toast Katherine had made.

"Julia made the jam from local island berries," Katherine said. "Isn't it delicious?"

"Yummy. Tell me more about Julia. How did you meet her?"

"Oh, it's hard to know where to begin. When things were getting really bad with Josh, I almost came home—back to the mainland that is. The thing is, I love my work with the whale study group and ..."

"Sorry to interrupt, dear. But you never did tell me exactly what you're doing here. All your sister and I know is that you are working on some sort of a research project about the orcas."

"I'll tell you more about that in a minute," said Katherine. "First, I want to tell you how I met Julia, and how she has filled a void I always felt in my life. You know how I always made bad choices in partners. Josh was just the tipping point. Somehow, he made me feel less than him, not good enough, and I succumbed to that for way too long. Knowing Julia, seeing her strength, her confidence and dynamic way of being, as well as her support for me in our whale research, made me realize I didn't deserve that poor treatment from Josh. I didn't have to take his guff, his put-downs, any longer."

Angela sighed with long-awaited relief, like finding something you thought you would never see again. She listened intently as her daughter's story unfolded, a story of intimidation and verbal abuse by her boyfriend, and then her epiphany and the realization she loved a woman. The reality of her daughter's bisexuality surprised Angela, but she prided herself on not being judgmental, at keeping an open and tolerant mind. Now was a good time, she told herself, to practice what she preached.

"I'm glad, Kate, that you saw Josh for what he was, a bully, and you kicked him out. Julia sounds lovely and maybe just the person you need in your life now." To lighten the conversation a bit, Angela added, "and she makes good jam."

Katherine laughed and seemed to relax now that

she had gotten her "truth" out and felt her mother's acceptance. "Oh, thank you for understanding. I know you and Daddy worried about me. I always wished I could be more self-assured like Arial. I guess each of us is on our own path, and mine has been a rocky one. I think I've finally found what I want to do, where I want to live, and who I want to be with."

"When am I going to meet this new love of yours?"

"Today. I'm taking you to the whale-watching station, and you'll learn more about our research. Julia will be there. We thought we could take you out to dinner after she gets off work. Tomorrow, when I go back to the station you can borrow my bike, or just hang out here and maybe work in my garden. It needs a little weeding."

"I get it. That's what you really wanted me to do while I'm here, right? Be a garden helper?" Angela chided her daughter, adding, "Of course, you know how much I love to garden, and don't worry, you don't have to entertain me. Besides, I can only stay for a couple of days. I have lots to do back in Seattle."

"Now we have to talk about *you*," Katherine said, looking very serious all of a sudden, "about your trip and other stuff."

Angela hesitated. It's the "other stuff" that worried her. "I think I know the 'other stuff' you are referring to."

"How about getting dressed first," Katherine said. "We can walk out to the point and sit on the rocks and talk more there."

"Good idea."

An hour later Angela and Katherine sat on a rocky

promontory, looking out at the small boats bobbing on the bay, admiring the water as it glistened and sparkled in the sunlight. The sound of the gulls engulfed the two, as the birds swept down and grabbed the small crumbs Katherine and Angela tossed to them.

They sat quietly for a few minutes, breathing in the sea air, and then Katherine said, as she looked straight into her mother's eyes, "As I mentioned on the phone, Moma, Arial told me about the letter. I must admit, at first, I was shocked, but after she read the whole thing over the phone, I was *mostly* curious. Who were you writing to? It's obvious you never sent the letter. It sounded sad, not just a *love letter*, as Arial called it."

"Thank you, dear, for not jumping to conclusions and thinking the worst of me, judging me for deceiving your father. I'm afraid your sister is feeling a bit ambivalent about me right now. In some ways, I don't blame her. I guess I disappointed all of you. I'm not the Virgin Mary, you may have thought me to be—of course, I'm being facetious. What I mean is, I believe it's normal for children to think, or at least want their parents to be totally faithful to one another, to adore and honor their marriage vows. And mostly they just can't believe their parents really have sex, with each other or with anyone else. I never planned on being unfaithful to your father. When I married him, I was terribly in love with him. He was a wonderful man, and I'm glad he was the father of you and Arial."

Katherine looked out at the sea, fidgeting with the ties on her sweatshirt and listening intently to what her mother had to say. Her red hair blew in the wind. Angela appreciated her prescience and willingness to listen.

"You may remember your dad worked a lot, and I got more and more wrapped up in my art career. Once we had raised you girls, and then had grandchildren, we seemed to grow apart. Oh, we loved each other, but much of the passion had left our relationship. I think we both sensed it, but didn't quite know how to reignite the fires."

"Sorry for interrupting," said Katherine, "but in spite of being very wrapped up in my own problems, I noticed the changes between you and Daddy. I was worried and tried to talk about it to Daddy once, but he seemed to be in denial. I decided to drop it."

Surprised, Angela realized she hadn't had a clue, how her and David's unhappy behavior affected the girls.

Angela continued, "Well, it was about that time that my old activist ideals and desires to help out again in Central America kicked in. When I went on the El Salvador trip with Sandy's friends from California, I felt something I hadn't felt for a long time. Helping the people down there, speaking Spanish, and discovering another culture made me feel alive again. It's hard to explain." She paused.

"I think I understand," said Katherine.

"I realized later that my secondary reason for going was to take a break from your father, to think about the next stage of my life with him, and how to mend the tears in our relationship. We're not in control of our destinies. Life happens one small thing at a time. While in El Salvador, I met a man—Liam is his name—who had been doing humanitarian aid work there for several years. We seemed drawn to one another by some kind of magical force. Without knowing how, we slipped and fell in love. It was incredible. We both felt dismayed that we could feel the kind of passion and love we once felt for our spouses, and we even commented that we felt like teenagers first discovering love."

"Wait a minute, Moma. I'm trying to take this all in. You mean he had a wife? You were both married? I don't mean to sound naïve, I know it happens, but …"

Angela interrupted. "I know. I know. How could I take up with a married man? How could I hurt another woman? And possibly break up a family—two families? Those questions seared my heart every day as we became more and more entangled in our affair. We had only two weeks with each other, not long enough, but enough to change my life, or at least my perceptions. We ultimately decided we could not hurt our families. The letter your sister found was one I wrote many months later, after Liam and I had unsuccessfully tried to meet in secret. It was really my final good-bye to him, when I finally released the lingering dream we would someday get together."

"But why didn't you ever send it?" Katherine asked.

"I decided it would be too much of a risk. His wife might find it, and it would destroy their lives. I truly forgot about the letter, but I admit, I never forgot about Liam."

"About that time, your dad retired, and we took more time to enjoy life together. I don't think he ever knew about my affair, but if he did he was sensitive enough not to ask about it. We took up salsa dancing and other activities that renewed our friendship, but it was never the same. We learn to live with disillusionment, especially when the price we must pay for complete honesty means bringing pain to many others."

Katherine wrapped an arm around her mother and looked into her eyes with empathy, "Oh, Moma."

"There was no point in making a confession of my trespass. I never expected that one of you would find the letter. In fact, I'm not even sure why I saved it. I forgot I had put it in the bottom drawer of my desk in the studio where, as you know, Arial found it."

"Yeah. She was pretty upset when she called me after discovering the letter. I didn't know what to say, other than she shouldn't rush to judge, but wait until she could talk to you."

"Yes, and now I have her upset over another development. While I was on my trip to El Salvador this past month, I ran into Liam, totally by accident."

Katherine's eyes opened wide in dismay. "Wow, that's amazing. Arial didn't say a thing about that. It must have been your destiny, as you called it. I sometimes feel it was mine to meet Julia. Go on. What happened?"

"We hadn't spoken or communicated with each other in ten years. I was looking up at the San Salvador Cathedral where we first laid eyes on each other ten years ago—and there he was again. It was an unbelievable coincidence that he should be there at the same time as me. Serendipitous, I guess you could say. In two days I was leaving for the Bajo Lempa to see Adriana and her family. Do you remember me mentioning them and showing you photos?"

"Vaguely," said Katherine.

"Well, Liam and I spent a couple of days together getting reacquainted." Angela decided it wasn't necessary to tell all the details of their romantic reunion. "The upshot is that Liam wants me to return to El Salvador at the end of the summer and assist him with his project aiding a small orphanage there, which was started right after the civil war."

"Oh, now I understand why Arial sounded so enraged when she called the other night," Katherine said. "All she said was 'wait until you hear what mother is planning to do next.' I begged her to tell me, but she said it would be better to hear it from you. So are you going back to El Salvador?"

After the past week's discussions with Arial and Maggie, Angela was more secure in her resolve. She knew, in spite of the risk of losing the love and respect of her one daughter, she had to follow her own path, as Katherine had acknowledged. She had no choice but to return to Liam in El Salvador and find the new meaning for her life she had been seeking, helping the children at the orphanage. All she could do, at this point, was to hope that the girls would eventually understand.

"Yes, dear, I *am*."

Angela pulled a handkerchief from her jeans pocket and wiped her wet eyes. She had been pouring out her thoughts and confessions to Katherine, and now her emotions got the best of her. She couldn't hide her tears any longer.

"Oh, Moma, I'm so sorry for the years you had to keep this to yourself. Knowing how I feel for Julia makes me understand how important love is in our lives, in whatever form or whenever it comes. I loved you and Daddy together, but I understand you were two separate people following your own trajectories. Knowing your truth doesn't diminish my love for you."

Angela collapsed against the shoulder of her daughter with a sob. It came with a rush like a backed-up dam, released by the flip of a lever, the truth.

"Thank you for understanding," said Angela. "I love you and your sister so much, but I have to be with Liam now, and to try to help the people we have both grown to love in El Salvador. My dream and hope is that you can eventually come down and meet them, and Liam, too. Then, maybe you'll be able to better understand."

"I will definitely try to do that, Moma. I hope you have a photograph of this Liam guy. I would love to see him. But for now I think we'd better get back to the cottage. I promised Julia we would pick her up about four and hang out together before going to dinner."

They embraced and Katherine held on to her mother's arm to help her descend from the rock. In silence, they walked back to Katherine's cottage.

Two days later, Angela boarded the ferry in Friday Harbor. She looked back at her daughter with her arm around Julia, standing on the quay waving and blowing kisses. Their faces glowed, and Angela felt the rush of remembrance of herself, young and in love so many years ago with David. How lucky she was to have experienced love twice in her lifetime.

Crossing the Straits of Juan de Fuca on the voyage

back to the mainland gave Angela time to reflect on the past two days with her daughter, their discussions of love, and the revelation of Katherine's new feelings for another woman. Angela felt humbled by her daughter's trust and couldn't help but admit that her own life, too, had been blessed with a series of fortunate circumstances—random acts and reactions. She seemed to have been always at the right time or if not "right," the propitious one, the one that opened a door to excitement or something interesting. Now in the autumn of her life, she was finding that time was running out. She sensed she no longer could rely on random chance that the rest of her life would be as interesting as the past. Her intuition moved her to pursue this new adventure with Liam, to offer service to others, before the leaves of her life's story became dust, swept back into the earth.

An hour and a half later Angela slid into the driver's seat of her rather dilapidated Toyoto, parked at the Anacortes harbor lot. Just as she began to start the car her cell phone rang. She reached for her purse, and grabbed the phone to stop its persistent ringing.

"Hello."

"Angela, *mi amor*, I miss you." It was Liam.

She gasped. "It's so good to hear your voice. It's been hard to resist calling you. I was so busy getting unpacked and wanted to have a chance to talk to my girls about our plans before I called."

"Well, I couldn't wait any longer to hear your voice, said Liam, "Where are you, what are you wearing? Is it sexy? What are you doing?"

In her mind's eye, Angela could see his wry smile;

she knew he was teasing her.

"Well, if you really want to know, I'm dressed in a sheer summer top, walking on a sandy beach under the moonlight, thinking of you." She knew she could get away with the different time of day. It would be night time in Boston by now.

"Um, wait. Did you say a sheer blouse, showing off your soft skin and round breasts, pointed upward to the stars?"

Angela giggled and with a self-conscious blush, said: "No, really, darling, I'm sitting in my old car in the Anacortes parking lot. I just visited my daughter, Katherine, on San Juan Island. I'm headed back to Seattle."

"Great—that much nearer the Seattle airport. I want you to come sooner than we talked about—back to El Salvador. I'll tell you why later. Could you do that? Oh, by the way, I hope everything's going well with your girls, as you call them."

Angela felt her heart wrench with this new proposition. Yes, she had decided for sure to return to Liam and El Salvador. She missed him and she wanted to go as soon as possible. But could she get everything done sooner than they had planned? How much sooner did he mean?

"Angie, are you still there?"

"Yes. I told the girls about us, and that I plan to return, but I don't know, realistically, how soon I can get there."

"Why? I know it's easy for me to say, but I really can't wait all summer to see you and hold you in my arms again. I talked to Father Rutilio. Sister Agnes needs our help at the orphanage. I have to bring down a bunch of supplies my church is donating, and I'm planning on leaving in two weeks, if I can get the stuff all loaded by then in the great new vehicle I've bought. You'll love it—an old 1987 VW bus, in near perfect shape, great for transporting the older kids back and forth from San Salvador for their tattoo removal, and a good vehicle for longer trips, too."

Tattoo removal? What did he mean by that? And longer trips—what trips was he planning to take? Angela mused a moment.

"Liam, let me catch my breath a minute and think."

"No, sweetheart, I want to keep you breathless, breathlessly in love with me, forever."

Angela laughed. "You just may do that, but tell me the details. Why the van? You never mentioned anything about tattoo removal or transporting kids into San Salvador. Tell me more."

"I can tell you all that in person. You must tell me when I can expect to see you. I'll pick you up at the airport. Just tell me when."

"Give me a day to think about it and—"

"Don't think with your head, just with your heart," Liam said. "You said yourself, 'the best journeys are of the heart.' Keep it open."

"I promise I'll call you tomorrow. I'll think about this all the way back to Seattle. I better get on the road now. As it gets later in the day, the traffic going back into the city can be atrocious. Oh, I forgot to ask about *you*. Is everything going well? Are you getting to your personal business, as you called it?"

"Sure, it's going fine."

Somehow, that didn't reassure Angela. She couldn't help but feel Liam was keeping something from her.

"Good. I'll call to you tomorrow and tell you when I can come."

"Perfect," Liam said. "I'll be hanging out at the phone. You have my number, right?"

"I do. Until tomorrow. *Ciao*!"

"*Beseme mucho*," Liam said. "*Ciao*!" The phone clicked off.

Angela sat stunned for a minute. How good it was to hear Liam's voice, how much she wanted to be with him, but could she really go sooner than the end of the summer? After all, she had only been home two weeks, and he wanted her to join him in another two. How would she explain it to the girls? She had hoped to have the whole summer to soften the blow she had already dealt them.

She started the car and tried the best she could to keep her eyes and thoughts on the road as she drove back to Seattle, wondering how she could really be back in El Salvador in less than a month.

Angela's Decision
Seattle

Upon arriving home, Angela found two phone messages: one from Maggie and one from Arial. Tired and not wishing to confront another argument with her daughter, Angela called Maggie.

"Hi, Mags."

"*Hola, mi amiga,* what's up? Things going better with the girls?"

"Well, yes and no," Angela said. "I just got back from a visit with Katherine, and she's great. It was fun to be in San Juan Island again, and Katherine's finally doing well. She got rid of Josh and has a new love in her life, a woman."

There was pause. "Whew, that's a bit of a surprise, but if she's happy, I'm happy. You remember I told you about my hairdresser, who married her lover, another woman. I went to their wedding while you were in El Salvador. It was *bee-uti-ful,* and they are darling and so in love."

Angela knew Maggie would understand and didn't think Katherine would mind if she told her. Maggie and Katherine had always been super close, like two peas in a pod, both redheads. Maggie had been a role model for Katherine, striking out on her own to open a business and never making her life dependent on finding a man.

"So what's up with Arial?" Maggie asked.

"Haven't talked to her yet, and I'm kind of dreading it, though I think she'll be happy I've decided *not* to sell the house. The ferry crossing gave me time to think. I had a call from Liam, and it was so good to talk to him. I've made my decision. I'm going back for sure to El Salvador and this is the part the girls won't like—I'm going sooner than they think. After ten years of being apart, I can't miss this opportunity, a second chance to be with Liam now and do the work I want to in El Salvador."

"I'm glad you've decided to put your own happiness on the top of the deck right now. The girls will be fine, and in time they will understand."

"I sure hope so. I will miss the grandkids, but even they don't need me as much now that they are all nearly teenagers and totally wrapped up in their own lives. Hopefully, I can get them all down to El Salvador eventually. They could learn a lot from the experience."

"So, what can I do to help you most, dear friend of mine?" Maggie asked.

"Well, I think I'll rent out the house, on a month-to-month basis. I'm still not sure what's going to happen or how long I will be down there. I'm having some doubts …"

Probing, Maggie said, "Hold it. Are you having

doubts about your feelings for Liam?"

"No, I love him, Maggie. We have a lot in common and share a desire to work with the people in El Salvador. I guess we both fashion ourselves as some kind of saviors of the poor, but it's true, we get a lot out of being with our friends there, perhaps more than they get from us. My doubts are more about what I will be doing. Will I really be able to make a difference and …"

"And what?"

"Well, Liam has become very involved in helping immigrants who want to re-connect with their families in the US, and has suggested that I help him. I'm not totally sure what I'm getting myself into."

"Wow, that's a hot issue. Lots of folks are not too happy with the immigrants coming into the country, claim they're taking all the jobs and costing the economy too much. The border is becoming militarized with the construction of the 800-mile wall and border patrols are growing in numbers like rabbits, I hear. They're everywhere. Of course, you know my opinion. This country was built on the labor and contributions of immigrants. Funny, I read the other day that Washington orchardists are really hurting this season with not enough workers to pick a record crop of their apples. In the meantime, the government keeps deporting all the migrant workers."

"I'll have to admit I agree with you on some points, but I have seen the terrible way the migrant workers often have to live here. It's hard on their families, too, being separated and not knowing if they are going to come back alive or not. Do you remember me telling you about my friend, Adriana, and her daughter, Cici?"

"Yeah," said Maggie, "I remember you showed me their pictures when you came back from El Salvador the first time. Sweet."

"Cici is twelve now, and Adriana worries she won't see her father again," said Angela. "It's a complicated issue, one of the few that may cause conflict between Liam and me. I think he has promised to take Adriana and Cici to the border, and I'm worried about that. We didn't get enough time to discuss it when I was down there. So enchanted at finding each other again, we set our differences aside. I guess we'll have to get more real when I return."

"That's for sure," Maggie said, "but you didn't tell me how I can help."

"I'm not sure how long I will be down there, so I'm wondering if you might act as a property manager, and try to rent the house at the end of the summer. In the meantime, I want the girls to be able to use the house for summer parties, and Heather can come over and do clay work in my studio during the break."

"I wouldn't mind doing that, at all. I can't guarantee we'll find renters who want a furnished place though."

"Don't worry, I'm planning on putting a lot in storage and I can box up stuff and store it in the studio. I want you to know, too, that I plan on paying you."

"Well, we'll talk about that later," said Maggie.

"Let's get off me, now," said Angela. "How are you? You mentioned something about meeting a new man the last time we saw each other. I want to hear more about him."

"Oops, you reminded me. I've got to get off the phone and get home to change. I promised Rick I'd go out to dinner with him tonight. I have to go. I'll tell you all about him later. We might both be finding love late in life."

They laughed. "Let's talk again, soon," Maggie said. "I'll be thinking about you and this new venture of yours."

"Don't worry, Maggie. I'm confident I'm doing the right thing. It's never too late to fall in love, and besides, someone once said, "You only grow old when you stop falling in love."

"I like that. Well, got to go so I don't grow old. *Ciao*, for now."

Saturday morning, holding her mug of hot coffee in her hand, Angela phoned her daughter.

"Arial, honey, I'm back. Sorry I didn't call you yesterday. I was exhausted after the ferry crossing and the drive home in traffic."

"How was the trip? How's Kate doing?" Arial asked. "Is Josh definitely out of her life? She sent the boys some cool postcards of the orcas. Did you find out more about her work with the whales?"

"Whoa. I can't answer all your questions at once." She was glad that Arial was at least talking to her. "My trip was great. You know how I love the islands. Kate's doing fine. Josh is definitely out of her life, and she has a new love, who I liked very much. I'll let *her* tell you all about that, when she's ready." Angela had promised not to disclose Katherine's relationship with Julia to Arial.

"She's living in a cute cottage, and I loved staying there with her. We had fun walks on Agate Beach, and some good talks."

"Did you talk about your plans to go back to El Salvador to be with your new love, Mother?"

Angela decided to overlook the slightly sarcastic tone in Arial's question.

"Yes, we talked about Liam and my plans to join him in El Salvador. In fact, I have to tell you something." Angela had decided not to avoid the inevitable. It was better to share the decision she made, while driving back to Seattle, directly with the girls, to tell them the truth. They would be glad, at least, that she wasn't going to sell the house right off. It suddenly seemed simple, the right thing to do. Time to stop pushing the river and just flow with it.

"After much thought, I've decided I'll be going back to El Salvador sooner than I originally planned."

After a long pause Arial responded. "Are you *sure* you know what you're doing, mother? I kept hoping you might change your mind. I know it's your life but …" she paused in mid-sentence, as if to muster her arguments. "I don't understand why you have to traipse off to Central America and live like a dog to change the world. You have your art, you give beauty and meaning to people's lives here and …"

"No, stop right there," Angela said. "All I do here is create icons of and for the wealthy. I don't believe in being sucked up and consumed by corporate wealth. Do you know that Sammy— you know, the guy who owns Sloan Gallery and my biggest promoter—told me the other day that most of my buyers are corporate CEOs. I want to bring brightness and light into the little guy's life. I have spent my life creating for the haves, not the have-nots. That bothers me now that I know so much more than when I started my career. Your dad and I often talked about that. His best clients desired castles to show off their wealth, but didn't care that much about his achieving great design, let alone helping the less fortunate in the world."

"Oh, Mother, don't get so dramatic," Arial said. "We know you love the poor, and we support you in that, but that doesn't mean you have to suffer, too."

"For some, real life *is* more melodramatic than Hollywood clichés. Arial, I don't suffer when I go to the Bajo Lempa. I live simply, but with joy each day. When I wake up, I feel like I'm truly living, something I can't say is always true here. I need to know I'm contributing to the world at large. In fact, you are part of that, for if I can be a beacon of how to live your lives—oh, does that sound self-righteous?"

"Yes, just a little, Mother." There was a long pause during which neither of them spoke.

"I don't mean to be sanctimonious," Angela continued. "What I mean is: maybe someday, Jessie or Joey will be inspired to reach out to a Latino farm worker and remember what his grandmother said once about who puts the food on our tables. Maybe, by my doing what I'm doing, I will give a glimmer of how we can all act out our deepest moral values, what we care most about. Maybe my artistic talent can help bring joy to the children at the orphanage, for example, lead them to find a better way to express their feelings than through violence and anger. Maybe. I don't know what the results will be, but I have to try. For me that is more gratifying than adorning someone's already plush dwelling with show-off works of art for their wealthy friends."

"Mother, you sound like you hate anyone with money. That means you hate what Dennis and I are trying to build, a comfortable life in which our children can thrive and have opportunities for the best education available in America. You and Daddy once said that was why you worked so hard. Do you really know what you are saying now?"

"Yes, I *do* know, honey. I'm proud of you and your success, but that's not where I am now. I hope you will eventually learn to accept my decision and be happy for me."

Angela knew she sounded abrupt, but Maggie had encouraged her to state her case. "It's not like I've stopped loving you. You, Katherine and the grandchildren are still very precious to me. You're in a different stage of your lives than me. I understand that. I've already told you the reasons why I feel I have to do this, carpe diem, and all that. At my age, these decisions are important."

There was another long pause before Arial said, "Perhaps I've been a bit selfish, wanting you to stay here and not being very accepting of this new relationship of yours so soon after Daddy's death. I'll admit that, but you've got to understand what a shock it was finding your love letter, and then hearing you disclose the affair you had while you were still married to our dad. It's been hard." Angela could hear the tear in Arial's voice.

"I understand. I know it was a shock. I'm sorry I disappointed you and that we had words. I regret I didn't tell you the truth a long time ago. All I can hope for now is your forgiveness. I know you will like Liam when you meet him. I hope you and Katherine will come down and join me in El Salvador for a week or so. In the meantime, I have made another decision I think you will be happy about."

"What's that?" Arial sniffled and sounded skeptical.

"For the time being, I'm not going to sell the house. I'll store some things and then you, the kids, and Katherine can use the house during the summer. Maggie's agreed to be my rental agent and manager."

"Oh, Mother, I'm so relieved you're not selling the house. It felt like you were selling away our childhoods. We had so many good memories growing up there. We know Daddy left you with a pretty good insurance policy, so you don't need the money."

"Yes, I know that, honey, and I think I understand, now, how you were feeling. Plus, maybe I shouldn't get rid of the house, yet." Angela thought for a minute, biting her lip, "Since I'm not *really* sure how long I will be down in El Salvador."

"Mother, are you having doubts about Liam?"

"No dear, not at all. I'm just not sure how long the orphanage will need us, nor what we'll be doing next," Angela said.

"Well, I'm glad you're not thinking of staying in El Salvador forever. I'd better go. Dennis is waiting for me. We're going to the boys' soccer game. See you later in the week. Bye." The phone clicked off.

Angela stared at the phone and realized she'd just had another sign that it was time to rebuild her own life. The girls were busy with theirs. Perhaps, sharing the truth finally, about her love affair, had been the best thing to do. Now, she just hoped they would someday come to like Liam.

After another night of wrestling with her demons and the guilt she felt leaving her family again, Angela finally got up and made herself a cup of strong coffee, knowing she couldn't put off any longer getting ready for her next adventure. It was coming up sooner than she had anticipated. She pondered why Liam made it sound so urgent. She tried to tell herself not to worry, to set aside her need to control, and to trust that all would be well once she and Liam were together, but Maggie's questions haunted her. How well did she really know Liam—and what he expected her to do, once she returned to El Salvador?

PART THREE

This is how she now believes life happens. One small thing at a time. A series of inconsequential junctions, any or none of which can lead to salvation or disaster. There are no grand moments where a person does or does not perform the act that defines their humanity. There are only moments that appear briefly, to be this way.

—Steven Galloway, *The Cellist of Sarajevo*

All things tend to stay inert unless an external force comes along to push them in one direction or the other.

—Newton's Law of Inertia

Return to Liam
El Salvador 2010

When she arrived at the hostel, Nueva Vida, in San Salvador, where Liam had reserved a room, there was a message from him. He apologized that he hadn't been able to meet her at the airport and had to send a taxi to fetch her in his place. There was an additional letdown: he would not be able to see her until the following day.

"Angela, sweetheart, get some shut-eye, and I'll see you bright and early tomorrow morning."

Though disappointed, Angela reassured herself that she and Liam would have lots of time to spend together while they worked at the orphanage. In anticipation of their reunion, she resolved to get right to the bottom of her concerns about Liam's promise to take Adriana and Cici across the border.

Awakened the next morning by the loud city noises and the hotel staff working outside her small window, Angela heard a tap on her door.

"*Señora* Larson, you have a message."

She quickly pulled on her cotton robe and tripped over the clothes she had dropped on the floor the night before, as she walked, still half asleep, to the door, speaking as she went.

"Just leave it under the door, please. *Gracias.*"

"Now what?" she whispered under her breath, and reached down to retrieve the message. It was from Liam.

"Sorry, Angela, I cannot make it to the hostel, but a driver named Felipe will be there at 10 o'clock to pick you up and take you to our surprise rendezvous."

"Surprise rendezvous?" That was almost titillating enough to help soothe her initial irritation. She stifled her disappointment as she shuffled back to bed, crawled in under the sheet, pulled her knees up to her chin and, with arms wrapped around them, simmered a moment.

Oh, well, she would see him soon. She reread the message to make sure she hadn't misunderstood, and then looked at her watch on the bedside table, and realized that it was nine thirty-five. She had just enough time to get dressed and pack up her things.

Twenty minutes later she pulled her wobbly-wheeled suitcase down to the lobby and heard a pickup drive into the parking zone in front of the hostel. Perfect timing. A Salvadoran man sauntered in and asked the young woman at the desk for *Señora* Larson. He looked up and saw Angela and smiled.

"*Señora* Larson?" he asked.

"*Si*, that's me*! Hola*. I have to get my backpack. I'll be right back. I have a big box, too."

"Can I help you, *Señora*?" said the man, in heavily

accented English. He told her his name was Felipe.

"Sure, that would be great. You can call me Angela."

Felipe followed Angela up the short staircase to her room and lifted her backpack onto his broad shoulders, picked up the box by the rope wrapped around it, and headed down the stairs. Angela followed. She stopped a moment at the lobby desk, wondering if she should pay the bill. The girl there seemed to read her thoughts.

"Oh, *Señora*, no problem," she said. "*Señor* O'Connor has already paid for your room."

"*Gracias*," Angela nodded, and grabbed the handle of her suitcase to walk out into the heat of the bright San Salvadoran sunshine. Felipe hoisted the heavy backpack and box into the pickup.

"It's heavy isn't it?" Angela said. She usually took more than she needed. Always be prepared for the unexpected, her father had taught her.

"*No, está bien*," Felipe graciously replied, slipping back into his comfortable Spanish.

Friends, who knew Angela was going to El Salvador to work in an orphanage, had stopped by the day before her departure with their donations to the cause, first aid supplies, toys, and toiletries. After thanking her friends, Angela had mused: *If only their goodwill gestures could be translated into putting pressure on the government to change immigration policies.* Pondering this, she jumped into the cab of the old blue pickup, next to Felipe.

At first, they drove along the busy streets of the city as if carrying a third passenger, the awkward silence between two strangers. Angela felt anxious about what lay ahead. The many questions she still had crowded out her usual positive nature, and optimistic embrace of a new adventure. As they weaved in and out of San Salvador traffic toward the open highway, known as *El Literal*, and headed toward the coast, she felt her body begin to relax. They whisked past the roadside *pupuserias*, run-down gas stations and some "no tell" cheap motels. Along the road, people set out coconuts to sell to passers-by, piling them high on makeshift wooden counters made from old boxes. Through the open window the air smelled of gasoline and trash, but she felt comforted by the warm breeze that blew through her hair.

"Would you like some music, *Señora* Angela?" Felipe nodded toward the pickup's radio.

"*Sí*," Angela said. "And feel free to speak Spanish. It's good practice for me." She smiled at Felipe, who responded with a shy grin, as he switched the radio on.

The Latin music brought back romantic thoughts of Liam. For a while she just listened, lost in her memories of their recent reunion. Finally, Angela broke the silence between her Salvadoran driver and herself, tentatively starting to speak in Spanish.

"*Tiene una familia, Felipe?*" Angela asked about Felipe's family.

"*Sí.*" Felipe began to tell her his story. His speech was laced with shy smiles, awkward laughs, and a few words of English.

"Where did you learn English?"

"Oh, I speak only *poco*. I learned when I was in the States," said Felipe.

"Ah, how long were you there?"

"For two years. I worked to send money to my

family in the Bajo Lempa. I was in Virginia, then New York where I worked in a restaurant. I finally had a good job," he said with some pride. Suddenly, Felipe swerved sharply to avoid a mangy dog, which ran out into the highway. Angela could hear Felipe cuss softly under his breath. He looked over at her.

"*Lo Siento,*" he apologized.

"No, that's okay. Boy, that was a close call, wasn't it?" Picking up where their conversation had left off, Angela continued her query into Felipe's life.

"Why did you come back to El Salvador if you had a good job in the States?"

"I was an *illegal,*" Felipe said. "I didn't have papers."

Angela winced at the word *illegal.* It bothered her senses. How could a human being be declared *an illegal?* Why not instead, just an *undocumented worker?*

A look that seemed like a mélange of embarrassment and anger crossed the face of Felipe. Angela tried to decipher the tone in his voice.

"Immigration guys caught up with me," Felipe said, "and I was deported."

His words were packed with all the dread and fear the memory of being sent back to El Salvador must have conjured up for him. Angela felt almost ashamed she had asked such a stupid question.

"I'm sorry. That must have been hard," said Angela.

"Oh, yeah, it was, but I was glad to be with my family again and to return to my community."

"Do you wish you could go back to the States?"

"Only for my kids. I worry about my kids and how they will get an education and have opportunities for a better life," he said.

"You mean your kids here?" Angela asked.

With hesitation, Felipe shifted in his seat.

"My kids here, and *there*, too."

Angela sucked in her bréath, and let it out, sighing knowingly. How often had she heard how the boys and men who went to the States in search of work so they could send remittances back to their families became lonely and depressed, met a woman and then began a new family in their temporarily adopted home. She remembered how she had worried about that happening to Adriana. Would Cici loose her dad to another stepbrother or sister in *El Norte*? She remembered how terrified Adriana was when she didn't hear from her husband, Jorge, for long periods of time. What could she say to Felipe? The air between them grew heavy. Again, there was an awkward silence. How could she possibly reassure him that all would end well, that he would get to return to the north, his family here would be able to go with him, and everyone would live happily ever after? This was not the truth for the immigrant. It was a hard road ahead, she knew, for everyone involved. The Spanish conquistadores had found gold and silver here in the New World, but there was no gold to be found now for those they had conquered. Most were left to survive on the small bits of land they could eke out of their historical past.

Finally, Angela offered, "It must have been terribly frightening when you got picked up and sent back."

"*Sí*, but not near as frightening as when I went to the States."

"Do you want to tell me about it? How old were you?"

"My big brother went first and then tried to talk me into going when he came home, and realized there was still no work here for him. I was sixteen. At first I didn't want to go. I was afraid. The *muchachos* in our village, who had crossed over before had many horrible stories to tell about the *coyotes*, the guys who they had to pay to take them over the border, and riding the rails in Mexico, either on top of trains or underneath them. They talked about walking for miles and miles across the hot desert, not having enough water. The scariest part was when they arrived and bright lights were shined in their faces, and they could hear the noise of the helicopters overhead. It was too frightening. I didn't want to go."

"What changed your mind?" asked Angela.

"My father died, and I knew my mother and two sisters would not be able to survive without someone providing cash income. Our small plot of land was not enough for growing food for the whole family, only a little corn. My older sister was married and had two children, and they lived with us. Her husband was in *El Norte*, also. My brother traveled with him the first trip."

"So you went with your brother when he left the second time?"

"*Sí*, I decided to go. We traveled by foot, by train, and by bus. Riding the rails in Mexico was the worst. One night, my friend, who had come with us, fell from the top of the train." Felipe paused as if trying to hold back an avalanche of vivid and painful memories. "My *amigo's* arm was cut off as the train went over it."

Angela let out a small gasp and brought her hand to her mouth in shock. "Oh, Felipe, how horrible."

"*Sí*. I tried to save his life. The train slowed up as we were pulling into Huixtla, a town in Mexico. I climbed down off the train with my brother and two others, and we ran along the tracks to get back to my friend. He died in my arms. He was only sixteen, like me. We were friends since we were little."

"I'm so sorry, Felipe, *lo siento*." Angela didn't know what more to say.

Felipe continued: "Sometimes at night, when we tried to get some sleep on the train, gangs would rob the people. My brother and I were lucky. We managed to hide the little money we had, but others weren't as lucky. At times we awoke to find our neighbors with their throats slashed or a symbol of the *Salvatruchos* cut into their chests."

"Oh, that's awful. Who are the *Salvatruchos*?" Angela asked.

"One of the worst *maras*—you know, gangs. They prey on the people going to *El Norte*."

As if resigned to this truth, Felipe shrugged and continued to drive. He looked straight ahead at the road, not saying much for several kilometers. Angela felt bad that her questions had forced him to relive the nightmare. The two listened to the music and said nothing for the remainder of the journey. Angela dozed off for a brief while, her sleep abruptly interrupted as the pickup turned in through a large metal gate with a sign over it announcing, "*Bienvenidos a El Paraiso,*" and rumbled down a gravel path toward a large *palapa*, the typical palm frond-covered open air structure seen all over Latin American beaches. In the distance, through the palms and small buildings, she could see a slice of turquoise-colored ocean and even smelled it through the open windows of the pickup. A cooling breeze brushed her cheeks. The ride had been hot. Her skin felt sticky with sweat.

Somehow, this charming resort on the Pacific Coast of El Salvador seemed out of place. It was a reality she had not been exposed to on her previous trip there, a place where the wealthy vacationed. Affluent Salvadorans strolled along the paths to the beach. It was fancier than the place at La Liberdad where she had first met Liam so many years before. He was obviously trying to impress her. As Felipe pulled up in front of a bougainvillea-covered building, which looked like the reception office, two young men in white shirts and dark pants, with broad welcoming smiles on their faces, approached the pickup and greeted them.

"*Señora* Larson?" one of them said.

"*Sí!* That's me," Angela said.

"Welcome to Paradise."

Felipe had already jumped down out of the pickup and was getting her baggage out of the back, setting it carefully on the walkway, while the two hotel workers began to pick up the box, suitcase, and backpack to take them into the reception area. Felipe opened the passenger door, reaching out a hand to help Angela step down. She was dazed by her new surroundings.

"*Señor* O'Connor is waiting for you," the young man said.

Liam? He was there and waiting for her? She felt flushed, and stuttered.

"Oh, thank you," said Angela, trying to hide her excitement. Brushing her hair back, she glanced up at the truck's side view mirror to check if she looked presentable, then looked back at Felipe.

"*Muchas gracias*, Felipe, for getting me here with such speed." She hesitated wondering if she should tip him. Had Liam already paid him? What should she do?

As if reading her mind like the hotel clerk, Felipe smiled and said, "Don't worry. *Señor* Liam has already paid me. I will see you again. We work together."

"Oh, *gracias*, I'm glad. *Hasta luego.*" Angela turned and followed the Salvadoran hotel attendant.

"*Hola, mi amor!*" Liam's voice cut through the air of the lobby as Angela entered.

With a start, Angela looked up to see Liam leaning against the doorway to the patio, on the other side of the reception desk, dressed in swim trunks and a blue shirt with a towel in his hand. She couldn't keep from laughing out loud as she looked down at his feet with the same boots he had worn ten years earlier.

"I know, I know, I should get new boots, or maybe some flip-flops for the beach, but I have more important things to worry about—like you! Boy, am I *glad* you're here. How about a swim?" He smiled, she was sure, knowing this would remind her of their first meeting.

Their eyes met, and with a flirtatious response, she said. "I'm not sure I'm up to it. Besides, don't I have to check in?"

"I've taken care of that." Liam said, smiling. "Come on, I'll show you our room and you can change into your suit. I won't take no for an answer *this* time."

Ignoring the other people present, they moved simultaneously toward each other, as if pulled by that magnetic force they had experienced on the beach the first time they met. In a second, they were embracing. Whispering in her ear, Liam pulled her out the door.

They walked down the narrow, winding paths lined with palms and hibiscus bushes, in amongst the small *cabañas*, to their room. Bright magenta-colored bougainvillea draped itself across every arbor and pergola they passed. The fragrance of gardenias was in the air. Liam snatched a hibiscus bloom and handed it to Angela.

"*Gracias!*" She smiled to herself as she acknowledged his romantic gesture. "Trying to make up for not meeting me at the hotel in San Salvador, eh? Well it works."

Grinning, Liam pulled her suitcase behind him. The bellhop followed with the backpack and the box. "Bellhop"—did they call them that anymore? Angela realized a lot of years had passed, but she felt like a young woman who was falling in love for the first time. They arrived at their small *cabaña* near the beach. The bellhop opened the door and pulled back the curtains to let in the bright Salvadoran sunlight. Sensing the intimacy of the moment, maybe feeling the electricity between the two foreigners, he quickly slipped out and closed the door behind him.

Without stopping to look around Angela fell into Liam's arms.

"It's so good to be back here with you. I have to admit I was nervous and upset that you weren't at the hostel."

"I know. I was upset that I couldn't be there when you arrived. It was something I couldn't avoid," Liam said. "At least now we're together and have some time to relax before leaving for Suchitoto. Let's make the most of it."

Liam held her at arm's length and his eyes ran over her face and body. She could feel the pulse of her heartbeat and suddenly felt shy, knowing what they were both thinking. He gently undid her bra from under her lightweight blouse and slipped the straps from her shoulders. His hands moved knowingly to caress her back, and then her breasts. Lifting her blouse over her head, he pulled her close to him. Their deep breathing joined into one breath. He sighed and she melted into his embrace. He coaxed her toward the bed with its bright-colored woven bedspread, and they fell together, tasting each other's kisses.

"Oh, Liam."

The afternoon slipped away under the sheets of their bed, two mature adults rediscovering each other's bodies and their love, redesigning their lives as they went along. They fell asleep after their lovemaking, and the afternoon passed. Awakening later, their bodies were warm and moist as they embraced. Liam rolled over and smiled.

"We sleep well together. That's good."

Angela opened her drowsy eyes and smiled into his "Yes. Yes, we do."

Strangely, for an instant, she remembered David, how their bodies had melded so well together in bed like puzzle pieces that had found their match, the ins and outs conforming perfectly to each other. Though their lovemaking had grown less frequent and passionate, as the years passed, they had still enjoyed the comfort of sleeping together. Would it be like that with Liam? She wondered.

"So, what do you say about catching the sunset and then getting something to eat?" Liam asked. "We can swim tomorrow."

"Um, sounds good to me. Now that I think about it, I'm starved. I was so excited I haven't eaten a thing since I arrived in San Salvador last night."

"You mean you weren't dreading meeting up with this guy, and being dragged off kicking and screaming into the jungles of El Salvador?" Liam asked. "I admit, I suffered a little guilt asking you to do this just when your life was getting back to normal. I mean, after your husband died and you were getting used to being alone."

Liam sounded worried, and Angela sensed it was his self-doubting mode.

"Liam, I came on my own volition. I came to be with you and to help you and Father Rutilio at the orphanage. I won't look back. Remember, this is our second chance. You said that would come, right?" She snuggled into his arms again and their bodies fused into one.

"Sure, and we are going to make the most of it. I have a lot I want to show you, to share and experience with you. But let's go see that sunset now."

"Yes, good idea. On second thought," Angela started to sit up, "let's talk a bit first." She remembered her resolve to clear up some questions that had been pressing at the back of her mind. "You promised when we talked on the phone a few weeks ago that when I came down here, you would explain what you meant by needing the van for taking kids into San Salvador for tattoo removal. What's that—another project of yours? I feel I don't know enough about what we'll be doing, for instance, taking immigrants to the border. Is that the *longer trips* you referred to when we talked?"

"Don't worry, sweetheart, I'll explain all of that soon enough. Now this is our time, you just said it." Again, Liam was evasive, but managed to distract her as he jumped up, pulled on his pants and shirt, and reached to pull her up out of the bed?"

Was he brushing off her concerns? Maybe, but she decided not to press the issue now.

"Oh, sure. I'm afraid, though, it takes me a bit longer to get myself together than it does you." She pulled the sheet around herself and grabbed her clothes, which had ended up in a heap at the side of the bed. As she walked toward the bathroom, she could feel Liam's eyes watching her. "I'll try to be quick about this."

He laughed. "Take your time."

Twenty minutes later, they left the room, arms around each other's waists, and made their way to the large *palapa* in the center of the courtyard near the beach. The sky was beginning to turn a light mauve and pink and the sea below looked like deep purple ink. Waves curled onto the sand, spewing white foam in the dusky light. Liam grabbed Angela's hand and began to sprint toward the beach.

"If we don't hurry, we'll miss it. Time passes quickly when we're having fun, to quote a famous writer. Well, I think it was from a famous writer." Liam winked at

Angela. "It's later than I thought."

How could it be, mused Angela, that just a little over forty-eight hours ago, she boarded a plane in Seattle, and now she was here in this land she loved, El Salvador, with the man she had been imagining loving for the past ten years? Now was so right, she couldn't yet bring herself to worry about what lay ahead.

Leaving for Suchitoto
El Salvador 2010

After swooning over a moonlit dinner under the *palapa* at *El Paraiso*, Angela and Liam strolled along the path back to their *cabaña,* drunk with the perfume of the tropical night in this exotic oasis, far from the harsher realities of El Salvador. It was like a honeymoon from the past they never shared and before the challenges ahead. Liam shut the door of the *cabaña* and pulled Angela to him, leaning to kiss her on the neck and guiding her gently to the bed. Clothes were shed, again, in a blur of passionate caresses as they gave in, finally, to their voluptuous fatigue.

The morning sun slanted through the bamboo blinds, casting shadows like stripes across their bed covers. Angela rolled over, her hand having fallen asleep locked under the heaviness of Liam's body as they fell asleep in an embrace. Her movement woke him. He groaned and gently pulled her back.

"Oh, I don't want to get up—not yet, at least," he said. "I could lie here with you all day long just to make up for all the years I missed being close to you."

"Then let's." Angela yawned and stretched her arms out.

"Let's what?" Liam asked with a wink of his eye.

"Lie here all day long." She smiled at him through half-shut eyes with a kind of flirtatious gesture of her body, cocking her head back against her pillow.

"Oh, if only we could," Liam said with a note of concern.

Angela could see a change in his expression, as if a grey veil slipped over his face.

"What's the matter, Liam?"

Liam hesitated a moment, and then began, "I didn't want to tell you this last night nor did I want to shorten this chance we've finally found to be together, but I must. I spoke with Father Rutilio yesterday, just before coming here. We are needed in Suchitoto, sooner than I thought."

"What do you mean?" Angela wondered if this was going to be more than she had bargained for.

"It's a long story," said Liam. "I'll tell you on the way. The thing is we have to leave this paradise sooner than I had hoped. Come on. Let's get our suits on and take that swim we missed yesterday. We can eat breakfast and then we'll pack up."

Angela lay there for a few moments digesting this new information. Somehow, she felt there were things Liam wasn't revealing. Why was he keeping the truth from her? What was she getting herself into? She had committed to helping with the orphanage. The question about Liam's taking immigrants over the border had not been brought up again since their first conversation. Was that the reason they had to leave so quickly?

As if reading her thoughts, Liam said, "I'm afraid I didn't tell you the whole story when I asked you to come with me to Suchitoto to work in the orphanage. I'm sorry. I didn't mean to deceive you. It's just that, at that point, I did not understand the graveness of the situation. Father Rutilio has just recently told me that the gang problem in San Salvador is spreading to the more rural areas. Gangs are recruiting the younger ones. He's afraid the youth at the orphanage are prime targets. He hoped that your talent as an artist could be brought to bear on this problem by distracting the kids and helping them to express themselves in a nonviolent way, giving them confidence to stay away from the gang culture. I hope that helps clarify some of the urgency."

"Some of it, yes, but not all," Angela said. "I still do not understand why a day or two of relaxation here would make a difference."

I promise I'll try to explain more as we drive up to Suchitoto," said Liam. "Now let's go for that swim. Those ocean waves are waiting for us, and remember, I'll hold on tight to you."

She knew he was alluding to their first meeting and their time in the ocean at La Liberdad. Again, he distracted her from her concerns.

Liam was already up and in his swim trunks, egging her on to get into her suit.

"Liam, just give me a little time," said Angela. I'll

jump into my suit and be with you in a few minutes. Why don't I meet you on the beach?" She reached up and gave him a wet kiss on the lips.

"Well, if I can count on more of those, yes, that's fine. See you there. I'm having flashbacks of how you put me off on our first swim date, at the beach ten years ago?"

"See you soon, *mi amor*." Liam slipped out the door.

After the swim and breakfast on the patio, they walked back to their room to pack. As they rolled their suitcases out to the front of the hotel, she caught sight of a bright yellow, 1987 Volkswagen van parked in front of the hostel. He had said it would be perfect for their work— she wasn't quite sure what that work would entail. After only one night together of romantic and passionate lovemaking, Angela felt cheated they couldn't have more time together before getting involved in the orphanage, and whatever else Liam seemed to have planned.

Liam interrupted her thoughts. "Surprise! Here it is, the van I told you about. Isn't she a beauty? She even has AC. We're going to get some good use out of her."

"It's really nice, darling," said Angela, "I can tell you are quite enamored with her. I'm jealous."

"Oh, I know I'm crazy, but after bringing nothing but pickups down here for so many years, it's kind of nice to have something a bit more spacious. I even slept in her on the way down from Boston. Of course, once I got to the border it was too dangerous to stay along the roads at night in Mexico," said Liam.

"I'm glad you didn't take chances," Angela said. "That would have been crazy. I've heard of some pretty gruesome holdups by gangs and drug cartels."

They looked the van over, and then the young men at the hotel helped them get the baggage, and Angela's big box, loaded into the back.

"You go ahead and get in, and I'll be right back. Just have to pay the bill," Liam said as he made his way to the hotel office. He came back in a couple of minutes, followed by one of the young Salvadorans who worked there.

"Angela, meet Chico. Chico this is Angela. Chico's joining us, as far as San Salvador. He has to go into the city to get some supplies for the hotel, and I promised we could give him a ride. Felipe will bring him back."

Another surprise, Angela thought. "*Hola*, Chico." The young man smiled broadly and jumped into the back seat.

They were off on the first leg of the journey to Suchitoto. What more had Liam not told her?

Liam's Secret
El Salvador 2010

When they arrived in San Salvador after a quiet and tension-packed ride, Angela was glad they were dropping Chico off and would be traveling on alone to Suchitoto, a two-hour journey from San Salvador. She would have more time to talk to Liam about her trepidations. They let Chico out in a small suburb and waved *adios.*

As they wove through the tangle of noisy cars, buses, trucks, and pickups, Angela reached her hand over to Liam and laid it on his thigh. He responded with a smile and seemed to loosen up, too.

Angela probed. "Liam, I have to be honest with you. I'm getting a bit nervous about the expectations you and Rutilio have of me. You really have not told me much about the orphanage, and what I will be confronting."

"What do you want to know, sweetheart? My eyes are on the road, but I'm all ears and willing to answer your questions, if I can. Admittedly, I don't know everything. Even though I have been bringing supplies down to the orphanage, I have only visited it a couple of times. Rutilio and I usually meet in San Salvador, and Felipe delivers the stuff to Suchitoto. I did meet sister Agnes, the *jefa* who is running the orphanage along with two other Catholic nuns about six months ago. I think you're going to like them and they're going to *love* you. They will share their story with you. It's profound."

"What do you mean by 'profound'?" asked Angela.

"They lived here during the war and suffered much along with the people. They have many stories of the sacrifices made by the people of Suchitoto. I'm going to let them tell you about it." Liam reached down and squeezed Angela's hand.

"I guess I still feel you are holding something back from me, Liam. We have really known each other such a short time, and though we felt the deep connection ten years ago, I hope you can give me time to digest all that is happening now that we have reunited. I admit I'm feeling somewhat insecure."

"I understand," said Liam. "I have to confess to you."

Puzzled by his use of the word *confess* she turned away from the scenery, unfolding on the open road, and towards him with a questioning look in her eyes. Was this what she had been waiting for?

"What are you saying? What more have you not told me, Liam?"

"I had hoped to save this for later, but time seems to be pressing the issue. Remember when you left to return to the States, after our reunion in San Salvador?"

Angela slipped her hand off Liam's lap and turned toward the window, feeling as if a bomb might be dropping and sensing the need to prepare. She pulled the lightweight woven shawl she was wearing around her shoulders, as if for protection. What was he going to tell her now?

"Yes?" she replied.

"I told you, while you were in Seattle, I had to return to Boston to attend to some personal business there. Well that was not the whole truth. I had to return to get the results from some tests I had, before I left to come back to San Salvador to meet Father Rutilio, and our fateful reunion."

"Tests? What kind of tests?" Angela's mind raced ahead. Was Liam ill? Why hadn't he told her?

"Angela, I have a rare form of blood cancer. It's called myelodysplastic syndrome, or MDS. It has remained in a chronic, nonlethal state for some time, which is typical. Eventually, it transforms into a …"

Shocked, Angela interrupted, "Into what?" She asked this, fearing the worse. Part of her didn't want to know the truth.

"Well," Liam hesitated, "it transforms into a lethal disease. I've been lucky, until now, that is. Tests have shown my disease is transforming, and I may have only a year to live. But that's the worst scenario. My doctor hopes to try a new experimental drug, when the FDA approves it. In the meantime, he's giving me another medication, which seems to be helping the fatigue, my low blood counts and the bruising. So far these symptoms are being reduced, and I'm feeling great, and …"

Angela grabbed Liam's knee, and her hand began to tremble. "Oh, Liam. I'm so sorry." Tears began to flood her eyes, and she did not know what more to say.

"The tests showed that the disease has progressed to a degree where there is not a lot they can do now, unless the new drug works. I'm confident they'll approve the drug, soon," Liam said with his usual reassuring tone.

Angela's chest sank and her shoulders slumped. "Oh, darling, you should have told me. I had no idea you were ill. You look so good and have so much energy."

"Don't worry. I feel fine and am determined to beat this thing. The doctor gave me some pills I have to take daily. You can help me remember. I have to return to Boston in three months to see if there are any changes. That has put the pressure on me because I want to get Adriana and Cici up to the States somehow before then. Father Rutilio knows this, and he realizes I will want you to go along. He's hoping you can get the art program started and train the Sisters to take over for a while when we go."

Angela bent towards the dashboard, dropping her head into her cupped hands and tried to keep from crying. Shaking her head back and forth, she said, "Liam, you really should have told me all this sooner." Suddenly, it seemed as if this whole new world she had been imagining, this new life with Liam, was cracking into pieces.

"I admit, I was selfish, and a coward," Liam said, shaking his head. "I was afraid if I mentioned this when we were in San Salvador, you wouldn't come back, and we would once again miss our chance to be together."

In shock, Angela tried to take in this news, to absorb it and understand what it meant for their future, for *her* future. Though she was a believer in many Buddhist prescriptions for living, she wasn't very good at just living in the moment and not thinking of the future. Being fully "present in the now" was something she had to consciously practice every day.

They rolled along the highway, north out of suburbs of the big sprawling city of San Salvador, into a landscape unfamiliar to Angela. It was completely different than the Bajo Lempa region. The small roadside stands were less frequent now, and soon they were in open countryside, where trees lined the road and rolling hills swept up in front of them. Finally, they came to a big lake, and Liam swerved into the shoulder of the road to stop.

"Let's stop here for a few minutes," Liam said. "The lake is pretty, and I think you'll like the scenery." They had been quiet the last few kilometers, neither one knowing what to say next. Angela had a mixture of emotions, worry about losing him and fear that she may be drawn into something she was not prepared to do, to attempt a border crossing with her dear Salvadoran friends, maybe risking their lives and hers, too, let alone possibly taking care of a man she loved for the second time in her life, and facing another loss. Things were unfolding quickly, and a fear of the unknown crept into her thoughts.

"OK, good idea," Angela said, "It'll feel good to stretch my legs and get some fresh air, even if it is hot." Her mouth felt dry, and she didn't know quite what more to say to Liam, this man she loved but might lose. It reminded her of the painful days before David died.

How could this be happening? She got out of the car, walked over to the edge of the lake and looked out at the still waters, brooding. Liam followed her, not saying anything. As he came up next to her, he slipped his arm around her shoulder and said,

"The weather here is much cooler from the breezes that blow off the lake. We'll sleep better at nights in Suchitoto, which is higher in the mountains." He pulled Angela close to his side.

The two stood quietly, looking out at the picturesque scene, both lost in their thoughts. It was late afternoon, and the light was changing. The sky glowed a soft mauve over the darker waters. A skiff with a fisherman in the distance revealed its silhouette against the sky. A heron flew over their heads, its call breaking the silence.

"Oh, Liam, this is lovely. The more of El Salvador exposed to me, the more I fall in love with it."

"With me, too, I hope," said Liam.

"Yes, of course, with you, too. I only wish you had told me your secret sooner."

"What good would it have done? You may not have come back down here."

"Well, to be honest, I have something to tell you, too," Angela said. "I was waiting until we arrived and began our work at the orphanage before I told you. But now, I guess I better let it out while we're making confessions." Angela cleared her throat.

"My daughters are concerned about me. They're not happy that I wanted to come back to El Salvador so soon. They found out about our love affair in an unfortunate way, and have felt deceived by me and confused. They may even come down to check you out and to see what

I'm up to. I would prefer they not know about this latest development."

A loud noise distracted them, and they turned to see a big truck barreling by, heading in the direction of Suchitoto. In the back, workers stood up, leaning against the wooden side rails.

Liam waved, and they waved back.

"Liam, you know everyone in El Salvador," said Angela.

"Oh, I don't know them. I'm just waving in solidarity. Salvadorans, as you well know, are friendly. This country is where I feel most at home these days," Liam said, "and where I hope someday to be buried, well, my ashes anyway."

Angela shivered with the thought of being the one to bury him. It wasn't long ago that she buried another man she loved. "Liam, let's hope that is a long time from now. You said the doctors might have found an experimental drug for your condition?"

Changing the subject, Liam grabbed her hand and said, "Come on. "We better get going. I promised Sister Agnes and Father Rutilio we'd be there at lunchtime, and it's already past two. "

They had no sooner started out again, than they rounded a bend, and Liam had to swerve to avoid a young boy on a bike, trudging up the steep hill.

"Let's see where he's going. That old bike won't make it far." Without waiting for Angela's response, he pulled to the side of the road, just in front of the cyclist, calling out as he opened the door and asked where the boy was going.

The boy responded a bit breathlessly, as he came to a stop. *"Suchitoto."*

Turning to Angela, Liam said: "I thought that might be the case. Let's offer him a ride in the back. Is that OK with you?"

"Sure, that's fine." Angela appreciated Liam's good heartedness, even when it sometimes cost her his full attention.

Liam motioned for the boy to jump into the back seat and went around the side of the van to help him get his bike up into the vehicle. Fortunately it fit alongside of all their bags. The boy looked relieved, but maintained a demeanor of reserve and suspicion. Noticing this, Liam commented quietly to Angela, when he got back into the car.

"I bet this guy is from the orphanage. He couldn't be over sixteen, but something tells me he has a sad and angry past."

"Liam, not to knock your deep perceptiveness, but I must ask, how could you have possibly deciphered that in such a brief encounter?"

"Maybe it's because of my own past. I was sometimes an angry boy, and then I had a son, who was also an angry young man. I usually pick up on those vibes pretty quickly."

"You've never told me much about your past," Angela said. "We've spent so much time caught up in our present, I realize that I still know little about you. Knowing about your illness now, darling, makes me realize I would like to know more about your growing up, you know, the details. We've never talked much about your son, either, the one you mentioned when we met ten years ago."

"Oh, you know the most important stuff." He smiled evasively.

"No, I mean it. I'm interested. Why were you an *angry young man*, as you just described yourself?" Angela decided to ignore, for the moment, their rider. He probably couldn't understand her English, anyway. She needed to have this conversation with Liam.

She saw Liam look up into the rearview mirror as if checking on their passenger. "The kid's asleep," Liam said. "That was a pretty hefty climb he was making on that old bike. Guess it tired him, out. Now back to our conversation."

"Maybe I overstated the angry young man part, but I'll tell you a little bit of what I remember. My mother brought me to the States from Ireland when I was only seven, escaping my dad, who was an alcoholic and an abusive husband to boot. I don't remember him much, just some vague recollections of his coming home from the pub late at night and screaming at us. The worst were the times I had to listen to my mother cry. Finally, she up and left my dad with me, the only child, rare for a Catholic family—having only one child, that is. I think my father was so inebriated most of the time, he couldn't, well you know, pardon the expression, *get it up* to make any more kids."

"I'm sure it was hard having an alcoholic for a father," said Angela.

Liam brushed off the sympathetic remark. "Oh, it's a long time ago, and I really don't think of it much. But you asked about my childhood, and as you can see, it was rather dysfunctional."

"You couldn't help that. You were just a boy," said Angela. "But tell me, when your mother left, where did she go? How did you get to the States?"

"Well, I think I've blocked a lot of that out. Things were tough. It was post depression, late forties, and my mother made it to England first and then somehow got passage on a ship and came to the States. We landed at Ellis Island, and after a few days of quarantine we were able to disembark in New York City. My mother didn't much like the city. Luckily, she had a distant relative that put us up in her flat, and soon the two of them came up with a plan to move to Boston, where they had more friends in the Irish immigrant community. My mother used to try to convince me that we were just as good as anyone else. After all, she had a third cousin, who was a south end ward boss in the growing Irish political machine. Unfortunately, that didn't prevent me from suffering abuse and prejudice from the kids at school who considered me a *mick*. They used to call the Irish that when the poor, flea-infested Irish immigrants arrived, escaping the potato famine."

"I've read about that terrible period in Irish history. I also learned a lot about the Irish from a book my friend Maggie gave me, *Angela's Ashes*. It was beautifully written, but terribly sad."

"Yeah, my mum suffered like that Angela, but she was a hard cookie. She defended me, and our rights, to the bitter end. I remember once when the nuns at my Catholic school sent home a note saying that I could not attend communion if I didn't have better shoes and a decent coat. My mother wrote them back something to the effect that, 'if they wanted me to be dressed more decently, then they needed to find it in their hearts and pocketbooks to buy me the clothing, because she could not.' She was working as a washing woman at a local laundry and moonlighting in a pub at nights, of all things, after having endured the trauma of my father's alcoholism. I had a paper route in the south end and that helped bring in some small change. I vowed that someday I would be as rich as the Kennedys." Liam laughed. "Well, I didn't make it that high in society, but my life has been vastly richer and different than that of my poor mother, not to mention my father, who died in a ditch back in Ireland." Liam paused. "You wanted my story and there it is, in a nutshell."

"That's a fascinating story. We're both immigrants, in a way. My background is Italian, and I know my ancestors suffered from a great deal of prejudice, too, when they immigrated to the US in the late 1800s. We have much in common."

"Yeah, I guess we do. Maybe that's why our hearts go out to the new wave of immigrants coming over the border from Latin America."

They were approaching the outskirts of Suchitoto, and just then Angela looked up to see the boy tapping on Liam's shoulder. Angela looked around at him.

"*Hola*, you woke up." She smiled, but he didn't smile back.

"Liam, I think the boy wants to tell us something. We better pull off here. Maybe he needs to get out. I was so engrossed in your story I didn't even remember he was there."

Liam steered the van off onto the narrow shoulder of the road and stopped.

"*Que tal?* Do you need to get out here?" he asked the boy.

"*Sí,*" the boy said.

"I'll help you get your bike out." Liam jumped down from the van and walked around to the sliding side door, where he helped the boy lift out the bike. Without a word, the boy peddled towards Suchitoto.

"*Adios,*" Liam said, but the boy did not respond.

"I'm sure he lives at the orphanage, at least part time," said Liam. "I think I recognized him from my last visit there, when Father Rutilio took me to meet Sister Agnes and the kids. Did you catch a glimpse of the tattoo on his arm? He's part of one of the *maras*, the gangs we are trying to get out of the town. They are having way too much influence on the kids at the orphanage. He seemed very troubled and even a bit afraid. Maybe he's escaping a gang that's after him, a rival gang member perhaps. Who knows?" Liam's furrowed brow reflected his worried tone.

"I see you're worried about it," Angela said. "I hope that I'm going to be able to help the situation at the orphanage. I'm beginning to wonder if I have the skills, let alone enough fluency in Spanish, to really make a difference." Self-doubt began to wash over her usual confident manner. "On the phone, when we talked back in the States, you mentioned something about using the van to take the kids into the city for tattoo removal. Tell me about that."

"Don't worry. You'll be great with the kids, and the sisters will appreciate any contribution you can make," Liam said. "And I will, too. As for the tattoo removal program, we started it a year ago, and my church has been funding it so far. I take a few of the kids who have opted to remove the tattoos they acquired in the States when their parents were exiled there during the war. Removal of the tattoos is a long and painful process. Those kids came back and can't get jobs, because they are thought to be gang members, even if they opted out. They also risk getting arrested. Most of the kids are not orphans but have families who returned, and like the people of the Bajo Lempa, they're poor, underemployed and need their kids to help with the family expenses."

They were pulling in to what looked like a small town. Ahead was the typical large central plaza and across from the road Angela caught a glimpse of a beautiful white church, the central focus of the square. Liam turned down a cobbled side street and then pulled up to a long, low, tile-roofed colonial-style building, with its old mesquite double doors facing out to the street.

"Well, here we are," announced Liam.

Before Angela could say anything, one of the doors opened and a tall, imposing woman with gray hair cut short, dressed in slacks and a cotton, embroidered shirt, stepped out to the van and looked through the open window to greet them.

"Well, you finally made it. We've been expecting you. Rutilio sends his regrets he couldn't be here to welcome you. He's in San Salvador. Come on in and introduce me to this pretty woman you've got with you."

Angela wondered if this was one of the nuns. She certainly wasn't what Angela expected, and in fact, she made Angela blush with her reference to a "pretty woman."

Liam jumped out of the van and came around to the passenger side, shaking the woman's hand and then opened the passenger door.

"Welcome. You're Angela, I presume," the woman said. "We're glad to have you here at the *Casa de los Niños*."

"I'm glad to be here," Angela said. "Liam has told me a lot about your efforts here at the *Casa*. I'm looking forward to learning more."

"Hey, I've been rude. Excuse me, ladies, I did not even introduce you. Angela, this is Sister Agnes Clare, the head honcho here. Sister Agnes, this is Angela, a humanitarian, and a friend of mine and Father Rutilio's."

"*Hola, mucho gusto*," Sister Agnes said, as she reached out her hand, big for a woman's, and showing the signs of a life of hard work.

"Nice to meet you, too." Angela said. She wondered how much Liam and Rutilio had told sister Agnes about her.

"Come on. I'll show you two to your rooms and then we can sit down and have some coffee and lay out our game plan. The kids are all off at school, and some of the older ones are helping in the kitchen and out back in our small garden."

They entered into an interior courtyard of the former convent, well kept up but with obvious signs of age and past abuse, the remnants of poverty and war. Sister Agnes led the way and showed them to their adjoining rooms not far from a communal dining room.

"Um, something smells good," said Angela.

"Yes, we're preparing supper for you. The children will come in later after they return from school. We're glad you'll at least get to meet them before they have to get their homework done. I hoped you would arrive in time to join them at lunch, when they have a two-hour break."

"We hoped to arrive earlier, too." Liam said, "but stopped along the road to pick up a young kid, I believe from here."

Sister Agnes looked puzzled. "Oh, that might be Santos. We've wondered about his whereabouts. Well, if it's him, I'm glad he's back in Suchitoto. I'll tell you about him later. Why don't you two get settled in your rooms and then join me in the dining room."

Sister Agnes
Suchitoto

Angela and Liam had adjoining rooms off the central courtyard. Sparsely furnished with an ascetic atmosphere befitting a convent, Angela's room had little decoration other than a crucifix over the bed. The tile floor had one small hand-woven rug in a dull color. The bedspread was also hand woven in brighter colors with geometric patterns. One small window to the street let in fresh air.

Glad to have a chance to freshen up, Angela tried to digest what Liam had disclosed during their trip. The thought of losing him now, when they finally had found each other again was overwhelming. *Why had he kept his illness from her for so long? What was this going to do to their plans?* Questions and doubts bombarded her. She tried to brush these thoughts to the back of her mind now, as she ran her hairbrush through her long hair. Anxious to know more about the orphanage and Sister

Agnes, she hurried to wash and to change into a clean blouse. Her room was connected to Liam's by an interior wooden door. She could hear him whistling in the next room. She tapped lightly on the door.

"Liam, I'll meet you in the dining room, OK?"

The door flew open and Liam pulled her to him. "Not until I get to embrace you."

Angela felt as if her breath had been taken away, and she came up gasping with a laugh.

"Shh! Liam, the Sister might hear us."

"Oh, don't worry about that. You'll see. She's a very broad-minded nun."

Still feeling uneasy, Angela gave Liam a quick peck on the lips. "Well, I think we should go to the dining room to meet her. I'm anxious to learn more about this place." She pulled herself reluctantly from Liam's arms and walked toward the outer door. Liam closed the interior door and met her in the arcade surrounding a garden.

The air was laden with scents of tropical flowers and sounds of birds. A hummingbird flitted in and out, poking its long beak into the bright red tubular flowers, which draped themselves over the arcade. Angela began to relax and looked with anticipation to the dining area where Sister Agnes waited.

"Well, there you two are. I've been looking forward to meeting you, Angela. Rutilio has told me much about you. What a great story, you and Liam meeting after ten years of separation, I mean. Sounds like it's been good for both of you."

Angela was surprised that Sister Agnes seemed so

familiar with their "love story." *How much had Liam told her and Rutilio?* She felt embarrassed.

"Yes, it was quite a coincidence that we ran into each other a few weeks ago in San Salvador," said Angela. "Liam probably told you I was on a pilgrimage back to Central America to see the many friends I met here long ago." Wanting to avoid talking more about herself and Liam, she continued, "I'm looking forward to learning more about the orphanage and how I can be of value here."

"Whoa! Let's get to know each other and then we can flesh out the details. We already know you will be of great value." Sister Agnes was forward and frank. Angela could see right away, that she would like her.

Liam sat down on one of the hard wooden benches that flanked the long table on either side, across from Angela and next to Sister Agnes. "I haven't told Angela near as much about you, Sister, as I did you about her. I imagine she would love to hear your story."

"Well, Angela, is that true?" Sister Agnes asked.

"Oh, yes I would. Liam has told me you have been here since before the war. I'd love to hear some of that history."

A woman emerged from the kitchen and set down a big plate of *pupusa*s, rice, and beans in front of all of them. She was about thirty years old and seemed shy and reserved. Her long black hair was braided, and her cotton dress was crisp and clean. She wore a yellow apron over it.

"*Gracias*, Loraina. I'd like to introduce you to Angela, who is going to be here helping with the children's art program. Angela, Loraina supervises our kitchen, and she will be happy to discuss with you any dietary needs you may have."

"*Mucho gusto*, Loraina, and *muchas gracias*. Fortunately, I can eat anything," Angela said. "Or maybe that's unfortunate. I usually put on some pounds when I'm in El Salvador."

"Don't worry about that. Looks like you could use some extra fat on that skinny body of yours," Sister Agnes said, with her usual bluntness.

Usually proud about her slender frame, Angela glanced at Liam, a bit abashed by Agnes's comment. He just smiled in agreement. They all laughed and began to eat while Sister Agnes launched into her story.

"I came here in 1979, with a group of Mary Knoll nuns. We were doing outreach work for the poor in Central America and had a special calling to come to El Salvador. You may know that things were really heating up then, and a civil war was threatening to break out."

"Yes, I do know that. About that time, my husband, David, and I were taking an interest in Latin American affairs. Concerned about our government's policies vis-à-vis Nicaragua and El Salvador, we became active in a peace group and spent a lot of time researching what was happening down here, especially after the Sandinista revolution of 1979, followed by the 1980 assassination of Archbishop Oscar Romero here in El Salvador. Let's just say, our antennae were up."

"I'm glad you know some of that history," said Sister Agnes. "I liked these humble people and was ministering to their health, since I had a nursing degree. I felt needed.

As things heated up, the battles between the opposing forces, the FMLN and the government-sponsored paramilitaries and national army, began to get closer to San Salvador. People here were frightened. Father Rutilio, then a young priest, was dragged one day from our church in Suchitoto and tortured. He was left for dead in the hills near the lake." Sister Agnes pointed in the direction behind the convent. "They didn't like him teaching liberation theology to the people. Small boys of twelve years old were being extracted from schools by the army and conscripted into the battle. It was getting hard to get food. One day, right about that time, two of my fellow Mary Knoll Sisters were viciously raped and murdered. I'm sure you heard about that in the news."

Angela nodded, and recalled the film she had seen in the Bajo Lempa, ten years earlier, about how the young boys were taken from their families to fight in the war.

Sister Agnes continued.

"I was seriously thinking of returning to the States until a group of people came and asked if I would accompany them to another, more secure part of the country. They felt somehow, that with a Catholic nun in the vehicle, they would perhaps be safer and have more chance to come out of the journey alive." Sister Agnes laughed to herself. "In their eyes, I was the one who had the direct connection to God. I could not say no." Sister Agnes paused. "Well, that's a good stopping point. Go ahead and start eating. You're being too polite, and the food is getting cold."

Sister Agnes continued: "Though I felt as much fear as everyone else, the people saw me as a force to be reckoned with. They respected me. It was probably just because I'm so goddamned tall."

Angela nearly choked on her food as these words came out of the Catholic nun's mouth. She certainly was not Angela's stereotypical impression of a nun. It was evident that this woman commanded a lot of respect and had no fear of standing up to just about anyone, even the pope, if she had to.

As if reading Angela's mind, Sister Agnes asked, "Did I shock you?"

Embarrassed, Angela smiled and shrugged. "Well, a little. Let me admit I don't know a lot of Catholic nuns these days, though I'm Italian and my parents sent me to a Catholic school. In those days, perhaps, I had the mistaken impression that most Catholic nuns didn't swear."

Liam and Sister Agnes laughed in unison.

"You have a lot to learn, Angela, about us servants of God. For that matter, the Catholic Church has a lot to learn, too. The Sisters and I represent a more liberal arm of the church. We followed the message of Vatican II and the theories of liberation theology. But I won't get into that now."

The three of them continued eating in silence, captive to their own thoughts, as they finished their meal.

Loraina came into the room to clear their plates.

"*Está muy rico*, Loraina," Angela said. Liam nodded in agreement. Loraina appeared pleased with their compliments about her cooking.

Sister Agnes looked up at Loraina and said something in Spanish and then turned to Angela. "Loraina is going to serve you some of her delicious flan for dessert, while I finish my story."

"Oh, yes, please do. I'm fascinated," said Angela.

"Well, as I said the people wanted me to go with them to another place that was safer. So, I agreed, vowing that right after I got them to safety, I would probably return to the US. I was still terribly shaken by the loss of the other sisters. I agreed to ride in the big truck, and try as they did, to convince me to ride in the front cab, I chose to ride in the back. It was open with nothing but wooden railings around the two sides. It was a rather long and arduous trip to the north to the border near Honduras. The day was hot, and we were all on alert, fearing for our lives. A little girl sat next to me on the wooden bench they had set at the rear of the truck bed next to the rearview window. She looked very frail, and I quickly surmised she had not eaten much in the past month. She clutched a small handkerchief her mother had handed her. As we drove out of Suchitoto, she opened it slowly to peer at the contents, three small grapes. She turned to offer some to me. That was an epiphany for me. I knew then that I would stay in this land of such humble people, where, even in her starving state, this young child was ready to offer me the little she had to eat."

Angela felt tears come to her eyes. She hesitated, before saying, "It's such a touching story. Please go on."

"Well, the rest is history. As you already know, the war dragged on, many people were killed, in fact about 85,000 that we know of. Of course, there were those we refer to as "the disappeared," the ones we could never find any evidence of and who are missing to this day. Their mothers and loved ones still display their photos every year on the plaza in San Salvador during the ceremonies commemorating the death of their martyred Father Romero."

"Yes, I've witnessed that," Angela said. "In fact, it was at that very spot on the plaza, near the steps of the cathedral, that Liam and I saw each other for the first time. Maybe he has told you about our meeting."

Liam and Sister Agnes exchanged nods and smiles.

Angela wondered what else he may have told her and looked down, self-conscious of the truth of their affair.

"Well, enough about my history. Let's get to what's important now here at the orphanage."

"Yes, I'm very interested in learning more about that, how you started the orphanage and about the children who live here."

"*Sí*. Where to start?" Sister Agnes reflected for a moment. "Well, right after the Peace Accords were signed and the people began to pick up the pieces of their lives, Father Rutilio, no longer a priest, returned. You've met him." She smiled. "Oh, not from the dead—he survived the beatings and was exiled in the US for the next twelve years. "

Angela nodded. "Liam told me about that, and how he and Rutilio met and returned here together."

"We were good friends and began to talk about what we could do to help get the people back on their feet. We had set up a makeshift health clinic here at the convent, and some of the other sisters, mostly Salvadorans and I, were fantasizing about how we could make this place benefit the community more. We wanted to start a community center here with literacy classes, art workshops for the children, and a place for the lost and dispossessed after the war. Many children had lost their families and were literally wandering the streets. Some were small, having been born during the war, some were the poor boys who were returning from battle, physically and mentally wounded, and some were just lost teens, who had escaped conscription, but were very poor and damaged. The problem was funding. Where would we get the money needed to renovate the place? The structure was crumbling, and when Liam takes you on a tour after you meet the kids, you will see some of that."

"I'm looking forward to that." Angela glanced toward Liam with a smile. "Liam has told me some things, but there is still so much I have to learn."

"Well, to make a long story short, we have accomplished a lot with the resources we have been able to scrape up through NGOs, the Mary Knoll Sisters, and others, over the past twenty years, but there's still much to do. Many of the original orphans have, of course, grown up and moved to the city to find work. We've continued being a refuge for abandoned children, not only those who have lost their parents, but others whose parents just don't have the money to support them. Our biggest concern is the safety and well being of our youth. The gang problem, as you already know, is a huge one in El Salvador. No longer confined to the big city, it is starting to affect the outlying regions, including our small town of Suchitoto. On the surface, the town looks beautiful and untouched, but scratch that surface and you will uncover some disturbing things. The gangs are infiltrating and trying to recruit more members amongst the local youth, including the orphans."

"I'm not sure how I can help, other than by giving the children some tools for self-expression and esteem through art. That may delay their need to find misperceived security with the gangs," Angela said. "I worked for a short while, in fact, with gang members in a special program in Seattle for inner-city kids."

"Yes, Liam mentioned that to me. Tomorrow I'll show you the makeshift art classrooms we have set up, and you can throw in whatever ideas or changes you want to make. Let me tell you a little about our population here. They range in age from five to twenty. I know that might sound unbelievable, but we provide room and board for just about all the 'lost kids' of Suchitoto, not only the ones directly affected by the war. The biggest problem now is poverty—how to get enough food to eat and clothing for a population of people who have been disenfranchised for generations. At least the Peace Accords offered all the families two hectares of land where it was available. Many who can farm in the surrounding countryside do so, but many are still dependent on the informal economy, like the small street vendors and food wagons."

Angela tried to conceal a yawn with her hand. With embarrassment she said, "Oh, I'm so sorry. It's so interesting, but suddenly I'm feeling very tired."

Liam had been quiet throughout Sister Agnes's story and looked totally absorbed in his own thoughts, nodding politely from time to time to show he *was* listening. Now, he looked up and said, "Yes, I bet you are. Why don't you take a short *siesta*, while Sister Agnes and I take care of some business before the kids return from school."

"That's an excellent idea," Sister Agnes said. "Please feel free, Angela, to leave us, and we'll fetch you when the kids arrive."

Relieved to have some respite, Angela stood up and said, "I think I'll take you up on the nap idea." She thanked the two of them before heading back to her room. As she caught Liam's eye, he winked.

Santos
Suchitoto

Just before falling into a deep sleep, Angela's mind flashed back to the boy they had picked up on the road. *Did Sister Agnes say his name was Santos? Yes, that was it.* He appeared to her in a dream, but it was hard to make out the details other than that she had some unpleasant contact with him. She awoke with a start and wondered what role he might play in her future here at the orphanage.

The sound of birds, mingled with children's laughter, came through the door, which opened onto the courtyard. Angela was startled to see that it was getting dark and probably time to meet the children. She got up and tapped lightly on Liam's door, wondering if he was in his room napping. There was no answer. She brushed her hair and examined her face in the small wood-framed mirror on the wall. She still looked tired. It had been a long trip to Suchitoto, and her worries about Liam and what lay ahead were written all over her face.

Angela stepped out into the courtyard and started to walk around the old adobe arcade, which surrounded a pretty garden of hibiscus, bougainvillea, and palms. She followed the trail of children's voices from where they seemed to be coming. She had an eerie sense that someone was watching or following her. Looking back over her shoulder, she detected someone in the shadows of the arcade, near the large wooden door. She looked closer and realized it was the boy she and Liam had picked up on their way to Suchitoto, the boy in her dream.

Angela stared right at him and said, "*Hola.*" She added in Spanish, "Aren't you the guy that we picked up in the truck earlier today? I'm glad you made it safely here." She walked toward him with her hand outstretched as if to shake his. "I'm Angela, the new art teacher here. Do you like to draw?"

The boy had a stern expression and made no attempt to shake her hand. Instead he shrugged and turned away, as if to leave. He looked back with a scowl and then opened the large old wooden door of the convent and walked out into the cobblestoned street.

As he left, Angela called out, "I hope you'll join our art class." She sighed and under her breath said, "Well, so much for a great start as the art teacher." She turned to go back toward the voices she had heard, but realized they were all quiet now. Where were Liam and Sister Agnes—and the children?

Suddenly it was as if the bushes and trees came alive, their leaves and boughs shaking and shifting. Small and medium-sized bodies popped out from everywhere, and with a thunder of voices welcomed her: "*Bienvenido, bienvenido, Señora* Angela!"

Her mouth dropped open, and her eyes expressed her surprise. Recovering from her astonishment, she said, "Oh, *muchas gracias, amigos.* I'm so happy to be here."

At that moment, Liam and Sister Agnes appeared from around the corner of the dining area. They laughed and approached Angela with a big bouquet of paper flowers that the children had made for her.

"*Para usted*, Angela, from the *niños!*" said Sister Agnes, handing her the flowers.

"*Muchas gracias!* I can't believe this wonderful welcome. Please tell the children how happy I am to be here and that I will work very hard to learn their names and to speak better Spanish."

"The children are glad you are here and are looking forward to your art classes. Why don't I introduce them now, as they have to get back to their studies."

"Oh, yes, please do," said Angela. "I want to learn all their names, though I have to admit, it may take me time to memorize them. I hope they'll be patient with me."

Sister Agnes translated Angela's comment for the children, and they all laughed and nodded their heads in agreement.

A noise came from the other end of the courtyard, as the big front door creaked and opened. Everyone turned to look in the direction of the door. The boy Angela had just talked to, entered and walked slowly forward, then hung back behind the others. Sister Agnes continued. "This is Margarita and Caridad—and oh, this is Santos," she said, pointing to the intruder. She paused. The teens seemed to know him, but looked surprised. Santos nodded his head, but still hung back.

Angela anticipated the challenges she was going to have with Santos, but put that aside for the time being. Now, all she could think of was how great it was to see all the children's smiling faces. Liam remained in the background through the introductions, as if he wanted her to be the star. When Sister Agnes finished the introductions, their eyes met and Liam winked and smiled at her.

The nun continued to direct the orphans. "Now children, it's time to go with the older ones off to do your homework. Tomorrow is another day and you'll have plenty of time to get to know Angela, when her art classes start next week. She'll be joining us for meals, and I'll make sure you all get a chance to talk with her." Agnes spoke in heavily accented Spanish, but the children seemed to understand her. It was apparent that they had a great deal of respect for this irreverent and aging nun, who had played such an important role in their lives during the years since the war.

All Angela could think to say was, "*Hasta mañana, chicos y chicas*! I'll look forward to seeing you tomorrow." The children slowly filed off to their study room.

Liam came up to her and slipped his hand into hers. Embarrassed in front of Sister Agnes, she pulled away.

"Oh, I know you two lovebirds have a lot to talk about. I have some paperwork to do in the office. Why don't you show Angela around the orphanage and then take her for a walk into town, Liam? It's beautiful in the moonlight."

"Good idea, Sister. Let's go, Angela."

With Sister Agnes's offhanded but frank admission

that she knew about their romance, Angela felt surprise and relief at the same time. There didn't need to be any more secrets.

"*Buenos noches*, Sister Agnes," Angela said. "It's wonderful to be here."

"It's fine to have you," the nun said. "I'll see you in the morning."

As Angela and Liam turned to walk to the other wing of the old convent, Sister Agnes called out to them, "And, by the way, you can just call me Agnes. The 'Sister' part isn't necessary. God doesn't worry about titles."

"I'll remember that, Agnes." The two women laughed.

When Angela knew Agnes was out of earshot, she said, "I like that woman, Liam."

"Yes, I knew you would. She doesn't beat around the bush. She has high expectations of everyone here and will always tell you when you're meeting them and when you're not."

Angela hoped she could live up to those expectations. She began to relax and looked forward to the days ahead. In the back of her mind, though, she worried about Santos. She could tell he was disturbed, and she hoped she could get to the bottom of it.

"Liam, I want to talk to you about that boy who came in at the last minute, Santos. He's the one we picked up, remember?"

Liam nodded his head, "Yeah, I realized that."

"I had a strange dream about him, and when I woke up he was standing near the door to my room. He scowled at me and when I asked him if he liked to draw, he disappeared out the door. Do you know his story?"

"No, but I intend to ask Agnes about him. I could tell by the way she introduced him that she knows him well. Don't worry. You won't be able to save all the lost souls here, sweetheart."

She was glad to hear this term of endearment from Liam's lips. He had seemed distant ever since they arrived. She wondered if it was going to be awkward sharing rooms next to each other. At the same time she wished they were in a room together but imagined this was not possible at the orphanage. How were they going to handle their relationship in front of the children? Obviously, Sister Agnes was not concerned.

"A penny for your thoughts?" Liam said. . "You seem off in another world. Well, I guess you are. This is all new to you, isn't it?"

"Forgive me, but I was thinking about us and being selfish. I was wondering how in heaven's name we're going to find time and privacy to be together, as we discussed, here in this place with all the children surrounding us." Angela blushed at her own disclosure of desire.

Smiling, Liam let out a loud whistle. "Wow, so that's what you're looking so woebegone about. You lustful woman…I'm flattered." He pulled her to him in a dark corner of the arcade.

"Liam, no, not here," Angela whispered. "The children might see us."

Liam moved away. "Don't worry, we'll find a time and place to be together. In fact, tomorrow I'm taking you over to Father Rutilio's small house in town. He is returning tonight from San Salvador and is anxious to talk to you about the orphanage and other things. We may stay at his house from time to time, when he is gone."

"I'm glad to hear that, but, if you want to hear the truth, I was also worrying about your health. You haven't told me much, like how long the doctors think the new drugs will prolong your life."

Liam avoided her eyes and grabbed her hand. "Come on and let me show you around this place. Don't you want to see where you're going to teach the art classes?"

Liam toured Angela around the old eighteenth century convent with its thick adobe walls, most in need of repair. They walked into the voluminous chapel with its sacristy and antique wooden altar. There were no benches, and it was dark and dank from the humid air surrounding the convent. The most picturesque parts of the place were the inner courtyard gardens with their many tropical plants, crumbling adobe walls, and small niches with iconic biblical figures, some with their limbs broken off. Off of the courtyard, the one next to the dining room, was a row of what looked like classrooms. On the walls were some children's drawings tacked up with duct tape. Angela peered in through a halfway-open door of one room.

"That's going to be your classroom," Liam said, pointing to one of the biggest of the rooms. "All you have to do is say what you need, and I'm at your service. I'll be getting the supplies in the next couple of days, and you can arrange the room however you'd like."

Angela's mind began to whirl. How spoiled she had

been at home with her own studio and all the equipment she needed for painting and sculpting. How could she possibly transform this crude space to accommodate the needs of the thirty or forty children who would be taking her classes?

Liam seemed to read her mind. "Don't worry, you don't have to have as fancy a studio as the one back in Seattle. The children are very good at improvising. That's the gift of poverty—ingenuity."

"How did you know what I was thinking? You're right. But, I'll need paper, drawing pencils, and charcoal sticks. I brought some materials with me, but there isn't nearly enough for this number of children. I haven't met a kid yet, who didn't love working with clay. Do you think I could find some here?"

"Whoa, wait a minute. You'll have to make a list for me. Let me worry about where everything will come from. My church gave me a nice donation for supplies before I came down this time. I told them about you. We're part of the nationwide Sanctuary Movement. But I will tell you about that later."

Funny he should bring that up now, Angela thought. She knew the Sanctuary Movement helped undocumented immigrants find shelter and safety when they came over the borders. Well, she was going to have to wait to get her answers. Liam was already walking away and pointing to something in the next courtyard.

"There stands the sculpture of the Mother Superior, who was the head nun of this Dominican Sisters convent when it was first started in 1776. Can you believe that it dates back to when our founding fathers signed the

Declaration of Independence?"

"I know the history of this country is very painful, such as the killing off of the indigenous people and, of course, most recently, the civil war. Will things ever get better for the people, Liam? Do you really think we can make a difference?" That same old question nagged at the corners of Angela's mind.

Liam sighed and shrugged his shoulders. "Well, it depends with whose standards you are comparing their lives. If you are asking if they'll have what we have in the States, probably that will take another hundred years. The important thing is how we can help them find sustainable ways to make a living for their families. This is mostly an agricultural country, and many clever people here know how to live off the land they *now* have, thanks to the Peace Accords. Others making up the economy are the school teachers, small trades people, and civil servants. If the US keeps its hands off for a while, I think these people have the chance to do quite well with the resources they have. Take the example of our friends in the Bajo Lempa. With sustainable farming methods, they have come a long way. "

Angela admired Liam's optimism, and knew she had to work on that in herself. She found herself getting discouraged before she had even started to try to make a little difference. She remembered the metaphor Liam had once mentioned: that they were just small grains of sand, but, together, they could make a difference.

"You're right, darling. Thank you for your optimism and the opportunity you've offered me to contribute this small thing, art for the children." Angela took Liam's hand and they continued their stroll through the convent, finally stepping out into the cobbled streets to wander down to the main plaza. It was dusk and the moon cast its soft light on the white church, which crowned the north end of the square.

Pointing in that direction, Liam said, "That's where Father Rutilio used to give his sermons on liberation theology, the reason he was tortured just before the war broke out. You know the story. The priests became disenchanted with the way the church had kept the people believing in a life hereafter, and they were preaching to the people that they deserved more than what they got from years of an oppressive regime ruling them ever since the Spanish conquistadores." Liam spoke with passion. It was contagious and Angela listened intently, taking in his words.

"Oh, there I go spouting off like I know it all. Forgive me. I'm sure you know all about liberation theology."

"I know some of the history, but when *you* talk about it, it takes on even more meaning. I'm looking forward to hearing what Rutilio has to say."

They had been making their way across the big plaza, and as she said this, Liam guided her into the door of the church. She always felt a bit uncomfortable in churches, since she didn't practice her childhood faith much anymore. She had lost faith that prayer did any good; wasn't it just the heart's longing to be heard? David was Lutheran and neither of them felt a need to go to church. The icons meant little to her, and she felt resentful for the decorative opulence displayed in churches, when the money could better be spent on food and shelter for the people. The money used to make these religious relics could feed so many, she thought.

As they entered the church, and she began to walk down the center of the nave, she was reminded that Liam was more devout than she. He first stopped at the entrance, crossed himself and looked down a moment in silent prayer. "There's the altar from which Father Rutilio preached," he said, as he pointed to the large pulpit at the end of the nave. "Catholicism has played a big role, both positive and negative, in the history of Latin America."

"I realize that," she said. "Thank you for showing me the church. Now can we see where Rutilio lives when he's in town?" It was hot and stuffy in the church, and she was glad to step out into the cool air of the approaching night. Suchitoto was in the highlands where there were some gentle breezes, unlike along the coast where the high humidity was often sweltering. As they stepped out into the plaza again, Liam put his arm around her, and they walked down a narrow side street to a doorway. Liam pointed to a squat whitewashed and tile-roofed house, simple, with few distinguishing features other than a wooden cross hanging to the side of the door.

"This is where we will meet with Father Rutilio tomorrow. He'll explain more about the orphanage to you and our work here. Let's get back now so we can get some rest. We have lots to do tomorrow."

Just as they rounded the corner to go back across the plaza, they caught sight of Santos, hanging out with a group of very tough looking young *muchachos*, all sporting tattoos on their arms. They were huddled in a circle and seemed to be discussing something important.

Liam caught sight of the group and steered Angela in the other direction. Angela could tell Liam was nervous.

"Let's take a different route back to the convent," Liam said. "I don't feel like confronting those guys now." He nodded his head in the direction of Santos and the group he was with, and took Angela's hand to walk back down Rutilio's street. They wound their way through backstreets leading to the convent. Slipping quietly into the inner sanctum of the old edifice, they walked toward their rooms. Everything was quiet, and Angela detected only one small light on, under the door, which was Sister Agnes's office, next to the dining area. They approached their doors and Liam said with a beguiling smile, "I'll meet you on the other side. Remember, we have adjoining rooms."

Angela put the dark thoughts of Santos out of her mind.

Angela's Art Classes
Suchitoto

Angela and Liam worked hard to set up the art room. It soon began to look like an art studio with wooden benches and tables and some sculpture stands that Liam built. She enjoyed the discovery of his many talents. Together they arranged bottles and tin cans with paints and brushes. Liam had managed to bring plastic sacks of *barro*, the Spanish word for clay, from the outskirts of San Salvador. Angela was glad she had brought down some of her ceramic tools. They would come in handy.

From time to time, Liam had to be gone for a day or two, to help Rutilio track down some of the teenage boys who would catch a pickup ride into the city and be gone for days at a time. Sister Agnes always feared the worse: that the boys were being enticed into one of the gangs, and might even end up in prison. The government was cracking down on the gangs, and little tolerance was applied, such as consideration of their age. They were treated as hardened criminals, and by the time they were released, they were tough and cynical. For months they would end up thrown in with a bunch of thugs and no one to defend them. Sometimes all it took to be arrested was an arm with a tattoo and hanging out in the wrong place at the wrong time. Angela worried about Liam's safety, knowing more and more how the young men, even small boys, became entangled in a world of crime and violence. She feared for them, but even more for Liam.

When they managed some time alone, Angela and Liam strolled into the central square, talked to the shopkeepers and got to know the village as if it were their own. Angela loved this open space crowned by the old white church. The two even managed some romantic time together with their adjoining rooms, walks up the hill to the lake near the town, and an occasional tryst at Rutilio's house.

Day by day, Angela came to know the kids and appreciate their winning ways. Some of the teens, like Santos, were aloof. Some had jobs in the fields, which is why they wouldn't be in class, Agnes explained. When they were lucky enough to get a job, they helped the farmers for minimal wages. Some worked in the small shops where they earned meager amounts selling trinkets, cokes, and other sundries. At least, she said, it gave them a sense of independence, even if false.

A month after arriving in Suchitoto, Angela received an e-mail from her daughter, and approached Liam with her news. "I have something important to tell you. I received a message from my daughter, Arial. She hopes to come down to visit us in a few months."

"Great," said Liam. I'll finally meet some of the family. I hope I'll pass muster."

"I know she'll like you," said Angela. Down deep she was worried that Arial's forthright nature would cause Liam to be uncomfortable; she doubted Arial would be able to resist mentioning their illicit affair under the nose of her beloved father.

Liam continued, "When is she coming? I've got to make a trip down to the Bajo Lempa and want be sure I'm back for her visit. "

"What?" Angela was shocked. "You didn't tell me you were going to the Bajo Lempa. When are you going and why?"

The two of them were outside the classroom. "Let's talk about this over coffee after your class, said Liam. "I can see your kids are starting to arrive. We'll go for coffee at Alejandro's café on the square."

Angela's children started to stroll into the room, at least the young ones. She was discouraged that she couldn't get more of the teenagers involved. The girls seemed to respond, especially to her figure drawing classes, but most of the boys just hung out in the courtyard, watching through the open door. Angela suspected they were more interested in watching the girls than in her art demonstrations. Oddly, the one person who did come into the class from time to time was Santos. Though he rarely smiled and usually looked bored, he did pick up the charcoal and draw. His drawings were often dark, and of mean-looking male figures, but he showed talent, and Angela told him so. At that point, he'd usually wad up his drawing, toss it in the wastebasket and leave the class. She couldn't seem to connect with him, and it bothered her.

"Yes, you're right," said Angela, "I have to go now. We'll discuss the Bajo Lempa and Arial's visit later—I'll take you up on that coffee date after class."

As she started to say *adios* to Liam, someone bumped up against her side. It was little Maria, who accidentally ran into her on her way into the classroom.

"*Lo siento, Señora* Angela." She looked as surprised as Angela was and very embarrassed. Her dark, obsidian eyes started to fill with tears. Angela embraced her and said, "*No problema*. You didn't mean to run into me. It's OK, Maria. Now run ahead and get your paint apron. We're going to do something really fun today."

The little girl looked up at her with a smile that made Angela's heart melt. She was falling in love with these children and felt she found her niche. She had always been so wrapped up in her own art career she had rarely taken time out to teach, except for the one brief stint with the juveniles in Seattle, and an occasional lesson for her granddaughter, Heather. Now, she realized maybe this was exactly what she was looking for in this stage of her life. "There's a time for everything," she remembered Liam quoting from Ecclesiastes, during one of their more serious conversations.

Liam laughed. "I better let you get to your charges. It's obvious they love you." As if on second thought, he added, "Almost as much as I do."

"Well, some of them, at least," Angela said. "That reminds me; I have to talk to you about Santos later. Please don't let me forget."

"Something in your tone sounds ominous," Liam said. "I won't let you forget. So, it's coffee at four?"

"*Sí*, I'll see you then. *Adios.*"

He winked at her as they waved good-bye and Angela closed the door of the classroom.

Liam's Plan
Suchitoto

Liam and Angela walked to the central plaza and found seats at their favorite small café, *Alejandro's*.

"*Hola, amigos.*" The heavy-set café owner waved to them from the kitchen. "How are you?"

"*Bien gracias,*" said Liam.

"And you, Angela?" Alejandro made her feel like an old friend, at home in Suchitoto.

"*Muy bien,*" said Angela. She and Liam smiled at each other. Their Spanish *was* improving.

Carlotta, Alejandro's wife, came out from behind the counter, wiping her hands on her red-and-white apron. "*Que quieres?*" She asked them for their order.

"*Dos Americanos, por favor,*" Liam said.

Maria walked back to get their coffees, and they reached across the table to hold hands.

"Now, what is this problem with Santos. Tell me about it," Liam said.

"First you have to tell me what these big plans are

you have for Bajo Lempa. I hope I can join you. I really want to see Adriana, Cici, and the family again."

"Of, course. I had hoped to take you along, but if your daughter—what is her name again?"

"Arial. Katherine is the other one, but she can't get away from her job right now. It will just be Arial. She hopes to come down over the Thanksgiving break, which is two months from now. She'll take vacation from her job at Microsoft. I think she wants to check you out. She's very skeptical about you. Just before I went home to Seattle she discovered a letter I had once written to you and never sent. It was a love letter. I had always managed to keep our brief affair secret until Arial found the letter. Now the girls distrust me, or at least Arial does. I understand. She feels angry, and disillusioned. To be truthful, it was hard for me to come down when you asked me. I felt I needed more time to mend the fences, but I knew I wanted to be with you, and now that I know about your illness …" Angela stopped, a catch in her throat, and wiped the back of her hand across her eyes, which were tearing up. "I'm sorry, but I worry about losing you just when we finally found a time for each other."

Liam reached over and wiped the wetness from her cheeks with the back of his hand and mouthed the words, "I love you." Then looking serious he said, "Don't worry, sweetheart, I'm sticking around for a while."

"But you're going to Bajo Lempa. Why, may I ask?"

"Well, now that you have told me your secret about your daughters' opinion of me—and by the way, do I ever get to read that love letter?"

With a flirtatious smile, Angela cast her eyes downward and said, "I'm not sure. It may depend on your answer to my question."

"Ah, bribery. I knew you were a wicked woman. Don't worry about the timing. We'll be there and back, way before your daughter's visit."

"Yes, but why are we going? Just to visit, I hope." Angela's voice dripped with suspicion.

"To be honest, I've had a longstanding promise to Adriana," said Liam. "I know you are not going to be pleased, but be patient with me."

Angela squirmed in her seat and felt flush. Her suspicions about Liam's role in getting Adriana and Cici to the border were verified.

Liam ignored her attempt to interrupt and went on. "This is very important. My promise is to take them to the border and help them cross to join up with representatives from my church's Sanctuary Movement, who will take them from there. Adriana has begged me. She misses Jorge and wants Cici to know her father, and have the chance for a better life with an intact family. He finally got a job there with an employer he trusts after all these years going up with the H2-A visa…"

"Wait," said Angela, "I know all about this. Adriana told me the story."

"Good, then you know how those guys who recruit the workers in their own country have a bonanza here," said Liam, "and make big bucks off these poor people. I can't stand it."

Angela reached over and touched his cheek, moved by his comments. She knew his heart was in the right place, but she didn't agree with the way he wanted to help Adriana and Cici.

Liam continued. "But, now that Jorge finally has a decent employer in California, who likes him so well that he's going to go out on a limb for him and make him manager of the flower fields, and help him get his green card, it's important that the family is together. Eventually, if all goes well, and we get a new amnesty law, Jorge will be a naturalized citizen. It's a chance for the whole family. I can't let them down."

"Liam, of course, I want the same for them, but taking undocumented immigrants over the border is a dangerous proposition for both you and them. Besides, it's illegal."

"Do you think I don't know that? Of course I do, but I *must* help them."

"Tell me this," Angela continued, "what makes you so driven about this and about the kids here who are getting tied up into the gang world. Do you think we can really make a difference? The problems are so huge; sometimes I feel overwhelmed. My heart aches to think of these kids' lives, but at the same time, I really wonder if I have the power to change things. I remember how idealistic David and I were when we went to Nicaragua in 1985; we were going to help the Sandinistas create a new Nicaragua. Look what happened: even the Sandinistas became corrupt, and the land reform they fought for really didn't make life much better for the majority of the people. Sometimes I feel there will always be this huge gap between the rich and the poor, and there's nothing we can do about it."

"Angela, where's my freedom fighter, peacemaker, dreamer of a better world? Don't give up on me now. Together, we can do small things but they add up, and we *can* make a difference. Remember Father Rutilio talking about how each of us is a grain of sand, and if there are enough of us working for change we can change the world?"

"I want to believe that, but I guess as much as I want a cause to fight for I have an angel on one shoulder and a devil on the other. I'm always trying to figure out which way to fly. I don't understand what keeps you going. You never seem to get discouraged, burnt out, or suffer from compassion fatigue, like I do."

"You really want to know why?" Liam looked down and when he looked up he had tears in his eyes.

Angela had never seen him like this, upset and so vulnerable. To her he had always been the picture of cool, always seeming to know what the next step was. Now he seemed unsure and at the same time, determined to move forward with his plan to get Adriana and Cici to the border and, at the same time, save every kid at the orphanage that he could.

She put her hand out to touch his, as he reached for his coffee cup. "Liam, I'm sorry I've upset you. It's just that sometimes I realize there is still so much I don't know about your other life. We are beginning to make a new life *together* and I love it. I love being in your arms. I love the way you make me feel, the way I'm needed by you and yes, the kids here, too. But I'm not sure I always agree with your plans, especially when it comes to taking Adriana and Cici over the border."

"OK, I have to tell you, Angela. I've been unfair. I admit I have not disclosed all. Do you remember when we drove up here in the pickup and I played the old sixties rock tunes on my portable CD player? And we reminisced about those days and the anthems of our generation?"

Laughing, but at the same time a bit puzzled, Angela said, "Yes, what's that got to do with any of this?"

"Angela, I was one of the *heads*. I hung out with all the rockers of that time. I read Ginsburg, smoked pot, dropped acid and tried to deny that I was an addict like my dad had been. I met Mary at Woodstock, and we hit it off. She got me on the straight and narrow, and I went back to school, got my journeyman electrician's license and built a successful business. Oh, I still loved listening to Jimi Hendrix, Dylan, Pete Seeger, and Joan Baez. I still believed that a better world was possible, but I realized it wouldn't come out of a needle or a bottle. Why do you think we always just have coffee and when you order a Corona, I order lemonade?"

"I figured that out, Liam. I know you told me your father was an alcoholic, but now I realize there are other reasons as well. Tell me more about Mary, your wife."

"We wanted kids desperately, but probably because of my drugs and drinking, I was impotent. So we adopted our son, Robbie. I told you about him once when we first met. I was so busy building up my business and trying to keep Mary happy by making up for what I couldn't give her, I ignored our boy. She became angrier and angrier. She tried to reform me, and the more she did the more I worked. Thank goodness for our church. Working with our peace and justice committee was the one thing Mary and I did well together. Then she got MS and she went downhill quickly. By that time, Robbie was almost out of high school, but he took a wrong turn with the wrong group of friends." Liam stopped. It was like he couldn't go on any longer.

"Mas café, Señor Liam?"

"*Si, gracias, Alejandro. Un poco*," Liam said.

"No, *gracias*," Angela put her hand over her cup. Too much coffee in the late afternoon meant trouble for her at night. Besides, she was so distracted by Liam's emotional state, that all she could do was look at him and listen. "Go on. Tell me what this has to do with your work down here."

"Forgive me. This is hard, but I know I must tell you because I love you and I need your trust," said Liam. "When Robbie was twenty-one he got in trouble with the law. Oh, it wasn't a big deal, just petty theft for the drugs he was using, you know, marijuana, but he ended up in the clinker. This almost killed Mary. Her MS was getting worse and she was in a wheelchair. Thank God, my business was doing well enough by then, that I could leave it to my employees and take care of her much of the time. And thank God for Father Rutilio. When he came and spoke at our church, he shed a new light on my life. By that time Mary was living at a care facility and I tried to be with her as much as possible, but I also needed to get involved in something bigger, to feel my life had even greater purpose." Liam looked down again, rubbing his hands together as if in anguish.

He continued, "I felt I had failed the two people I

loved the most. That's when I started coming down with the pickups, and it gave me a kind of high. And that's when I met you, Angela. You were the final narcotic. I fell in love again and knew this is where I wanted to be. Mary died two years later. Robbie got out of jail and straightened himself up, but didn't want to spend any time with me. That's probably my fault. I tried to relive the role of a father through these Salvadoran kids. And when I met Sister Agnes and she shared her dreams for them and her deep desire to keep them out of the gangs, things just happened. As I got to know more of Adriana and Cici and their wonderful family, thanks to you, I knew that was my mission. I got my church to agree to send humanitarian aid down once a year. At the same time, our church became involved in the nationwide Sanctuary Movement."

Angela breathed in deeply, a *yoga breath*, as she liked to call it, hoping it would get back her equilibrium, as Liam's story unfolded. "I'm beginning to understand you more, Liam." With each day they were together she saw him more clearly—like the emergence of a Japanese brush painting: with each stroke of *sumi*, more of him was revealed. "I guess I just don't understand your drive, your dedication. I, too, am coming to love these people, but at the same time, I must admit I miss my daughters and my life in Seattle." There, she'd let it slip; she was homesick.

Liam reached over and put his hand on hers.

"There's more to my story," Liam said.

"Oh, go on," Angela said.

"I kept coming down, and got more and more

entangled in the lives of the people. It was almost like another addiction, helping people, that is. Call it self-centered altruism, or my escape with altruistic side notes. I don't know why exactly, Angela, but if I wanted to get religious about it, I would say it felt like a calling. I can't expect you to have the same calling, but I had hoped we could be in this together, share the load and warm each other's bodies at the end of sometimes hard and sometimes sad days. Maybe I was wrong to drag you into this."

Liam's voice dragged off into nothingness as he looked up at Angela with an almost pleading stare. She'd never seen this side of him, almost frail, and with some fear in his tone. Maybe this is what knowing your days are numbered does to one, she thought. She longed to pull him close and wrap her arms around him. Instead she just squeezed his hand and said: "I'm sorry. I do love you and want the same things you do. I'll try to be a more cooperative partner and support your longing to get Adriana and Cici safely over the border. But, I admit, I'm scared. I sometimes lie awake looking over at you as you sleep, and wonder how long I have with you. I guess my worries are selfish when I say I don't want you to risk the dangers of getting undocumented immigrants over the border. I even worry when I know the risks you're taking in San Salvador to pick up the kids and bring them back here. You put yourself in harm's way so often."

"Come on, let's get out of here," Liam said, changing the subject. He slipped some change to Alejandro with a sideways smile as they left, and grabbed Angela's hand, pulling her out into the waning daylight. A few streetlights were just coming on to cast a mysterious glow on the central square.

Angela realized that for Liam, the subject of taking Adriana and Cici to the border was no longer a subject for conjecture.

"I have a plan," Liam said, "and it's a good one, but let's talk about it later. Good thing, by the way, that I bought the old VW van in Boston. Not only will it come in handy for the trip north with Adriana and Cici, but it will also be great to travel around in with Arial when she visits. We can show her the country."

Angela laughed and it felt good to lighten the conversation.

"Oh, yeah, I almost forgot," said Liam. "You mentioned wanting to talk about Santos."

"Yes," Angela said, "I'm really concerned about him. It feels as if he's rapidly slipping out of the fold of the orphanage. I felt better when he began to come to the drawing classes more. He has talent, and even though his drawings are a bit dark—he likes to draw portraits of gang members and popular tattoos—I've ignored that, seeing how engaged he is. He's apparently selling some of his drawings to his *homies*, as he calls them."

"Yeah, I'm worried, too. Sister Agnes and Father Rutilio feel it's time for some kind of intervention. We've seen Santos associating with what appears to be members of one of the worst gangs, the *Mara Salvatruchos*. Those are the guys you saw him with on the square with the tattoos all over their arms. In order to feed themselves and their *brothers* in jail they continually recruit more of their kind to steal, embezzle and intimidate. Worst of all, they prey on the poor immigrants who are trying to get to the border on the trains through Mexico. They have *homies* all along the line, like the drug syndicates. I'm fearful Santos is in too deep and may not be able to get out, even if he wanted to."

"That's my fear, also. Do Agnes and Rutilio have any thoughts on what to do about this?" Angela asked.

"They're not sure yet. They hoped that you could help by engaging him so much in his art that he would not be tempted by this evil attraction. They saw early on that he had some talent in drawing. Now, I have serious doubts that the art is going to keep him here. I want you to be very careful around him. I'm not sure if you might be in some danger, too."

"I don't think he'd hurt me," Angela said. "He even gives me a smile once in a while, but then, without warning, he walks out of the class and I don't see him for several days. His drawings are good, but I know he wants to leave the orphanage, and I can understand that. He's almost eighteen and wants to be on his own."

"That's the problem," said Liam. "He can't be on his own because there's no work for him, and he only has a third-grade education. The more tattoos he gets on his arms the more any potential employer will turn him away. His parents both died in the war, and he basically grew up on the streets until Sister Agnes found him. She's now in competition with the *maras*. They promise to be like a family to these street kids, to feed and defend them to the bitter end. They suck them in and then won't let them leave. If they try, they suffer penalties, which are often severe beatings and torture, until they're in so deep it's the only way of life they know. You haven't seen what I have in San Salvador, and I'm glad you haven't."

"I've got a pretty good imagination," Angela said, as a shiver ran down her spine.

Liam continued. "The police don't help much, often extracting bribes from them or severely beating them and then hauling them into the prisons, which are rife with disease and filled with even more nefarious criminals. Some of these boys are kids, eleven and twelve years old. Unfortunately, they look up to the leaders, and prefer them to living with their poor mothers and grandmothers in horrid slum conditions. They have the idea they're going to be "big shots" and get their families out of poverty. It's a long road of self-deception that often leads to an early death from a gang shoot-out or a police crackdown."

"Well, I'll keep trying to engage Santos," Angela said. "My Spanish is getting better, but half the time I don't understand the street slang he uses."

"Be careful." Liam had a worried look on his face. "By the way, I have to leave for two days to pick up some supplies for the orphanage. Please promise me you'll stay clear of Santos."

"Aye, aye, captain," said Angela, with a smile.

When they arrived back at the orphanage, they slipped into their room and shut the door. Liam pulled Angela close to him and began to unbutton her blouse, and she grabbed his shirt and pulled it over his head. Pressing her bare breasts to his chest, he pulled her toward the small bed they shared when the door between their rooms was trespassed. Their night was filled with lovemaking, and Angela secretly thanked God that she had one more night with Liam.

Santos' Threat
Suchitoto

Liam left for San Salvador the next day. Life went on at the orphanage as usual. Angela continued to teach classes and get to know the children, becoming more and more attached to them.

One day Agnes and Angela had to go out to *Señor* Fernando's farm, to pick up dried cow pies, which they were collecting for the pit kiln the older kids were building. Angela had explained to them that this was the method they could use to fire the clay figurines that the children made. *Señor* Fernando, an old friend of Sister Agnes, had promised to stack them up by the fence at his farm, where they could dry.

The two women drove out together in Agnes's old pickup, taking two of the twelve-year-old boys along. The road was dusty and dirty.

"Angela, the *chicos* are really enjoying your art classes. I can tell you've already made a big difference in their lives." Agnes veered suddenly to avoid a cow in the road.

"That was a close call. I admire your driving ability, Agnes," Angela said.

"You think this is good, you should see me in the San Salvador traffic," she said and chuckled. "I'm like a bull after cows in heat."

Angela smiled to herself. This Agnes was certainly not like the nuns she had ever met. She couldn't wait to tell Maggie about her. She wouldn't believe it. Maggie was always saying the nuns at her school were so uptight they couldn't empathize with a cow giving birth.

Changing the subject now, Angela asked, "Did Liam tell you of our conversation about Santos?"

"Yes, he did, and I share your concerns. As soon as Rutilio returns from his trip to Guatemala, I intend to approach him about Santos. He made a promise to these boys that things would get better, that he hoped to raise money from one of the NGOs in the States to start a job training program for them. This was months ago, and they're getting restless and impatient. Can't say I blame them. Rutilio is such an idealist. Sometimes he's not in touch with their everyday reality. The threat of them being recruited into the gangs is the most worrisome thing of all for me. I'm afraid I don't have the solution yet. If you can keep them engaged in the art program along with Sister Maria's helping them write about their lives and frustrations, maybe we can keep them in school and out of the gangs. The thing is, then what? If they can't find work, we're back to ground zero. That's the sad thing about the teens now. But there's always hope."

"You sound like Liam," Angela said. "How you and he keep your optimism beats me. I have to admit, I get pretty discouraged at times."

"I understand, Angela, but if you had seen what I saw during the war and the difference now—how the people are building a new future—it would give you hope.

"There's a quote, and it's not in the Bible. For all I know it's from a sinning poet. '*Hope is the thing with feathers, that perches on the soul, sings the tune without the words and never stops, at all.*' That's what keeps me going."

"Agnes, I know that one. It's from one of my favorite poets, Emily Dickinson."

"Well, she had a good thought didn't she? Never give up hope*, esperanza*, Angela."

Before Angela had a chance to reply, they were pulling up to an old metal gate crossing a rural road, which led to a run-down concrete-block structure, covered with corrugated tin. An old man emerged, and Pablo and Luis, the boys who came along, jumped down from the back of the truck.

"*Hola, Señor* Fernando," they said in unison.

"We came to get the *caca de vaca,*" Luis said. The boys laughed with each other and Luis kicked the dirt and wiped the sleeves of his cotton shirt across his face, as if to hide his embarrassment, while Pablo just looked down. Ever since Angela had taught them this expression for the cow pies, they loved to use it.

"*Que?*" Fernando liked to tease them as if he didn't understand what they were talking about. After a minute, he pointed to the huge stack of dried cow pies. "You mean that ugly, smelly stuff over there? You can have it!"

The boys began to load the cow pies onto the truck bed, Agnes chatted with Fernando, and Angela listened and enjoyed the opportunity to learn more quotidian Spanish.

They got back to the orphanage just in time for Angela's afternoon drawing class. Caridad and Patricia waited by the door of the art room, sketchbooks open, as they practiced drawing each other.

"*Hola,*" they said as she walked up with her keys out and opened the door.

"*Hola, chicas.* How are you?"

"*Bien,*" they said in unison.

As Angela opened the door a few of the young boys shuffled in along with the two girls. Others followed. Angela set out the charcoal, paper, and drawing pencils and began the demonstration for the day. She hoped that Santos would join them, but he never showed up. When she dismissed the class she felt hot, tired and in need of some exercise. She decided to take a walk as soon as it cooled down a bit.

Around six o'clock, an hour before suppertime, Angela slipped out the convent door and up the street toward the trail to the lake. She loved to go up there and watch the sky change colors as the sun set. Dusk was her favorite time of day. She climbed the trail, huffing and puffing a bit, her breath coming with more difficulty due to the high elevation of Suchitoto. When she arrived at the lake she plopped down on an old wooden bench. She sat quietly, watching the pale moon's glimmer as the daylight faded and the sky turned pink.

Lost in thought, she didn't hear anyone approach until she looked up, and caught sight of the glint of something steel-like out of the darkness of a nearby bush. Before she knew it, Santos stepped out in front of her, brandishing a switchblade knife. Standing rigid in front of her, fierce like some kind of a wild animal, his face scowled at Angela.

She struggled to keep her calm, and with a whisper, said: "*Santos, que quieres*? What do you want?"

He moved closer, and Angela began to tremble as she slowly rose from the bench. Santos glared at her and spoke gruffly, "You, the great artist. You think you are so smart. You're just like Rutilio, always promising things you can't produce. Tell the Father, to hell with him. He promised, if we didn't join the gangs, he would find work for us. You fill us with expectations of our greatness as artists. You are all the same, while we go on with nothing."

All the while Santos was talking, waving his knife about, and moving closer to Angela, she was slowly backing up, her feet groping the ground to make sure she didn't fall.

"Now, I have no choice but to kill you to keep my honor with the *maras*. They are my family, and I must prove to them I am worthy to be a *Salvatrucho*."

Angela felt her throat constrict. She was too scared to scream. She slowly backed away, tripped on a rock, and fell backward to the ground as Santos approached and raised his hand with the knife over her.

"Wait, Santos." Liam's voice came seemingly from nowhere. "You don't have to do this."

Distracted, Santos whirled around to face Liam. "So it's you. You're one of them." Liam motioned to Angela to get up as he tried to distract Santos away from her.

"Santos, Angela and I can help you find work. You have too much talent to waste. Don't throw your life away for the *maras*. They can't give you anything." As long as he could keep talking, Angela could see Liam might be able to grab the knife from Santos. He was slowly moving toward the youth.

Like a human scream, a heron's cry pierced the silence of the lake, just enough of a distraction to cause Santos to turn his attention away from Liam and Angela, for a moment short as a breath. Liam lurched forward and knocked Santos down as he grabbed the knife from his hand.

"Be happy, my man. I've just saved your life and your future," Liam said.

Santos curled up in pain, wailing, "They'll kill me now, you *puta. Damn you!*"

"You'll thank me for this someday, Santos. Now get up, brush yourself off and come with us. Angela, are you alright?" He grabbed Santos by the shirt collar, lifting him up.

Angela stood up, trying to regain her composure, still shaking, "*Sí*, I'm OK. I'll ask you later how you happened to get back a day early and come to find me here. Thank God. I'd hate to think what might have happened, if you *hadn't* arrived."

Santos gave her a scowl and tried to slough off Liam's tight grip. Then as if overcome by a sudden change of heart, he fell to the ground, shaking with sobs, his head in his hands. Liam and Angela could both see the new tattoos he had acquired with the name of the gang on his five fingers of his right hand. Liam reached down and lifted the young man up by the arm, and pushed him ahead of them, as all three walked down the trail and back to the convent.

Preparing for Good-Bye
Suchitoto

Santos could not be Angela's primary concern now. In a few days, she and Liam would be leaving for the *Bajo Lempa* to pick up Adriana and Cici for their journey north. As the time drew closer for their departure, she knew she would not dissuade Liam from this mission. Her thoughts were unraveling like balls of yarn dropped from a knitter's basket as they rolled around in her head, finding one problem after another for which there were no immediate answers. She told herself that it would all work out, but she was not so sure. Ever since the incident with Santos she had been wondering what she was really doing here.

She knew the children loved her, and their artwork was creating quite a stir in the community. People loved the drawings she displayed in Alejandro's café and when she walked in the streets of Suchitoto, people waved to her and smiled.

"*Hola,* Angela," Sister Agnes said as she opened the

convent door one day when Angela returned a little later than usual from her Spanish class. Angela had forgotten her key and had to ring the bell outside.

"*Que tal?* How was your Spanish class? I was just getting a bit worried. You're late."

"Oh, Agnes, I'm sorry, I forgot to tell you I was going to stop by Rutilio's house to talk to him about Santos and the other teenage boys."

"Ah, a good idea. And what did he have to say?"

"Well," Angela began, "as usual, Rutilio had a solution, or at least, a *temporary* one."

"You don't sound convinced it will work, whatever it is," said Agnes.

"Well, it's a first step toward a solution. I guess I have to start realizing that progress here is made in imperceptibly small increments."

"Good for you. You're getting it. One doesn't come here and change the whole country and the culture overnight, or for that matter, at all. The people here own their own problems, and *they* know best how to fix them. We are just here to show them that we care, to be in solidarity with them."

"Rutilio wants to help the kids start a radio station and evidently, the funding is being provided by a small NGO in the US."

"Oh, he's spoken to me about this for several months now. I hope it will soon come to fruition. I think it may be a very good catalyst to keep the kids here, to encourage them to stand in opposition to the gangs, and to give them some empowerment over their own lives," said Agnes.

"Agnes, I know I can learn a lot from your optimistic attitude. I want to talk more about this with you, but would you forgive me now? I'm exhausted and tomorrow we are getting up early to leave for the *Bajo Lempa*. Is Liam back yet?"

No, but he called and he should be here soon. He had lots of things to pick up for the orphanage before you both leave. I'm glad you spent time yesterday showing the other nuns what to do in the classes. They will try to keep the children occupied until your return."

"I know and I'll look forward to being back," said Angela. "I better get some sleep before our big day tomorrow. Good night."

As Angela finished putting the last things together for their journey, she recalled a recent conversation she had had with Liam. Every time in the past month during the planning, when she had tried to talk to him about her concerns, he had told her not to worry, he had everything under control.

"My partners with the Sanctuary Movement have had luck before getting women and children to safety. I don't expect it to be different this time," he'd say, putting an end to their conversation.

"I know, darling," Angela demurred. "You've assured me of that." She added under her breath, "but I still have some doubts about what we're doing." As much as she cared about Adriana and Cici's desire to be reunited with Jorge, she thought there must be a better way.

A few moments of silence passed between them. Leaning his elbows on his knees, Liam rested his head in his two large and calloused hands, as he sat on the edge of his bed. Then looking up and staring into her eyes, he said: "I know you think I'm crazy for wanting to do this, but I really must. Maybe I believe, like one of my favorite writers, Toni Morrison, when she says: 'the function of freedom is to free someone else.' Call it my search for freedom, release from life's bondage—that's going to happen soon enough, I know." His voice trailed off.

Angela realized he was alluding to the possibility that his potentially terminal illness would not be quenched by the medicines still awaiting approval. She shuddered at the thought and decided then and there she wanted to help Liam do what was so important to him, in spite of her doubts.

Departure for the Bajo Lempa

Angela heard a light tap at the door. "Are you ready? I have the van all packed, and we should try to get an early start. Adriana and the family are expecting us sometime later today."

Now as they prepared for the big trip, she hurried to zip up her backpack.

"Yes, I'm all set. My backpack is ready to put in the van." She opened the door between their rooms and threw her arms around, Liam. "I do love you and thank you for helping me to be more optimistic about the outcome of this journey. I have to admit though, I was restless last night after our late night together, as I thought about the unknown and what lies ahead."

"That's your problem, sweetheart. You forget to live in the moment. You're worrying so much about tomorrow you can't enjoy today—an old Buddhist tenet. Well, it's something like that. Now come on, let's go say *adios* to Agnes and the kids. The children have to get to school, and they're all waiting to say good-bye to you.

They're sad you won't be teaching the art classes for the next two weeks, but I have assured them we'll be back."

As Liam swung Angela's backpack over his shoulder, they walked out into the courtyard where Agnes, Marie, and the other nuns were standing, surrounded by all the children. The older youth stood back but also looked eager to say good-bye. Rutilio had found the funds to help pay the kids for mentoring the younger ones and helping build the pit kiln. It would be ready when Angela got back. Emotional, she looked around at all their eager faces.

Agnes stepped forward with outstretched arms. "Angela, we're going to miss you. Liam has promised to bring you back to us in two to three weeks. *Buena suerte*, on your mission, my dear. It's a good thing you're doing."

"*Gracias*. Liam and I will miss all of you at the casa, also. I'll try to send you word of our whereabouts from time to time, if I can get through on my cell phone." Turning to the children, Angela said, "Children study well and finish your projects and I will be back soon. *Te amo, todos*. I love you all."

The children broke out in smiles and ran to embrace her and Liam, some laughing, some crying. How could she have ever thought she did not make a difference in their lives? Angela brushed the tears from her eyes, and Liam helped lighten the moment by jostling with the small boys and pinching the cheeks or pulling the braids of the girls.

"Don't worry, we'll be back, maybe sooner than you think," he said. "Loraina, *muchismas gracias* for the picnic lunch you packed for us."

"*De nada, Señor* Liam. It was my pleasure," said Loraina, looking down with her usual shy restraint.

"Now come on, enough of these long good-byes. *Adios, amigos.* We'll see you again soon." Liam began nudging Angela toward the big wooden door as the children followed. The van was parked in the cobbled street outside the *Casa*, fully packed with all the things they would need for the drive to Bajo Lempa and then to *El Norte*."

Angela jumped up into the front seat at Liam's side, rolled down her window and waved to the group as they pulled away, ready for the next part of the odyssey.

"*Adios, amigos.* We shall return!"

Adios Amigos
Bajo Lempa

When they arrived in Juiquilisco a few hours later, Adriana's whole family was there to greet them. *"Bienvenidos, amigos."*

Liam and Angela jumped down from the van and embraced Isabel, Jesús, Adriana, and Cici.

"*Hola, hola.*" Everyone laughed and talked at once.

"*Que tal?*" Jesús asked as he shook Liam's hand in the double hand grasp he had taught him years ago when they first met.

"*Bien,* Jesús, *gracias, y tu?*" Liam said. "It's good to be back. Angela and I have been looking forward to our reunion with you and the family."

Angela wondered how Isabel and Jesús were facing up to saying good-bye to their one remaining daughter and granddaughter, as they anticipated their departure to the US. She watched the two men pat each other on the backs and wander off together.

"Adriana, I know you must be excited, and Cici, too,

" said Angela. "Do you have your bags all packed for our big adventure?"

Adriana nodded with a smile and Cici's dark eyes sparkled in the bright sunlight, the eyes of a young girl on the edge of puberty with, Angela imagined, unfathomable dreams of what was awaiting her in the US. She could not foresee her future, where her father had worked off and on her whole childhood, a place he was eager to bring her to, so she could have a better life than his had been.

"*Sí*, Angela, *lista*." She looked down shyly, scuffing her flip-flops in the dirt, leaning on her grandmother, with her arm draped around her neck. She was taller than Isabel, now. Her dangling beaded earrings and the gentle rise of her newly blossomed bosom, peeking above a tight-fitting tee shirt, suggested maturity beyond the innocence of this Salvadoran girl. Angela could only hope the future that her father promised her in America would pan out as she dreamed. She knew there would be more hardships before the American Dream was hers.

"*Sí,* she's ready." Isabel smiled and hugged her granddaughter. Angela had always found the Salvadorans restrained in talking about themselves or their emotions, a shy and proud people. She didn't expect that Isabel and Jesús would mention their despair in watching the departure of their second daughter and granddaughter. They accepted with grace that it had to be. So many had left their village to seek work in the US, so they could send back remittances to their families. Until things changed and the farmers could earn enough from their land and compete against the subsidized agriculture of the US, it would be that way. Maybe it would never be any different.

Adriana stood off to the side, watching her daughter and her mother, with a wistful smile. Angela knew she must have thoughts about the long anticipated journey confronting her and her daughter, the possibilities of reuniting with Jorge, but the pain of leaving her aging parents.

Isabel pulled Cici toward the lean-to kitchen. "You're in time for *comida*, Angela. Cici, come help me put the food on the table. I bet Liam and Angela are hungry and thirsty."

"Ah, *sí*, Isabel. I could use some of your good hibiscus juice, and the food sounds good, too."

Adriana had walked over to peer into the windows of the big yellow VW van. "Wow, the van is really nice. Better than a pickup for our trip."

"Yeah, we'll show it to you after we eat. We can talk about how we're going to fit all our things in, plus an extra tire as well."

"Why an extra tire?"

"Liam doesn't want to take any chances that we'll have a flat, with no spares, on the long stretches of deserted highway we'll be traveling over, especially in Guatemala and Mexico."

Almost imperceptibly, Adriana shuttered and softly said under her breath, "at least we won't be riding the rails."

Angela remembered Felipe's horror stories of his experiences on the trains going north. "No, Adriana, you're right. Liam and I will keep you and Cici safe.

We've promised Jorge that, and your *madre* and *padre*."

They linked arms and walked toward the porch where the wooden table was now set with a typical Salvadoran meal. Just as they got to the porch, Liam and Jesús rounded the corner of the concrete-brick house, chuckling.

"Ah, smelled the food, I bet," Angela said. "What are you two laughing about?"

"I was telling Jesús," Liam said, "about how I gallantly saved your life a few weeks ago when Santos pulled a knife on you."

"That wasn't funny." Angela was indignant that Liam could joke about such a thing.

"No you're right, but Santos *was*, when I crept up behind him and surprised the hell out of him, he looked scared as a wet rat."

Jesús, who didn't speak a lot of English, looked puzzled. Angela was sure he didn't know what he was laughing at.

"Liam, I promised Adriana and Cici you would show them the van. They're curious about where everything is going."

"Do you want to see our packs and the boxes we are taking?" Adriana asked. "I even managed to fit Cici's favorite schoolbooks into the stuff we packed. We'll have school in the van. She promised to help me improve my English before we get to the States."

"No, that won't be necessary now. Come on, I'll show you all the van," Liam said. "Your mom and dad will want to see, too. We don't have to pack your stuff until tomorrow. Angie and I are going to stick around for another day, and we'll begin loading the van tomorrow night so we can get an early start the next day."

Adriana's parents and Cici were interested in seeing the van's roomy interior and the way Liam had outfitted it, so Cici and Adriana could sleep in the back during the long journey. He explained that they would alternate sitting in front, next to whomever was driving, either Liam or Angela. The upholstery was a bit threadbare in places. Isabel offered some old blankets to cover the worst spots. She ran to get them and returned with a smile, as she handed them to Liam. Angela was glad that Isabel could be part of the preparations.

"*Mi madre* wove them many years ago," said Isabel. "Adriana used to sleep with this one. It will make her feel more at home in the van on your long journey." She handed over an old multicolored woven blanket with frayed edges, and as she did, Adriana reached out and squeezed her mother's hand. Angela and Liam glanced at each other. They knew they were taking on a great responsibility promising to deliver these two people into the arms of their friends on the border, who would give them sanctuary until they could join Jorge in California.

The night was star-studded. Angela, Liam, and Adriana's family all sat around the front porch. Juan stopped by, and he and Jesús played their guitars and sang some Salvadoran folk songs. The clear skies and moon, and hot, humid weather foretold another good day. The dreaded hurricane season wouldn't start for another month. Liam had anticipated this to be the best time to make the long trip and to get Adriana and Cici safely north. He knew it would be hard for them to leave family and friends, especially with the possibility of another inundation like they had had with Hurricane Mitch a few years back. But the people had grown used to this looming danger and had the forbearance to survive and not to complain.

Angela awoke in the morning with the bright sun's light in the sky telling her it was later than she thought. She looked over to see that Liam was already out of his hammock. No time to loll in hers now. It was quiet. Where *was* everybody? What had she missed? She threw her legs over the side of the hammock, slipped out back to the outhouse and ran back, clutching her lightweight nightshirt around her legs as if to preserve some modesty. No one seemed to be around.

"Maybe they've gone down to the beach," she said to herself. She ran over to the van, grabbed her backpack and pulled out her clothes, taking them inside the house, where she dressed. She could hear voices in the distance as she skittered down the porch stairs and out to the concrete *pila* to wash her face.

"Well, sleeping beauty is finally awake." Angela heard Liam's voice loudly announce to the others. She looked up as he approached with Isabel, Cici, and Adriana.

"We've already had a walk on the beach, while you were off in dreamland. Jesús has been in the fields for hours, and it's almost time for lunch."

"Oh, be quiet," said Angela, with a smile, knowing how early a riser Liam was and how he loved to kid her about her patrician habits of sleeping in.

Isabel, Cici, and Adriana went along with Liam's joke: "*Sí,* Angela, *Está muy tarde.* There's no more coffee and tortillas left, just *fruta,*" Isabel said. Liam brought out her good sense of humor.

Isabel lifted the light tablecloth, which covered the breakfast items, and announced: "Surprise! Breakfast is ready."

They all laughed and Liam grabbed Angela's hand. "After we eat, I'll take you down to the beach and we'll go out to the mangroves to see the changes," said Liam. "Cici and Adriana have to help Isabel and Jesús with some field work, and we can help when we get back."

"Well, my dear, it sounds like you've got my day all planned," Angela said, with a hint of sarcasm. Sometimes, she felt Liam didn't really understand what she was truly capable of. He seemed to like organizing her life. The trip they had ahead of them would show Liam she was capable of more that he might think. She was mustering up all the courage and willpower for it to succeed. In the meantime, she would go along with his sometimes micro-management of her life. After all, he needed to feel he was the strong one now. She was coming to know how, down deep, he worried about his failing health. The signs were there, even when he tried to hide them. He was more tired lately, and sometimes she had the feeling he was holding back from telling her something.

Departure day was a flurry of activity. Jesús helped lift the spare tire into the back of the van, then covered it with a board where Cici could sleep on the soft blanket her grandmother had provided. Adriana would have the back seat to stretch out on, and the suitcases, bags, and boxes went on the floor.

"Do you have the thermos with the purified water,

Angie? And the big bag of mangos and *pupusas* that Isabel prepared?" Liam called out to her from the house.

"*Sí*, I put them in back of the front seat," Angela said. Cici started out to the van and then called out: "Oh, I almost forgot my hairbrush and comb, and my *scrunchies* for my pony tail. Sorry, it will only take a minute." She almost ran into her mother, as she headed back to the house.

Adriana handed Angela her small cotton bag, the one with the Salvadoran design on it, and string shoulder straps, that she used like a backpack.

"Angie, can you put this on the seat, while I go and check if I've forgotten anything?" She ran back to the house, her flip-flops making a clapping sound up the steps to her small room next to the porch.

"Liam, did you get that tool you wanted to borrow from Jesús?" Angela asked. Everyone scurried around in anticipation of the grand departure. Juan rode up on his bicycle, and the neighbors walked over to say *adios* to them. Word had gotten quickly around the village that they were leaving for *El Norte*. Some looked envious, others sad and more just resigned that two more were leaving their small community for what they perceived was a better future.

"*Sí*, got it," said Liam. "Are you ready, Adriana, Cici? We've got to get started."

Jesús appeared from around the back of the casa, carrying a small package, which he handed to Cici. "*Un regalo para ti, mi nieta*." Angela knew Jesús' gift was a carving of a turtle from Jiquilisco Bay he had made for his granddaughter, one to add to the collection Angela had started for her. He had shown it to Angela the night before, displaying a proud smile.

"Don't open it now but wait until you get to the States. It will help you remember your home," Jesús said. He hugged Cici, and Angela could see the tears in his eyes.

Liam jumped up into the driver's seat. "*Gracias, Jesús,* for everything. Don't worry. We'll take good care of them." One person was conspicuously absent from the farewell gathering—Isabel.

"Where's Mama, Papa?" Adriana asked, as she reached out to embrace him.

"*No se, mi chulita.*" Jesús looked back to the cooking lean-to.

With a sad look, Cici said, "I have to say good-by to my *abuelita.* Cici looked for her grandmother to appear. "Where is she?"

"Don't worry," Adriana said, "she'll be here in just a minute. "

Angela got out and went up the steps into the dark interior of the small house.

Several minutes passed and Liam called out to Angela, with some impatience, "*Ven mi amor*—we've got to get going." Just then Angela appeared at the door with Isabel, who was carrying something wrapped in old cloth. She looked determined to hold back her tears.

"Here, Liam and Angela, this is for you, for taking my two *chicas* safely to the El Norte. Don't open it until later. Not now. It's very small." She wiped her eyes with her apron and reached out to embrace Cici and Adriana. The three women hugged. Angela and Liam waited. The neighbors looked on. Finally, Adriana and Cici slipped out of Isabel's embrace, Jesús gave them a gentle pat on their backs and helped them up into the van. They closed the big sliding door and rolled down the windows. The neighbors began waving, and shouting, "*Adios, amigas! May you go well! Go with God!*"

Liam started the van, and Angela blew a kiss to Isabel. They drove slowly down the rutted dirt road to the highway.

The Journey to El Norte Begins

As the van rumbled over the rough road, the passengers and driver were speechless. Liam finally broke the silence.

"Are you *chicas* comfortable back there?" he asked, glancing up at the rearview mirror to check on Adriana, with her daughter curled up next to her, head resting on her mother's lap.

"*Sí,* we're fine."

Liam had explained the route, as they all pored over the big map of Central America, the night before. The map was crumpled and dog-eared, didn't fold right anymore and had several yellow highlighter marks and lines on it. It was the map he had used for years on his many treks back and forth from the States to El Salvador. Angela had suggested they buy a new map, but Liam insisted this one would bring him good luck. They would travel by day, and stop before dark at various small wayside motels that Liam had noted on the map. The goal was to drive, alternating between the two drivers,

Liam and Angela, for about eight hours a day. That way they would arrive at the border in about ten days to two weeks, depending on weather and road conditions. They would drive through Guatemala and Mexico. With luck they wouldn't have any trouble at the borders. Liam had made sure to have fake passports made for Adriana and Cici—who knew how? Angela had no idea. The less she knew, maybe the better. They would go straight through Oaxaca, Mexico, and up through the Central Highlands. Angela knew that area well, as she and David had visited friends there in the state of Guanajuato.

"Do you remember Sandy and Jake?" Angela asked Liam, as they drove towards the Guatemalan border.

"Names sound familiar."

They were the leaders of the brigade I was with when I met you in El Salvador. I've stayed in touch with them over the years. They're still doing good work, building schools now in Nicaragua and working on potable water projects. Sandy was the friendly one who was slightly suspicious of our relationship."

"Oh, now I remember them," Liam said, with a smile. "I don't think she liked me much."

"She liked you, but she was watching out for my welfare. You were a little *macho* and persistent," Angela teased, "pursuing me rather hotly while we were on the coast in La Liberdad."

"What do you mean? You pursued me. I just didn't have any resistance to your charms," Liam bantered back, and reached out for her hand, as he kept the other on the steering wheel.

Angela continued. "I wrote Sandy and told her how

we had run into each other in San Salvador, and that I planned on coming back down to El Salvador to join you. She invited us to stop by for a stay at their place in San Miguel de Allende in the central highlands of Mexico. Maybe that would make a good stopover on our trip north. It would give us a chance to clean up and rest before the day of reckoning at the border."

Liam's tone shifted to a defensive one. "Hey, what do you mean by the day of reckoning? I've got everything set up. We shouldn't have any problems with the passports and temporary visas I've had made for Adriana and Cici. But I think your idea is a good one. Let's stop at Sandy and Jake's, for an overnight, if that's OK with them. We can call them when we get closer to that part of Mexico."

Angela smiled, deciding her choice of words had been wrong, even though she questioned their ability to get Adriana and Cici over the border with fake papers. She loved Liam, and had decided she would do anything to be with him as long as possible. Their time, she knew, was limited. "I already talked to Sandy and told her we would be calling. So it's all arranged. They'll be in San Miguel de Allende around the time we are planning on getting to the Central Highlands of Mexico. She said no problem."

"Good," said Liam. I'm sorry I sounded edgy, sweetheart. I guess I'm getting a bit nervous the closer we get to pulling this off."

Angela's antennae went up. It was good to know Liam had some doubts also, but where was the cool confidence she had seen in him ever since he proposed this adventure to her—or was it a misadventure? She wanted to support

Adriana and Cici's hopefulness. *Esperanza* was all they had at this point.

Adriana called out from the back of the van. Angela hoped she hadn't understood the content of their discussion. "Cici and I are getting really excited," Adriana said. "We were just looking at the map that Liam gave us with the yellow line marking our route. We know we'll be with Jorge in just a couple of weeks. It's incredible."

"*Sí*, it's exciting," Angela said. She was still mulling over what Liam had said. Was it really going to work? Would the border guards accept the false documents? Much was unknown.

Angela decided to keep her mouth shut, and trust in Liam and all his good intentions. She settled back in the passenger seat and glanced at him. She knew they had a long and challenging journey ahead. She hoped it would all go well.

Liam's Folly

"Oh, shit," shouted Liam from the back of the van as he rummaged through his rucksack. He didn't realize Angela and the girls were within hearing distance.

"What's wrong? Are you okay?" Angela approached from the wooded area where they had stopped for a quick break. They were well into the second day of the trip and almost to Guatemala City. Liam seemed agitated, and Angela noticed that he looked a bit pale.

Adriana and Cici came back and climbed into the van. They seemed to sense the tension and scurried to stay out of the way.

"Yeah, I'm sorry. I'm just mad at myself. I seem to have forgotten my meds, the extra package I intended to bring. I left it at the orphanage."

"How could you forget it? Didn't you tell me you needed to take it in order not to have symptoms erupt from your blood condition?" Mad at herself for the scolding tone, she reached out to caress his back and looked into his eyes. "Darling, I know you need those medicines. Could we call Agnes on your cell phone and get her to mail the package to the next nearest town on our route?"

"I already thought of that. Don't worry. I'll be fine. I'll call Agnes as soon as we get out of these hilly areas. We'll have better reception."

"Why don't you let me drive now for awhile, so you can rest?" said Angela.

"Think I'll let you do that," said Liam. "I'm feeling a bit punk. Let's go."

Liam jumped into the VW's passenger seat and looked back at Adriana and Cici. "You *señoritas* alright back there? Either one of you want to sit up front, before we get to Guatemala City?"

"No, we're fine here," said Adriana

Liam showed increasing signs of fatigue and weakness, as they got nearer to the city. Angela had to help him down from the van when they stopped for gas. He had spotted a small roadside produce stand next to the gas station, and wanted to get some fresh fruit.

"You stay here, sweetheart. I'll walk over and get the fruit. Here's some money for the gas," said Liam.

"But Liam, I can do it. You are so tired. Why push yourself?" Liam was already on his way to get the fruit, waving at her from behind his back. Angela saw a new side to Liam, his stubbornness and unwillingness to listen to reason. Was there a bit of David in him? She smiled to herself. Maybe our choices don't change much when it comes to partners.

Adriana and Cici got out of the back of the van and

stretched their legs and arms. Angela struggled to not show her concern, but she knew they noticed how weak Liam was.

"Is everything alright with Liam?" asked Adriana, as she watched Liam walk slowly back from the produce stand, carrying the bag of fruit.

"*Sí*, he's just tired from the long drive," said Angela. She knew she was kidding herself. They had to get the medicine soon. Liam had called Agnes, and she and Rutilio had arranged for Felipe to bring the medicine to the border, a day-long drive, where a Guatemalan connection, another friend of Rutilio's, would meet him and bring it to Guatemala City. It would take two to three days. Liam tried to assure Angela he would be fine.

"Don't worry," he said. "Father Rutilio has a good friend in Guatemala City where we can hole up. Hey, we might even have time to take a side trip to Antigua, and show Cici and Adriana the *Volcano de Fuego*."

"Liam, you shouldn't be going anywhere the way you are feeling."

"Oh, I'll be fine," said Liam. "As soon as I get that 'juice' the doc sent, I'll be better than new. Since we have to wait a couple of days for my meds to come, might as well take advantage of the time. You'll like Guillermo. He helps the poor who live at the Guatemala City dump. It's a sad situation, but he's doing a lot for the children there. He's an old *curandero*, you know, a healer."

"I would love to see more of Guatemala. David and I once slipped over the border from Mexico, when we were on a vacation, and visited the amazing Mayan ruins at Tikal, but we didn't have the time to see more," Angela said. "I just want to make sure you don't overdo it." She smiled at Liam as she caressed his back and neck.

"Yeah, wish we could take the *señoritas* up there—to Tikal, I mean. It's pretty fascinating, but it's far up into the Pétan. I don't think we'll have the time for that trek. Antigua and its big volcano aren't far from Guatemala City. We'll get some pointers from Guillermo."

Angela smiled at the thought that they were going to be tourists. This was not what she thought would happen on their trek taking two Salvadorans to the US border crossing.

"Come on, let's shove off or we'll have to break my rule about traveling after dark, not a good thing to do especially on the outskirts of Guatemala City, one of the less savory places in Central America," said Liam.

Angela shuddered at this admission from Liam. It was unlike him to cast any shadow over their road trip.

"Ah, it's a piece of cake," he had said when she had expressed fear and doubt as they poured over the map back in Suchitoto. "I've done this so many times I could practically drive this route blindfolded. Don't believe the ugly things the US newspapers tell you about the dangers south of the border. We'll be fine."

An hour later, everyone was grumbling that they were hungry and why not stop to eat some of that fresh fruit Liam had bought. Liam agreed and pulled to the side of the road to get out and go to the back of the van to get something while Angela, Adriana and Cici began munching on papayas and bananas. When he came back he was holding the wrapped objects that Isabella and Jésus had presented them.

"I think this is a good time to open our gifts, don't you?"

"*Si,* good idea," Cici said, as she took the small wrapped package her grandfather had handed her, and began carefully to unwrap it. As the carved turtle slipped from the package almost falling to the floor of the van, Cici caught it and came up with a big smile.

"Oh, this is my favorite animal--*que bueno*! Remember when we set the turtles out to sea, Angela?"

They all laughed at Cici's enthusiasm.

"Now it's your turn, Angela and Liam," said Adriana, "Mama wanted you to have something from her."

Liam and Angela began to undo the cloth that Isabel had wrapped around the gift. As they unfolded the last section, they gazed at a small hand-woven basket Isabel had made. It had a lid and when they opened it, there inside were two beautiful brown eggs.

Angela let out a gasp! "How delightful!"

"How practical, too! We can share the eggs with Guillermo when we arrive," said Liam, with a smile. "I'm sure he'll appreciate them. Now, *vamanos*! We're not far from Guatemala City."

They made their way through the smoke-filled, polluted outskirts of Guatemala City and past its congested center, avoiding the dogs in the road, the people with their wares on their heads, Mayan women in traditional colorful *huipils,* with babies hanging on their backs, while they carried plastic bags of produce from the markets. Trucks jam-packed with workers on their way home from the coffee plantations sped past them. The rancid, gasoline-infested smells of the city wafted through the partially open windows of the van, as Liam, who was driving now, wove his way across the town, and down dark side streets, where questionable men gathered on street corners. Their glances belied their curiosity and their longings.

"Close the windows, Angie, and keep the doors locked," said Liam. "We're almost there. Guillermo will be waiting for us. I call him Memo. He's quite an interesting old Mayan who claims to have a shaman as a father. You'll like him."

"I don't understand, Angela. *Que pasa?*" asked Adriana. "Where are we?" Adriana and Cici had been sleeping for most of the past half hour, awaking now from the city noises surrounding them, as Liam drove them, rather wildly, through the congested and unfamiliar streets. They had barely ever seen even San Salvador, the capital city of their own country, except to pass through it once on an old bus to take Cici to the doctor.

"Don't worry," said Angela. "Liam has a good friend here in Guatemala City where we'll stay to wait for his medicine to arrive. We might get the opportunity to do a little sightseeing, too. It'll be fun for you and Cici."

"*Bien*. We'll both be happy to get out of the van for a few days." Adriana sounded relieved, as they pulled up in front of a small concrete-block house in a run-down neighborhood where one streetlight glowed against a night sky. They unfolded their way out of the van, glancing up at a full moon. The sounds of cicadas and barking dogs accompanied screeching car brakes, and, somewhere in the distance, a siren cut the night in half.

"*Hola amigos, bienvenidos.* Glad you made it." A

small man with long white hair tied back in a ponytail, bronze skin and an aquiline nose poised between high cheekbones and intensely dark eyes, approached them from the front porch of the house. He wore baggy blue jeans and a shirt of madras-like plaid stuffed into them. His pants were kept up with a piece of rope tied in the front. Around his neck was an old bandana. He had a strong-looking stature, and as he got closer to them, they could make out his warm smile.

"Get your things and come on in. Good to see you again, Liam. Rutilio has told me about your important cargo and journey to *El Norte*."

The two men embraced, and Liam turned to introduce Angela, Adriana, and Cici to Guillermo. "These are my traveling companions, Memo. I'm a lucky guy to be traveling with three such beautiful *señoritas*, right?"

With an intense stare, Guillermo studied the three women and broke into a slow smile.

"*Sí, amigo*. You're a lucky man. Now come on in and tell me about your trip. There's coffee on the stove and beer in the fridge. Take what you want." He patted Liam on the back, picked up one of the backpacks, and the two started toward the porch. The women followed. This was going to be interesting, thought Angela.

"Angela, you and Liam can sleep in there on the floor. I've laid out some blankets for you." Guillermo pointed to a small tile-floored room to the side of the combination kitchen and living room. Angela was glad to see the room had a bathroom next to it. She supposed it was Guillermo's usual sleeping quarters. It appeared he lived alone. Liam hadn't mentioned a partner.

"Cici, you can have a hammock on the back porch and your *madre,* also," said Guillermo. He pointed to the rear of the house. "Don't worry about mosquitoes. It's covered and has a screen around it."

"*Gracias, señor.*" Cici looked tired and a bit dazed by the new surroundings. Adriana put her arm around her daughter with a protective hug, as the two went to survey their room.

Angela noted that Guillermo's house was a lot like Adriana and Cici's in Jiquilisco, with its gray concrete-block walls. An old calendar with pictures of the volcanoes of Guatemala hung high on the wall over the cooking area. Photos were stuck up with tape. They appeared to be Mayan relatives of Guillermo's. In the corner was a small crudely built altar with a colorful old *rebozo* laid over it on top of which were some corn husks, small stones, and a sage stick. A stone mortar and pestle with a peyote pipe, some small dried plant material, and what looked like flower petals completed the collection of altar objects. A smell, a pleasant one, like burning sage, permeated the room, and a thin trickle of smoke flowed up from a dish where the sage was placed.

When Adriana and Cici came back into the room, Cici gazed at the corner altar with interest.

"Ah, I see you're interested in my altar," Guillermo said to her. "A curious mind is an intelligent one. We'll talk about those things later. Have you and your *madre* settled in on the porch?"

Adriana and Cici nodded their heads and stood awed by this man.

While Guillermo talked with Cici and Adriana, Liam picked up his and Angela's back- packs, noticeably wobbling under the weight, weaker than when they began the trip.

"Liam, no. Let me carry my own pack. You're not feeling well. Don't try to hide it. I love you," Angela whispered as she took her pack from Liam's shoulder, and he acknowledged her remarks, gently nudging her forward.

"Thanks," said Liam. "This will be a good stop on our road to *El Norte*. I think after a couple of days rest, I'll be back to normal, with energy to spare."

The two walked into the adjoining room that Guillermo had pointed out, and set their packs down. They noticed a blanket hanging over the opening between the two rooms, one side of which had been pulled back and tucked behind a nail in the wall. When they dropped it, they had some long-awaited privacy. Being cooped up in the van with Adriana and Cici had not allowed for much intimacy. Liam pulled Angela to him and they embraced with a long, deep kiss. Though she wanted to succumb completely to the sexy smell of his body, delicious taste, and tempting seduction, Angela pulled back from his embrace. "Liam, let's be discreet around your friend, and Cici and Adriana."

"Don't worry. Memo's a smart guy. He's taking care of them and letting us have a few moments to ourselves. Let's take advantage of it while we can. I may be tired but I'm never too weak to show my love. As if he heard them, Guillermo called out:

"You two want a *cervesa*? I bet you're hungry, too.

There's *frijoles* on the stove."

Angela and Liam laughed. "Guess we'll have to resist a bit longer," said Liam, as he buttoned her blouse. "Well, so much for time alone together. I have a date with you later."

"Is that a promise?" Angela flirted and pulled away, hot and electrified. "Come on, I'm looking forward to getting to know this friend of yours."

Memo's Story
Guatemala City

After a brief conversation, Cici began to yawn, and Adriana and Angela walked to the back porch with her to say goodnight. She crawled into her hammock and pulled her small *muñeca* close to her. Angela noticed how quickly she slipped the doll under the covers to hide it from her view. She could tell Cici was embarrassed. She was at such a fragile crossing, the age between childhood and adolescence. Angela remembered, with nostalgia, her own daughters at twelve. She hoped that Cici would survive the new world she was about to enter, far different from her rural village of El Salvador.

"Goodnight, Cici," said Angela. "You have been brave on this trip so far. You'll soon be with your Papa. You'll have many tales to tell him." Angela leaned down to kiss the young girl on her cheek. Cici smiled up at her.

"*Gracias*, I'm glad we're here with you and Liam's friend, Memo. He's a nice man."

"*Sí*, he is," said Adriana. "*Gracias,* from me, also,

Angela. Cici, go to sleep now, and may you dream with the angels. Tomorrow is another day on our trip north. Don't worry. We'll get there soon, and Papa will be so happy to see you." She leaned down to embrace her daughter.

"*Buenos noches,* Cici," said Angela.

"*Buenos noches,*" said the young girl as she rolled over and hugged her doll to her chest. She was almost asleep when Angela and Adriana walked back to where the two men were talking.

"Memo, why don't you tell Angela and Adriana what you were just sharing with me, about your work at the dump with the children," said Liam.

"First, you have to eat," Guillermo said. "Didn't the girl want something before going to sleep?"

"No, don't worry. She's very tired, and we had some fruit in the car earlier," said Adriana.

Guillermo brought bowls of hot frijoles and a basket of warm tortillas wrapped in a white towel over to the old wooden table around which they had gathered.

"Well, at least you three can fill your bellies before going to sleep tonight," he said. "Then we'll talk."

Angela learned that Memo came from a long line of shamans and *curanderos*, people who heal the mind and spirit as well as the body. She wondered if he might have some secret herbs, or spiritual connection to the ancient gods, that could heal Liam. She doubted it. She didn't know if Memo knew about Liam's illness, and she didn't feel right exposing it, at least not yet.

"Liam, *que pasa, mi amigo*? You look pale of face and

seem weaker in the legs than I remember the last time you and Rutilio stopped here. Was it a year ago?"

"*Sí*, it was. I'm fine. The road trip is just wearing me out a bit. I'm waiting, as Rutilio probably told you, for some medicines from my doctor in Boston, *gringo* medicine. That should do the trick, and I'll be fine." A wry smile crossed Liam's face and he continued: "Now tell the ladies about your work with the children."

Guillermo didn't seem convinced, as his eyes traced those of Liam's and he looked deeply into them— to his soul, maybe? Angela wondered how much he knew about Liam's illness. Then, he veered from the subject of Liam's health—maybe wise to the fact it was not Liam's wish to discuss it, at least, not now.

"Well, about my work." He took a sip of his *ochada*, a native drink made with rice, almonds and cinnamon. "I work with the most poor of our city, the children. Many who live at the dumps are orphans. They glean what they can there and survive on the meager diet. Some turn into mean little urchins, knocked around by their wicked conditions. They steal when they can, and eventually join the gangs. Others turn out pretty well, if they don't die of malnutrition or infection. Some of them even learn to be pretty good *curanderos* themselves. I guess you would call us medicine men or doctors. Infections, as you can imagine, are rampant in the dumps. Some of the children suffer from rat bites and other diseases from rotten food. I go there every day and set up a healing place, where they come and I give them salves made from natural plant materials, and other things to help. Most of all, I try to be the papa they don't have. This past year, a young *gringa*, Patricia, has come to our aid. She has set up a small school at the dump, and works with the children every day. We think she is an angel sent by God. The children love her, and she is helping to keep the younger ones from being recruited by the *maras*, the gangs that hang out on the fringes of this inferno."

Angela shuddered as she looked over at Adriana to see how she was taking this story. She suspected she knew about the *maras*. After all, they were rampant in El Salvador. Poverty breeds despair, despair breeds violence. Fortunately, the gangs had not yet embedded themselves into the rural areas of the Bajo Lempa, and though poor, the families there took care of their children for the most part, and they were not living at the city dump in San Salvador. She had heard there were cases like that there, too. She felt sick to her stomach, as Guillermo described a couple of the children and the conditions they had to endure. Liam appeared to have fallen asleep in his chair. His eyes were shut and Angela patted his leg gently under the table. He looked up, startled.

"Liam, why don't you turn in? We can tell you're tired, and much of what Memo is telling us is not new to you. Go ahead. I'm sure Guillermo won't mind."

"No, of course, Liam. Angela's right. Go to bed. We'll talk more in the morning, old friend. Now you need your sleep."

"Yeah, I guess I do. Sorry for falling off while you were talking, Memo. I'll say *buenos noches* and hit the hay, as we say in the States." He leaned over Angela and squeezed her shoulder, as he kissed her behind the ear. "Good night, my lovely lady. Don't stay here listening to this old guy too long."

"Good night, Adriana and Memo." He walked toward the small room and turned to the others. "Don't keep the *señoritas* up listening to your tales too long, Memo. I'm worried they might end up liking you better than me."

Memo chuckled and waved his hand, dismissing Liam. "Oh, don't worry about that, *amigo*. I'm too old for them."

"With age, comes wisdom," Liam called out from behind the blanket. "Women like that."

Angela and Adriana laughed and looked at Memo, eager to hear more about his work with the children, in spite of the sadness his stories imparted.

"Our biggest problem now," Guillermo continued, "is fighting the AIDS epidemic. Many of the children are infected from their mothers, who have been infected by their fathers, when they return from the work in *El Norte*. The *hombres* are lonely up there and get infected from the prostitutes, then bring SIDA, our Latin word for what you call AIDS, back with them. Eventually the fathers die, the mothers are infected and pass the disease on to their unborn children, who are orphaned early in their childhood. It's not a pretty picture. We have some medical teams that pass through from time to time, like Doctors Without Borders, but the epidemic is spreading in Guatemala."

Angela felt overwhelmed by the tragic tale, and whispered under her breath, "as if poverty weren't enough." This was another effect of immigration to the north. The US takes advantage of the migrant workers' cheap labor, and then sends them home to spread AIDS. Where would it stop? They either die of poverty without jobs in their own country, or of the dreaded disease. She felt confused. Here she was bringing Adriana and Cici to the north. Was it going to be better for them there?

As if reading her thoughts, Adriana touched her shoulder. "Don't worry, Angela, I know what you're thinking. Jorge is faithful to me. I know. We will be fine once we can be a family again."

Memo sighed. "Well, ladies, it's time to get some shut-eye. I'm up early to go to the dumps. Help yourselves in the morning to *pan, tortillas, frijoles, frutas*, whatever you like. I will return about noon, and we can talk about your trip to Antigua."

"Guillermo—may I call you Memo, too?" Angela asked.

"*Sí.* " Guillermo said. "*Como no?*"

"I wanted to ask if there is anything we can do to help, at the dump, I mean, while we're here waiting for Liam's medicines to arrive?"

"Gracias, but no. For now, Liam needs you most. Take care of him. I will see what I can do, too." He studied her with a deep, knowing look, as he disclosed he knew more about Liam's illness than she had suspected— maybe, even more than she. Her thoughts slipped back to their dreams of being together for the next chapter of their lives. Now that seemed like nearly an impossible dream. *Carpe diem*, she thought. She must enjoy him for as long, or as short of a time, as they had together.

Adriana stood and slipped out to the back, turning to say good night as she left.

Angela picked up the dishes from the table and helped Memo clean up; then they said good night.

The following day passed quickly as the four travelers took advantage of the time to wash their clothes, and get to know more about Memo and his work as a healer. That night after they ate dinner together, Memo answered Cici's curiosity about his altar. He explained to her that it was a spiritual center in his house, where he prayed for ancient wisdom. He explained to her how he prepared the complex world of herbs and plants he used to cure skin irritations, palpitations of the heart, and other illnesses. Then he demonstrated by preparing some herbal infusions for Liam, and conducting a short healing ceremony, which ended with passing of the peyote pipe.

Though fascinated with Memo and the ceremony, twelve-year old Cici was tired and said good night. Adriana excused herself, too. Angela and Liam joined Memo in passing the pipe.

Angela slipped into a kind of reverie of heightened senses, reminding her of *marijuana* experiences in the sixties. She and Liam liked the idea of getting a little high now together, to relax after the tensions of the trip.

"Not bad weed is it, Angela?" Liam said, with a smile. "I thought you were more pure than me."

"Oh, you don't know everything about me yet," said Angela, as she leaned back on a big pillow where they sat crossed legged on the floor.

What would her daughters say if they could see her now? Well, they were in Seattle and would never have to know. Was this a continuation of the path of deception she had started with Liam so many years ago? Sometimes, she rationalized, the whole truth is not necessary, particularly when the product of that truth might be misunderstood and serve no purpose of enlightenment for the better good. She no longer espoused the Catholic tradition of confession.

Angela and Liam soon slipped off to their room, saying good night to Memo. They knew they wanted to be up early for their trip to Antigua. Memo gave them a map, told them the road to follow and bid them a pleasant night's sleep.

The Road to Antigua
Guatemala

They awoke early the next day and began to prepare for their trip to Antigua. Angela and Liam reviewed the Guatemala map that Memo had drawn out for them. The trip would help pass the time while they awaited Liam's medicine. It would give Adriana and Cici some distractions, and it would be fun to be tourists for a day before they continued their journey north, through Mexico, to the border. While Liam and Angela discussed their plans, Adriana and Cici packed a picnic lunch. They had said good-bye to Memo earlier as he left for the dump, wishing them good luck. They would sleep that night at a small *posada* in Antigua. Memo knew the owner and had made reservations for them. After some sightseeing, they would return to Guatemala City the following day, and hopefully, Liam's drugs would be there. Liam was anxious not to delay longer than necessary, as he knew the Sanctuary group would be waiting at the border in a few days.

"Don't worry, Angie," Liam said, "I know they will be there for Adriana and Cici. My biggest concern now is getting them to the border by the time I promised. It didn't help that I left my meds at the orphanage."

Angela could see that Liam was suffering both physically and mentally for having left his medicine. "Oh, Liam, don't beat yourself up. It will all work out, darling. I think our side trip to Antigua will be a good distraction for all of us. Now, let's go. *Vamanos!*"

"Hey, *señoritas,* let's shove off." Liam walked out the door with their backpacks. Since Memo's healing ceremony, he seemed to have more energy and to feel better. Was it just the power of faith?

"*Shove off,* what's that?" asked Adriana, as she picked up the lunch she had packed in an old cloth sack Memo had lent them.

Liam laughed, "Oh, I'm sorry, Adriana, I use way too much slang, I know. You'll be picking up American slang soon enough from the streets of the US. "What I meant was it's time to leave: *Vamanos, Señoritas!*" Early in the trip, Liam had begun calling his three female traveling companions, *señoritas.* Angela felt flattered.

Cici replied with a smile, "*Sí,* let's shove off, " and everyone laughed.

As they continued an earlier conversation in the van, Angela spoke of some of her misgivings about the trip, her worries if they failed in their mission of getting Adriana and Cici safely over the border.

Liam explained to Angela: "It's always a gamble and dangerous, but I have hope and faith it'll work. My sanctuary group has helped others embed themselves into the US economy, finding them work and shelter. Immigrants are now contributing their labor to the economy and building a more secure future, taking a piece of the American Dream. For me, the most important part is reconnecting families. It's all about doing something for someone else, something that really counts, before I leave this fuckin' unjust world—'scuse my French." Angela rarely heard Liam talk with such cynicism. She was glad that Adriana and Cici could not hear their conversation in the back of the van. She reached over and touched Liam's leg.

"I'm not as good as you are, darling," Angela said. "I'm here for me. Helping you get Adriana and Cici to the States makes me feel needed and loved, with a purpose. It's a selfish act."

"That's the point. The real reason doesn't matter. We all have our self-interests. It's the action that counts. The result is the same. You do the work, which makes you feel good. They receive the help and feel good. You get to exercise your compassion muscle and everyone comes out ahead. Get it?"

Angela shook her head and slipped into her own thoughts, as they continued along the road to Antigua. Adriana and Cici played a game in the back seat and practiced their English. Liam pointed out a few sites along the way and finally suggested they stop for their picnic at a place he considered safe.

The place was by a cool stream, and it felt good to get out and wash the sweat from their faces and take a break. They didn't linger long there, as it was getting late in the afternoon, and they were anxious to get to Antigua before nightfall. Liam took the drivers seat and started up the van. It would soon be dusk. Angela struggled to read the map Memo had drawn for them. He had warned them about a place where the road split and had cautioned them to take the right fork. She thought they were almost there and warned Liam about the turn ahead when suddenly a band of men appeared, jumping down from the back of a pickup parked horizontally in the middle of the road. Liam put on the brakes and came to a halt. The men ran toward the van.

"Damn, what now?" Liam said. "Roll up your windows. They may not be up to any good."

Angela knew that he didn't want to frighten them but she could read an expression of fear on his face. She noticed the flash of a machete blade in the hand of one of the men who appeared to be the leader. She quickly did the math. There were six of them, and they were only four. Not good odds.

The band of disheveled-looking, mostly young men, but not with the usual tattoo markings of a gang, stood arm-in-arm across the road as if to signal that they should proceed no further.

"Let me handle this," said Liam. "Keep your cool."

Adriana called out from the back. "What should we do, Liam?"

"Don't act frightened, whatever you do." Liam said. "These guys are probably just looking for money. Don't worry. I left most of our funds back at Memo's, but I have a small amount stashed just for this purpose: a *mordita* or bribe. If they ask you, give them what you've got."

Liam knew that all Adriana had was some small

change. Angela knew that the problem was going to be getting rid of these guys if they weren't satisfied by what they could get. She felt her body tense. Her instincts told her what was coming was not good. Liam seemed tense, too, all the while trying to sound calm, as if he had everything under control.

Without warning, the group of *bandidos* rushed at the van, two of them jumped up onto the roof and hung over to peer in at the passengers, as if to assess the number in the car.

"There are four, Pancho."

The older one, the one with the machete, Pancho, said, "Get them out and on the ground, *pronto*! Check out the van for money."

As he said this, the others tried the doors, which had been locked by the frightened passengers. The men began to pick up some big rocks to break the windows.

"Oh, no you don't," Liam said under his breath, and opened his door to get out with his arms raised. "Hey, guys, no, don't do that? What do you want? Here, I can give you this," he said as he reached for his wallet in the back of his pants. He hoped to satisfy them with the small amount of money he had. Angela could see he was trying to stall the bandits. She, Adriana and Cici were frozen in their seats.

The biggest guy in the group grabbed Liam and shoved him over to the side of the road, taking the wallet as he did so. Two of the men grabbed Angela out of the car and began to laugh, as if they were making jokes about her. She could imagine what they were saying in their rough, *macho* Spanish slang. One guy grabbed the shawl she had wrapped around her shoulders and tied it around her waist, using it to pull her, like a cow, over to the road's shoulder where Liam stood with his back to the road. They had tied his hands behind him with a scraggly looking piece of rope. Another man pulled Cici, who was crying, from the van. A third grabbed Adriana. They shoved the two in front of them to the same place near Liam and Angela while the remainder of the surly bunch scrambled into the van, checking out everything and throwing stuff out the windows.

"Hey, there's some weed back here. Smells like good stuff," Angela heard one of them exclaim. The leader, Pancho, replied: "Take it and any other crap that looks good." Then turning to the four captives, he walked over and forced them to fall to their knees in a straight line, as he poked them with the tip of his machete.

Liam tried to reason with him in Spanish, explaining they were tourists returning to Antigua after a day trip, and they didn't have much with them. He stopped short of begging for their lives. It probably wouldn't do much good, thought Angela. Even though he had never told her the full story of his other trips down to Central America, she imagined he had experience with this kind of thing. She remembered he once mentioned that he had had a couple of run-ins over the years with *bandidos,* who just wanted money. He explained that he always traveled with dollars he could afford to lose expressly for the demanded bribes at the borders and in situations like this. She hoped he had them now.

As if taking a chance he could bargain with this guy, Liam squinted at the leader, Pancho, and said in his best

Spanish, "Make you a deal. Don't hurt the women, and I'll give you the last greenbacks I've got."

Angela watched Pancho look at Liam with a steely, suspicious stare and then a wily smile.

"*Por que*? I can have them both, *Señor*, the women and the *dinero*. He glanced over at Angela and surveyed her. Nearby, Cici clutched Adriana's arm while she pressed next to her mother, trembling and crying softly with fear.

"Shut the kid up." Pancho poked at Cici, and Adriana almost lurched at him, as she pulled Cici closer. Two of Pancho's sidekicks stood like sentinels, as they watched the road, while the others took whatever they could find from the van: blankets, bottled water, extra clothes and the bag of *marijuana* that Memo had given Liam to stash, just in case. Angela remembered hearing him say to Liam: "Better take a little grass. It might come in handy either for you or as a *mordita*. Won't hurt if you keep it well hidden. No one will search you until you get to the border. If you don't use it before, you can leave it with me when you continue the journey to El Norte. "

Pancho's words elicited contempt in Angela. At the same time she noticed memorable details, including a bright red bandana tied around his neck. It had an imprint of Che Guevera's face. How odd, Angela thought. Che had always been one of her heroes. Latin America was filled with contradictions.

His screaming at them flayed her nerves. Cici quietly whimpered as she clutched her mother's skirt. Pancho forced Liam to lie down, face in the dirt, and with one foot on his back, he motioned to his men, yelling out orders. The men moved toward the women while Pancho began patting down Liam. Terrified, as the men waved their arms at the three to move them further off the road, they hovered together. The three men forced the women to lie face down in the dirt, pushing their backs down with their boots. In a protective gesture, Angela carefully slipped one arm over Cici, in the middle, and reached to touch Adriana's shoulder. Somehow—she knew not how—she had to save them and herself. At the same time, she was thinking of Liam and feared what Pancho might be doing to him. She craned her neck to turn and look back at him. Adriana, succumbed to her fear, and began to weep, too, as she pulled Cici closer.

"Shut the bitches up!" Pancho shouted out orders. "Keep checking out the van's interior and see what you can find—documents, money—whatever we can use, and get the tires."

Angela was glad she and Liam had thought to leave their passports and ID back at Memo's house. She had tucked some money under the sole of her shoe. Now, her biggest fear was being strip-searched—or worse, raped. She was about to hand over the money from her shoe when she heard the sound of another vehicle, chugging up the steep incline. Howler monkeys directly overhead, in the dense jungle canopy, let out a loud warning scream. The bandits heard the sounds, too.

"Quick—let's get the hell out of here—*Vamanos*! Take the money and the weed."

Angela couldn't see what was happening. All she hoped for was that they wouldn't kidnap Liam. With her face pressed against the earth, she tasted the filth of the dirt, and felt its grit between her teeth. She kept her arms tightly around her friends and prayed—something she hadn't done since her childhood in Sunday school. Fear could change one's perspective quickly, just as hunger could make men into beasts.

"Oh, God, make them go and leave us. Take us out of harm's way."

She could hear a shuffling of feet, and one of the men kicked her with his boot as he ran by—"Good Luck, bitch." She heard them scramble into the pickup, while Pancho yelled epithets at them as he gunned the motor. They took off down the road in the opposite direction of a big tourist bus, which rounded the curve a few yards ahead. Angela could feel Liam leaning down by her, his breath brushing her cheek.

"Come on, sweetheart, it's OK now," he said. He had rolled over and scooted to her side. "Help me get this rope off my wrists. Cici, Adriana, don't worry. They've gone." Angela rolled over, got to her knees, and quickly undid the rope around Liam's wrists. He reached down to help them up off the ground. Cici's tear-stained face looked up at him with fear still engraved in her eyes.

The large tourist bus heading for Antigua came to a halt, as Liam ran in front of it, waving his arms. The bandits had pushed the van over to the road's shoulder and slit one of the back tires before they made their escape. The bus driver opened the door, slipped out of his seat and jumped down from his high perch, nearly tripping on the step. He looked annoyed at having to make the abrupt stop.

"*Que pasa, Señor?*" He addressed Liam, who was by

now wiping his face with his shirt and pointing to the van.

"Sorry to stop you, but we need your help. We've just been held up by a group of bandits. The women are frightened, and we have to get to Antigua before nightfall. Can you help us?" Liam rushed this off in his semi-fluent Spanish, and the bus driver looked at the four and then at the van.

"Wow, you guys are really in trouble," the bus driver said. "Come along with me, and I'll get you to Antigua, where you can find some wheels and get back here."

"No, that's not necessary. I have a spare. Luckily they didn't take that. It's in the back underneath a false floor," Liam said. "I don't want to leave the van."

"I've got a busload of tourists, man. I can't stop and help you now, but we can get the women to the town while you stay here with your vehicle. We're not far from Antigua, now. I'll send a couple of guys back to help you."

Liam turned to Angela. "You go with Adriana and Cici in the bus. I'll stay here with the van. You can make sure this guy's good for his word, and sends someone back to help me. In the meantime, I'll get the bugger jacked up and find some rocks to support it. We have a reservation at the *Posada Buena Vista*, in the center of town. Just give them my name."

Still shaking, Angela was dubious. It was already getting dark, and she knew Liam wasn't well. He looked more and more washed out, and she feared that he wouldn't have the strength to get the van jacked up, let alone gather big enough rocks to support it while he attempted to change the tire. The van was on a steep slope. What if the bandits came back?

"Liam, I'm staying with you. I may not have your herculean strength, but I can help. Besides, you're not well." She knew he hated to have her remind him, but she felt she had to insist on staying. Adriana and Cici would be fine with the tourists in the bus. She saw bewildered tourists looking out the window. They smiled at them, not fully understanding the gravity of the situation. In the meantime, the bus driver showed more and more impatience.

"Okay, okay, ladies, come on." He motioned Adriana and Cici up the steps of the bus, as he grabbed their arms to help them.

Adriana looked back at Angela and Liam, as she pushed Cici gently ahead of her. "It's okay, Angela?"

"*Sí,* it's okay. Go with the tourists. Liam and I will meet you at the *posada* in Antigua."

Liam protested: "No, you go with them, too, Angela."

She wouldn't listen—she wasn't going to leave Liam there alone.

Angela climbed up into the bus behind Adriana and Cici, and spoke with the two women and a man who sat close to the front. "Excuse us for stopping your bus. We were just held up by some robbers." A gasp came from the passengers. They all began to whisper to one another. "Thankfully, we are OK. The noise of your bus scared them off. They tried to make sure we didn't get anywhere soon by slitting one of our tires on our van over there." Angela pointed in the direction of the van. "We have to get to Antigua to find help for my husband. He isn't well." She took the liberty to call Liam her husband. It was less complicated than trying to explain things now.

Everyone in the bus leaned forward, curious to get the story. Some looked bewildered, others frightened.

Angela continued, "Luckily, my husband had a spare hidden away. Would you mind taking care of our two friends who are traveling with us? They have had quite a scare and need rest. We have a reservation to stay at the *Posada Buena Vista* tonight. Our reservations are under the name of Liam O'Connor. The bus driver has promised to send someone back to help my husband change the tire on our vehicle."

Two women in the front seat moved over and motioned for Cici to sit next to them. Adriana took the one empty seat behind them, still looking pale and afraid. She put her hand on her daughter's shoulder and gave her a reassuring squeeze. Cici clutched the small woven blanket she had pulled around her shoulders, the one her grandmother had given her. She lowered her dirt-stained face, streaked with tears, avoiding the stares of the two women.

The man sitting in the front seat spoke first.

"Yeah, no problem. We'd be glad to help. The little girl looks about the age of our granddaughter. We'll make sure she and her mother get to the *posad*a. I'll check that the driver sends someone to help your husband. In fact, why don't I just stay behind and help him? My wife can take care of …"

The woman next to him interrupted, "No, Jack. It's too dangerous. Let the driver get someone to come back."

Jack looked chagrin, having let his better self emerge only to be squelched by his wife's fears. "Well, anyway, maybe my wife is right. I'll make sure, though, that someone comes."

His offer to stay and help them was their best option, but Angela decided not to create a marital argument, given the frightened look on Jack's wife's face. "That's okay. We'll be fine," she said. "Thank you, sir." She stepped back off the bus and waved as she stretched to see Adriana and Cici's faces."

"Don't worry, *Señora*," the bus driver said. "I'll send some guys to help you. They should get here in about an hour. You'll have the light of the moon by then. *Adios y que vaya con dios.*" He pushed in the clutch, shifted into first gear and climbed up and over the hill to Antigua. Angela waved and then turned to Liam.

"Well, here I am at the ready. Give me something important to do, darling."

"You know, you're one amazing woman. I love you. I can't believe how well you held up to that experience, Adriana and Cici, too, for that matter. Let's just sit here together in the van for a minute and assess what has to be done. I'm sure glad I thought to hide that spare, and they didn't find it! God was watching over us."

Ever the contrarian when it came to religious proclamations, Angela said, "Or could it have been just luck?"

"Whatever it was, we're here. That's the main thing. I'll have to rely on your help. We can go in search of some big rocks. I think I saw some over that embankment," Liam said, pointing across the road, where the robbers had pinned them down to the dirt.

"Liam, just rest for a minute. I can lift the tire out of the back. Where's the jack? Underneath?"

Without a warning, Liam pulled Angela to him and gave her a passionate kiss. When they pulled away from each other she could see his eyes were wet with tears, and she felt a pang of worry shoot through her. Were these the last days they would have together?

Help Comes
Guatemala

Angela and Liam managed to get the van partially jacked up by the time a pickup with two guys rolled up an hour later. The moon had just crested, and the air was chilly. Liam showed signs of near collapse, and looked relieved to see the two friendly faces.

"*Hola, Señor y Señora,*" one of them yelled out as he jumped down from the truck. "We're here to help. Ramon, the bus driver, told us about your mishap with the robbers. You're lucky. Just last week one of the tour buses was held up by a big group of robbers and they made everyone get out, stole all their documents, stripped them of their clothes and left them here standing stark naked by the road. Several of the tourists were whiplashed. Fortunately, no one died, but it was a pretty horrid site. My *amigo* and I found them, and we were able to get help and take them to town."

"Yeah, guess we *were* lucky," Liam said with a haggard look on his face. "Thanks for showing up. We can use your help." Liam pointed to the rear of the van where he and Angela had struggled to get the rocks positioned under the jack.

"No problem," the talkative guy said while the other one headed back to inspect the situation. "The way you two look, I suggest you just sit here and get warm under this blanket. My *amigo* and I will get the tire on in no time. Don't worry." As he said this, he reached into the cab of his truck and pulled out a heavy hand-woven, multicolored wool blanket and handed it to Liam.

"*Muchas gracias.* What's your name?" Liam asked.

"Just call me Cheve. Everyone does, 'cause I like to drink beer. You know the word, don't you? It's slang for *cervesa* in my country, Mexico."

"Sure, Cheve. I'll buy you and your amigo a few beers when we get back to town."

"Gracias, but you don't have to do that. We're glad to help."

"Did you, by any chance, see a mother and child arrive in the tour bus?" Angela asked Cheve.

"Oh, *sí*, they told me to tell you they were fine. One of the tourists, a nice guy named Jack, took them to the *Posada Buena Vista.* They're okay and will be happy to see you, I'm sure. Sorry you've had this trouble, *Señora.*"

As they sat huddled under the blanket, Liam leaned close to Angela and whispered, "If I hadn't left my meds in El Salvador, we'd be half way to the border by now.

"Liam, don't beat your self up." Angela tried to be reassuring, all the while wondering what might happen next on this journey to El Norte. She leaned in close to Liam.

When the two men finished getting the tire on, Liam handed them a tip from the money that Angela had hidden in her shoes. He told them to buy some beer, thanked them and asked if he could follow them back to Antigua.

"Sure, *gracias*, *Señor*. It's not far, only about 40 kilometers from here. Follow us."

Once in town, Liam split off, waving to the two guys as he went down a side street and found the small *Posada Buena Vista*. He explained to Angela he had stayed at the modest *posada* many times before on his treks into Guatemala with Rutilio. They often stopped to help a women's collective just outside of town get their produce and coffee beans they picked to Guatemala City.

Adriana and Cici were fast asleep in their room next to Liam and Angela's. When Angela knocked lightly on their door, Adriana opened it slightly and peered out. She had a big smile of relief. "I'm so glad you got here safely. Cici was completely exhausted and fell right to sleep."

"That's good. I hope she doesn't have bad dreams. We're fine, and the van's got a new tire. Let's all go to sleep now. Tomorrow is another day. We'll have some time to look around this beautiful town and maybe take a short hike up to the volcano before heading back to the big city. See you in the morning. Sleep with the angels."

Adriana smiled. It was she who had taught Angela this poetic good night refrain: "*Que tu duermes con los angeles.*" It meant "May you sleep with the angels," and Angela always liked to say it.

Mexico and El Norte

Thankful they arrived back in Guatemala City without incident, Liam rejoiced that his medicine had arrived. They spent one more night at Memo's and then said their good-byes in the morning before he went off to the dump. It was hard to leave the comfort of Memo's house, and his kind and generous hospitality, but the border called.

"*Vamanos,* my lovely *señoritas,*" Liam said. "If we want to get to our next stop, Oaxaca, Mexico, in one day, we have a twelve hour drive. We've lost four days with my stupid mistake, not bringing my medicines. We'll have to make that up now, as my friends from the Sanctuary team will be waiting for us at the border."

"Are we going to get there in time, Liam?" asked Adriana. Her voice was filled with anxiety, as she lifted her backpack into the van. Angela knew how much emotion she had invested in this journey to rejoin her husband, Jorge, after four years of separation.

"*Sí,* we'll get there on time, but we have to drive

while we have daylight. You know our rule, no driving after dark."

The four piled into the van. They were all conscious of the long drive they had ahead, through Mexico to the US border. Liam and Angela took turns at the wheel as they followed CA-l to Mexico's 190, a journey that traced the route of the Mayan culture all the way to Mexico City. Their travel took them through a spectacular canyon and rarefied climes of the ancient Zapatec city of San Cristobal de la Casas. Adriana and Cici sat with their noses pressed to the windows, exclaiming at every turn in the mountainous road about the beautiful scenery.

"B-r-r-r, it's cold out there," said Angela, as she rolled up her window. "Liam you've driven all morning. It's my turn. Why not pull over for a minute and we'll change seats."

"Good idea. I'll pass around the lunch that Memo made for us and we can eat in the car. I'd like to make it to Oaxaca by dark where I have an acquaintance we can stay with, a physician named Dr. Mendez. He's a nice guy who sometimes rents out a room for a reasonable rate."

Angela wondered if Liam had checked in with him about his medical problem when he drove down the last time to El Salvador. Liam still kept so much from her. She knew he was probably trying to protect her from a truth too difficult to face, at this point.

"Did I hear you say Oaxaca?" asked Adriana, from the back seat. "Jorge nearly got caught up in a very bad riot there a few years ago when he was on his way back to *El Norte*. Cici was only eight then. There was a big protest, he said, and many people were killed and shot at by the National Police. I don't know what it was about, but he was glad to get out of there. Is it still dangerous?"

Angela and Liam glanced at one another and then Liam replied, "That was the 2006 teachers' protest. They were asking for better wages and more money for education. Purportedly, eleven striking teachers were killed by state security forces."

"Oh, Liam, I don't think I want to stop there," said Adriana, with a sound of fear in her voice.

Lowering hers, Angela said to Liam, "Let's not frighten Adriana and Cici. They've been through enough on this trip, so far. Please reassure them all is fine now."

"Things have calmed down for now," said Liam, "not that the issues are solved, but we'll be fine. Don't be afraid, Adriana. Mexico has its problems, just like El Salvador. I was just in Oaxaca a few months ago when I was driving the van down from Boston. Had a good time and stayed with Dr. Mendez. I told him I might be back again in a few months. You'll like him and especially his wife, Rosie."

For the rest of the trip, Adriana and Cici slept while Liam and Angela talked about the scenery, and their plans for the future. Angela appreciated the cooler temperatures, a relief from the heat of El Salvador. As night fell they were still on the road, several kilometers from Oaxaca.

"Guess we're not going to make it to Oaxaca today, after all," said Liam. "We better stop here." Liam pointed to a motel as he pulled off the road. "We'll go into the city tomorrow, and stop to say a quick hello to Dr. Mendez.

Then we can pick up some stuff at the local market for our picnics for the next couple of days."

The following day, Liam drove down a narrow Oaxacan street and stopped in front of an imposing two-story colonial house, painted the color of pomegranates. It was not far from the *zocalo*, the central square. He rang the bell several times. Finally a maid came to the door.

Liam nodded to her and said, "Dr. Mendez? Is he here, please?

"No, *Señor*. He and his wife are with their sons in Cuernavaca."

Liam looked back at the three anxious faces, waiting patiently in the van, and shrugged his shoulders. After a short conversation with the maid, he walked over to the van.

"Sorry, guess we're not going to see Dr. Mendez, but the maid has offered to give us each a cold lemonade on the patio. She remembers me from my last visit. We'll take a quick break, then hightail it to Mexico City and hope to get there in the next two days."

Their drive through windy mountain roads was accented with dramatic scenery and few stops, except at Pemex stations for gas. When they reached Mexico City, the traffic was a frenzy of noise and intermingling cars, trucks and taxis. Billboards, along the road's shoulder flashed garish advertisements. The three passengers remained glued to their seats, sometimes grasping them, when Liam swerved to miss another vehicle that didn't seem to know where it was going. The bustling sprawl of the this largest city in the Western Hemisphere was a nightmare to circumnavigate and they all breathed a sigh of relief when they were out on the open highway again, heading towards Mexico's central highlands.

Everyone in the van was anxious to reach the colonial city of San Miguel de Allende to spend a night with Sandy and Jake. Sandy had told Angela it was a beautiful town, full of artists and interesting people. Angela looked forward to seeing her friends again, and relished the thought of a day of rest in the aesthetic atmosphere of San Miguel, before continuing to *El Norte*. For now she tried to set aside her anxieties over what might happen at the border.

A Pleasant Respite
San Miguel de Allende, Mexico

F our hours later they pulled up to another brightly painted colonial house on a hill in San Miguel de Allende. Sandy and Jake had been expecting them, and were there to meet the four tired travelers.

"*Bienvenidos, amigos.* We're glad you finally arrived safely." Sandy embraced Angela as she climbed out of the van, glad to stretch her legs. Liam ran around from the driver's side, shook hands with Jake, and opened the van's side door helping Adriana and Cici get out.

"Cici, how you've grown," said Sandy. "When we were in El Salvador ten years ago, you were a baby. Now you're a beautiful young *señorita.*" Sandy reached her arms out to hug Cici, who looked down with shyness. "Good to see you, too, Adriana, after all these years. I'm sure you're being well taken care of by Liam and Angela on this important journey."

"*Sí,* Sandy. It's great to see you, too," said Adriana.

"Mama and Papa said to say hello to you. They remember well how hard you worked when you planted the mangroves and fruit trees. Too bad you can't see the fruit trees now. They've all grown so big, and the children love to eat the mangos."

"Me, too. I steal a few mangos off those trees every time I drive by their school," Liam said, gently tousling Cici's hair.

Cici took him up on the tease. "So you're the robber. We've been wondering who's been taking our *fruta!*"

They all laughed, and while Jake helped with their backpacks, Sandy ushered them into the inner courtyard of their Spanish colonial home, where they felt awash in the peace and quiet of a lush tropical garden.

"Oh, Sandy, this is beautiful," Angela said. "We may not want to leave."

"Jake and I love it here," said Sandy. "It always feels good to come back here, after we've been working down in Nicaragua. We regret we haven't gotten back to El Salvador for a long time. But, come on, we can talk about all of that later over some cold drinks. Let me show you to your rooms."

Jake and Liam came up behind them.

"That sounds good," Liam said. "I could stand to freshen up a bit. I feel like a ragged old dog scraped up off the streets of Mexico City, pretty smelly and dirty."

"Liam, you haven't changed. I'm glad you and Angie are finally together."

Angela blushed, knowing Sandy was in on their affair ten years earlier, and not too approving of it at the time.

"Adriana and Cici, you have the room right next to Angie and Liam's," Sandy said. "I hope you'll be comfortable here and get some rest before you have to continue the journey. By the way, can you stay for a couple of days, at least?"

"No, I'm afraid we're here for just one night," Liam hastened to say. He looked over at the disappointed expression on Angela's face. "We're already a few days behind schedule. I guess Angela may have told you, when she called, about our mishap in Guatemala."

"Yeah, in fact, she did," said Jake. "Sounds pretty scary. I'm also sorry to hear about your illness. Sandy and I are concerned for you. Maybe you should consider taking a rest here for more than one night. We have a friend in California who has been fighting the same blood cancer for several years. He gets really tired and needs lots of rest."

Liam put up his hands and said, "Thanks, Jake, let's not go there now, please. I'm fine, and I know I still have lot of life in me."

Angela regretted she had disclosed Liam's illness to Sandy and interrupted. "Come on, you two, I want to get cleaned up, and we can talk later." They had arrived at a door that opened into a spacious room with a big carved Mexican bed, referred to in Mexico as the *cama matrimonia*, marriage bed. The down comforter and soft pillows promised a good night's sleep.

"I hope you'll be comfortable here," Sandy said. "Take your time, and we'll have some drinks and snacks out on the patio when you feel ready."

Liam and Angela closed the door and fell into each

other's arms. Liam pulled her to the bed, sliding his hands down her hips as they fell onto it, wrapping legs and arms around each other as if ravenous for a meal of scrumptious delights. Then slowly getting up, Angela began to undress over Liam's gaze, slipping each garment off, seducing his every sense. Once nude, she knelt over him and began to undress him. He lay prone, kissing her when he could, and they fell into an amorous embrace, naked body to naked body enjoying to the fullest the slow and steady rhythms of their hips, until they both let out a cry of joyful release. Exhausted, they fell asleep and woke with a start, an hour later, to a light tap on their door.

"Angie, Cici and I are going out to the patio with Sandy and Jake," Adriana called out through their door.

"We'll be there in a few minutes," Angela said, wondering if they had heard her and Liam's passionate moans.

"No, we won't," said Liam, "not until I've had time to get more of you." Liam pulled Angela close to him.

"No, darling. We really have to go out to be with our hosts now." Though delighted Liam still had the energy for lovemaking, Angela pulled away from his embrace and headed for the bathroom to get dressed. "I'll take a rain check."

Liam laughed. "I'm sure we can arrange that."

The five adults had a good time that evening as they reminisced about their shared past in El Salvador. Cici enjoyed playing with Sandy and Jake's dog, Azul, a beautiful German shepherd, named for his unusually blue eyes. Big but gentle, he and Cici bonded instantly.

After a delicious dinner, Angela and Sandy escaped to the kitchen to talk over dishes, while Jake helped Liam roll out the map on the dining room table. Angela could hear the two men talking in the dining room.

"I'm sure you know the gravity of what you're attempting," Jake said. "The *migras* are cracking down hard on the undocumented immigrants crossing over the border. May I suggest you have a back-up plan, if you can't get through with Adriana and Cici?"

"I'm not taking my responsibility, lightly," said Liam. "My whole reason for doing this is to protect Adriana and Cici from the horrors most of our *compadres* face when they make this trip and then cross over, if they're lucky, like walking for days and nights across the hot dessert, nearly drowning in the Rio Bravo, and then being left, by the *coyotes* to whom they paid so much. If they're picked up by the border patrol they're sent back. It's even worse now since the 800-mile wall has been built."

"I know, Liam, it's terrible," said Jake. "I know your heart is in the right place; you care about Adriana and Cici, but I wonder if you have thought about the consequences for them, even if you do get them over. They'll be undocumented and have to live with fear for a long time, always worried about whether they will be deported and torn away from Jorge after all."

There was a long pause and then Angela heard Liam say, "You sound like Angela."

"Well, I have to speak my truth. I worry that, as well meaning as you are, you may have filled Adriana and Cici with false expectations."

"You might be right. But I can't let them down now.

I haven't told Angela yet, but I have an alternative plan if we can't get through the border crossing."

"May I ask what that is?"

"I've got an old friend who owes me one. I never planned on calling in the debt, but, if we need to, he can pick up Adriana and Cici off the west coast of Baja in his fishing boat. He's a trustworthy guy and has promised he will get Adriana and Cici safely to Astoria, on the northern coast of Oregon. Our only hitch there would be getting them transported by car down to California. There's a chance the Sanctuary people can pick them up there."

Eavesdropping on this conversation while she helped Sandy with the dishes, Angela unconsciously wrung her dishtowel, and fumed that Liam had never disclosed this to her.

"Hey, are you still here, Angie?" Sandy called out from the sink. "You look as if you're lost in thought."

"Sorry, Sandy. I'm letting you down on the job. I'll be honest. I was eavesdropping on Liam and Jake's conversation about the border. Liam was telling him something that was news to me. To tell you the truth, I'm getting scared and I'm wondering if Liam is really thinking clearly since he's been sick."

"Is there something more you're not telling me, Angie?"

"No, I'm just worried," said Angela, about what will happen at the border. Liam thinks the fake documents he secured for them will work, but I have my doubts, given the political climate vis-à-vis immigration these days. Like Jake, I worry that we may be taking Adriana and Cici on a dangerous road of unfulfilled expectations."

Sandy tried to reassure Angela. "I'd suggest you get some sleep, since you have to leave early tomorrow," said Sandy, "Things will look brighter in the morning and we'll think positive for the culmination of your journey."

"You're right. Maybe I'm just tired," said Angela.

The following morning after breakfast, they all said good-bye as Liam pulled out from the curb on the cobblestone streets in front of Sandy and Jake's house. Cici and Adriana waved and Angela called out from the open car window, "Wish us luck. We shall return."

The Border
Mexico

The next four-day's of driving were the hardest. They were all tired, a bit grouchy and the scenes of desert, dry mesquite and cactus, small dusty towns and roadside Pemex stations became monotonous. The closer they came to the border, the more palpable the excitement and the tensions became, in the van. Liam finally spoke to Angela about his reservations.

"I'm not naïve, sweetheart. I know we're attempting the almost impossible. I'm not at all that sure the visas we have for Adriana and Cici will hold up to the stringent inspection of the immigration agents at the border. With that in mind, I've devised a Plan B. I want to tell you about it."

"Liam, I have to be honest with you," said Angela. "I know about Plan B. I heard you talking about it with Jake. I think you need to tell Adriana about it, also. She has a right to know about what may happen."

"Well, that's a surprise, but I value your opinion. Of course, I had planned to discuss this with both you and Adriana when the time was right. We're only a day away now from the border. Let's stop at the next roadside café and have some lunch, and go over the details. Maybe Adriana can make a call to Jorge, while we're there, to let him know how close we are."

"Are we almost there?" Cici called out from the back

Angela and Liam laughed. "Yes, Cici, you have good ears and understand English better than we thought," said Angela. "Is your mother awake?"

"*Sí*, I'm awake," said Adriana. "I heard what you and Liam were talking about, and I hope you will explain to me what is going to happen when we get to the border. I'm getting a little nervous."

"Don't worry," Liam said. "We'll talk about the plans over lunch. You can call Jorge from there."

"He'll be so happy to know we're close to the end of our journey," said Adriana. "I know for him it was much more dangerous. I won't tell him about our problems in Guatemala. That's over now."

Angela felt a lump form in her throat. She feared that they had misled Adriana, and prayed that all would go well and without a glitch. She was angry with herself for going along with Liam. Somehow, he wielded a kind of invisible control over her. It was one thing to love him, another to give up her sense of what was right. Why had she completely lost herself to love?

"Liam," Angela turned to him and whispered so Adriana couldn't hear, "I really think you need to be honest with Adriana and tell her the odds of her crossing over successfully. Frankly, I think they are very slim, and I'm not sure your Plan B is going to work either."

Liam ran his hand through his hair, sucked in his breath and let his shoulders drop with an impatient sounding sigh, as he pulled the van to a stop, in a parking lot outside a small café. "Angie, I thought we already talked about this. Trust me, sweetheart."

Angela didn't respond, but instead got out and slid the back van door aside and helped Adriana and Cici jump down. "Come on, *amigas*, let's make it to the bathroom before we get lunch. We'll meet Liam inside."

Tensions mounted while they ate their lunch, and Liam tried to explain the plan to Adriana and Cici for the border crossing.

"May I please call Jorge?" asked Adriana. "I need to talk to him."

"Sure. There's a phone booth out there," Liam said, pointing to the booth by the café entrance. "Here, you can use my international calling card, and Angela will help you."

The two women got up and headed toward the phone booth.

"Can I go, too? I want to talk to Papa." Cici tried to follow.

"You wait here, Cici, it might not be easy for your papa to talk now since he will be at work. You'll be seeing him soon," said Liam.

A few minutes later, Angela and Adriana walked back into the café, their faces white. Shock and anguish were written all over them. Liam knew immediately something was wrong.

"Liam, it's good we called," said Angela. "We got hold of Jorge's employer. He was very upset. Jorge was picked up yesterday by police over a simple traffic violation, and Mr. Ricardo, his boss, fears he may be deported. He felt so bad. He has been working to get a green card for Jorge, and told the authorities that he could not find anyone as qualified as him to do the job managing the nurseries. He didn't know that Adriana and Cici were on their way to cross the border. Jorge hadn't told him. I guess he was afraid."

Liam's mouth dropped open, amazed. He lowered his head into his hands as he leaned his elbows on the table.

Tears welled up in Cici's eyes. "Does that mean we won't see Papa now? What will they do to him?"

Adriana, her face still stricken with shock over the news, slid into the booth next to Cici and wrapped her arms around her. "Don't worry, Cici. Your papa will be fine. Angela and Liam will help us find him."

Panic ran through Angela, as she looked at Liam, and questioned what they were going to do next.

"Mr. Ricardo said he was tracing the whereabouts of Jorge when we called," said Angela. "He thinks they took him to a detention center. He has connections, he says, with Immigration and he'll do everything he can to get Jorge released. At any rate, he will know more by tomorrow morning, and said to call back by nine o'clock. He suggested we go on to Tijuana and get a motel room there. We'll have to wait and be patient. He said it wouldn't do any good to try to get Adriana and Cici through the border now and might, in fact, hurt

Jorge's chances of being able to stay."

Liam cast Angela a long and apologetic look.

"Adriana and Cici, I'm so sorry," he said. "Perhaps I was wrong to think I could do this, get you over the border so you could be with Jorge again. Somehow, we'll help you reunite with him. I'm sorry my country seems to have closed doors to you and others like you, from our neighboring south."

Adriana looked up, her eyes filled with tears. It's OK, Liam. I know it isn't your fault. Now, all I want to know is that Jorge is safe. Please tell me they won't do anything to hurt him."

Liam got up abruptly, his fists clenched at his sides, as he strode toward the door of the café. Under his breath, Angela heard him say: "They better not."

He turned to them and said with resolve in his voice: "Let's go and we'll get to the border in Tijuana, and do as Mr. Ricardo suggested, get a motel room and then call in the morning. In the meantime, I can make some inquiries there."

The next twenty-four hours were difficult ones, with tensions between Angela and Liam, and anxious questions from their two Salvadoran friends, questions that they couldn't answer. They learned from Mr. Ricardo that Jorge was being deported, but he assured them that he was making sure that Jorge had enough money to start a new and better life with his family back in El Salvador. He had instructed Jorge already that, if this ever happened, he would wire money into a Salvadoran bank account in Jorge's name.

"Frankly," said Mr. Ricardo, "Jorge is like the son I

lost in an accident many years ago." Mr. Ricardo's voice cracked over the telephone as he spoke to Angela. "He has been a faithful and excellent worker this past four years, and my business has grown because of it. My only way now to thank him is to make sure there is enough money in the bank so that he can pay off the debt to the goons who got him his work visa in the past. His time is up on that, and it is partially my fault for not making sure he returned to El Salvador when he should have."

"Mr. Ricardo, what do you mean?" Angela was confused.

Jorge's employer continued, "When he came to me, as an undocumented worker he explained he owed a lot of money to the people who recruited him the first time he crossed. When I saw what a good and reliable worker he was, I promised to pay him enough so he could pay that off and then some. I talked him into staying, and he falsely dreamed he could one day, in the not too distant future, bring his wife and little girl here. I told him I would help him."

"I was wrong, I think," said Mr. Ricardo. "I built too many false expectations in Jorge. All he could think of was to get his wife and child here, and then everything would be OK. But it wouldn't be, not until the laws here have changed. In the meantime, I want to make sure he and his family can live. I plan to send a certain amount to him, call it his remittance, every month until the day I can help him come back, a legal immigrant with his family, if he still wants to."

Angela heard a quiet tremor in Mr. Ricardo's voice and knew he was sincere. She detected a slight Spanish accent from his childhood with immigrant parents, who had become successful and employed more than 125 workers in their nurseries and paid taxes to the US government.

"Just a second, Mr. Ricardo." With her hand over the phone, she tried quickly to explain to Liam what was happening. He was standing beside her with a worried look.

Liam took the phone and said, "*Gracias*, Mr. Ricardo. We appreciate everything you have tried to do to help Jorge and his family. We're on the same team and look forward to meeting you in the future. In the meantime, please keep us informed as to when and where Jorge will be crossing over and returning to Mexico. Please tell the authorities his friends will meet him. Then we'll take him and his family back to El Salvador."

"*Sí*, I'll call you as soon as I know, Mr. O'Connor. Please tell his wife not to worry. They will soon be together, and I'll look forward to meeting her someday, and Jorge's daughter, too."

Two days later a very tired and defeated looking Jorge Gonzalez walked over the border in Tijuana, past the border patrol and into the arms of his wife and daughter. It was a tearful reunion filled with bitter sweetness.

Once they had time to embrace and tears were wiped from the family's faces, Jorge looked up to Liam and Angela.

"*Muchas gracias,* for trying to get Adriana and Cici across to me. I guess it just wasn't meant to be. We are luckier than most. *Señor* Ricardo was good to me, like the father I lost when I was sixteen. He treated me well, paid me a fair wage and saved some for me to bring home to Adriana and Cici. Maybe this is for the best. Now I have enough to build a small house for us in Jiquilisco, and we'll be back in our own village again. In the meantime, I can help keep other guys from risking their lives to come to *El Norte* until there are better laws and ways they can earn their citizenship. Besides, it was not good, in spite of the money, to be away from my family."

Angela and Liam, arms wrapped around each other's waists, stood half smiling, tears in their eyes. The journey had ended differently than they all had hoped and expected, but they had succeeded in doing what Liam first set out to do, to reunite Jorge's family.

"Come on, you guys," said Liam, "we've got a long trip back to El Salvador. Cici knows the way, don't you Cici?"

Epilogue
Time to Go Home

Angela awoke, startled by the nearby church bells ringing and the dog barking. She tried to return to sleep, that wonderful escape from the new realities of her life. The birds were singing in the pomegranate tree outside her window. It was time to get up. Maybe an early walk would do her good. The sun streamed into the room, casting shadows of the curtains, gently blowing in the morning breeze, across the terra cotta floor. She arose from the soft, comfy bed that she and Liam had once shared on that fateful trip to *El Norte*, walked to the bathroom and splashed water on her face. It felt cool and soothing, like the tears she had cried the previous week, washing away sad memories. She dressed and brushed her hair while looking in the mirror. She was sure her hair was even whiter than when she returned to Latin America a year ago. So much had happened in such a short while. It seemed as if it was another time in another world.

She called softly to the dog, Azul. Sandy and Jake were still asleep. As she reached down to put on the dog's leash, strangely she thought about the letter, the one she had once written to Liam, professing her love. Maybe it would be nice to read it one more time up on the hill. She took it out of her purse and slipped it into her pocket.

Looking at Azul, she said "*Ven, mi amor*—Come my love." Liam had said that to her when they hurried to leave with Cici and Adriana to head north.

Once back in El Salvador Liam became so ill he had to be hospitalized. He had laid in her arms his last few days and died reassuring her that he'd see her in heaven.

"Sweetheart, even if you don't believe in God anymore, I know the guy will let you in after all the good deeds you have done. I love you."

Those were his last words to her. Angela brushed her hand across her tear-stained face, took the leash and walked out the door into the cobbled street.

It wasn't far to the *cerro*, the hill that led up to the *Cruz del Pueblo*, a tall metal cross. At the end of the street she walked up the narrow steps, and made her way to the top of the hill. She panted, and Azul's tongue hung out as the dog padded along beside her.

With a gentle tug on his leash, Angela helped Azul make the last step up as they arrived almost at the top. They scrambled over the rocks and reached the crest of the hill, even with the base of the cross. She turned and looked out over the vista of the city of San Miguel de

Allende. Sounds of crowing roosters drifted upwards, and the air was filled with early-morning birdsong. Finding a soft, grassy spot, Angela sat down and pulled the letter from her pocket. Azul plopped down at her side, resting his head on her thigh. A cooing sound caught the dog and the woman's attention. They looked up in unison to the branches of the nearby pepper tree, and saw a dove perched on one of them. Just then a louder sound pierced the air and another dove swooped down to the branch. Angela could not help but smile, wistfully thinking of Liam and how he had swept her off her feet. All the longing for each other and the sacrifices they had made to have this one last chance together seemed worth it. She had changed, and now she knew her heart better.

As she looked back at the letter in her lap, Angela began to slip the thin, tattered paper from its envelope. A breeze snatched it from her hand, and it drifted up and, like a kite, flew over her head southward toward Central America, where it had all begun. For a moment she watched, as it floated away, a tiny speck of white.

Angela knew now that it was as it should be. She had had two loves in her life, and she had found meaning and value, working with the orphans and through her deep friendship with her Salvadoran family. It was time to go home where she would advocate for changes to her nation's immigration policies. She had her purpose.

Azul looked up at her and their eyes met. The dog got up and began to walk toward the rocky pathway, taking the lead as Angela followed. The two descended the stairs and took the street home.

Acknowledgments

Under the Salvadoran Sun has been a labor of love, inspired by the people of El Salvador and also, by the many Latin American immigrants who struggle to cross the border into the United States, with the dream of a better life for their children.

Many friends, acquaintances and family members have listened to my stories about my interest in, and support of the Salvadorans. They have kindly contributed to the fund raising I have done to help the small villages of the Bajo Lempa, through EcoViva, a non-profit NGO based in Oakland, California. My deepest appreciation goes to Jose Alas, former priest and founder of the original NGO, the Foundation for Self-Sufficiency in Central America. It is he, who first introduced me to his country and its many wonderful people struggling for a better life after the Peace Accords.

My gratitude for permission to use the beautiful images, for my cover and for the chapter headings, goes to Salvadoran artist, Fernando Llort. His work graces the façade of the San Salvador Cathedral, a key place in my novel.

I would like to offer my heartfelt thanks to all those supporters, in addition to the many friends and family members who have given me encouragement and advice over the five years I have been writing this story. Amongst them are those who have offered to read the first and later drafts of the novel, and have given me insightful suggestions: Marlene K. Dalziel, Rosalie Hewins, Cindy

Stine, Sharon Leder, Milton Tichner, Lynda Schorr, Cecile Pineda, and my beloved daughters, Dawn Evans, and Tiffany Nelson.

To my copy editors, Holly Franko and Marlene K. Dalziel, I offer sincere thanks for helping to improve my manuscript. Literary Agents April Eberhardt and Jeff Kleinman also offered helpful advice and, for that, I am very grateful.

To all the many inspiring writing teachers with whom I have taken workshops at various writing conferences in Portland, Oregon and San Miguel de Allende, Mexico, as well as at Summer Fishtrap in Joseph, Oregon, I offer my gratitude for their guidance in helping me to be a better writer. They are Elizabeth Engstrom Cratty, Robert Dugoni, Jennifer Lauck, Jessica P. Morrell, Joanne B. Mulcahy, John Reed, and last but not least, Luis Urrea.

Finally, I want to thank my devoted husband and life partner for the sacrifices he has endured, while I have spent hours at my computer: the many meals he's cooked and the hours he's spent helping proofread my drafts and the final manuscript. I thank him from the bottom of my heart.

Permissions

My grateful appreciation goes to the authors of works that I admire and whose permission to use quotations from those works has been granted: Owen Sheers and Steven Galloway. Pema Chodrin's quote is taken from my notes of an interview I heard and thus are paraphrased.

BOOK GROUP GUIDE

Under The Salvadoran Sun

Sher Davidson

Introduction

Angela Larson, a Seattle artist with two daughters, had a brief affair ten years ago while working in El Salvador for a humanitarian aid effort. Now widowed and seeking a new purpose for her life, she returns to El Salvador where, by chance, she runs into her former lover, Liam O'Connor. Liam wants Angela to join him in helping Salvadoran orphans. When her daughters discover her past affair, by accident, and confront her, Angela is torn between their needs and her own.

She follows her heart to El Salvador and Sister Agnes' orphanage, where she is dealt a blow when Liam shares a secret, and she also has to deal with gangs recruiting the young orphan boys. She begins to question her presence in El Salvador but agrees to help Liam guide their friends, a young Salvadoran mother and daughter, to the United States to join the father, an undocumented worker in California. The four set out on a dangerous journey with no guarantee of success or survival.

Questions and Topics for Discussion

1. Comment on the push-pull duality of Angela's attraction to the exotic El Salvadoran culture and the impoverishment that she must confront.

2. Does the author succeed in giving you a sense of place?

3. Which side do you connect with in the ongoing debate between Angela's and Liam's points of view vis-à-vis immigration?

4. What are Angela's challenges, and how does she deal with them?

5. Do you find Angela and Liam sympathetic protagonists, and why?

6. Discuss what you like and dislike about the author's supporting characters: Rutilio, the ex-priest, Sister Agnes, the irreverent nun, and Memo, the Guatemalan *curandero*.

7. Is Santos a force of evil or a victim of circumstances?

8. Discuss Angela's relationship with her daughters and how she deals with their revelation of her past transgression.

9. Do you agree or not agree with Angela's decision to follow her heart and return to Liam in El Salvador?

10. Discuss what you learned about El Salvador and

whether it influenced your viewpoint towards the country and its people.

Deepen Your Book Group Discussion

The author suggests you deepen your discussion by seeing the following films, fictional and documentaries: *Romero* with Raul Julia, *Innocent Voices*, *El Norte*, *Sin Fronteras* and *The 800-Mile Wall*.